The Girl
IN THE
Photo

BOOKS BY CATHERINE HOKIN

CATHERINE HOKIN

The Girl
IN THE
Photo

bookouture

Published by Bookouture in 2023

An imprint of Storyfire Ltd.
Carmelite House
50 Victoria Embankment
London EC4Y 0DZ

www.bookouture.com

ISBN: 978-1-80019-705-3
eBook ISBN: 978-1-80019-704-6

*For Jane,
the writers' champion
who makes me stand taller*

PROLOGUE

OCTOBER 1944, THERESIENSTADT

The room is a functional place.

The walls are bare. The window is barred. The furniture is sparse and unyielding. There is no privacy. There is no space. Three rows of narrow bunkbeds jostle together. A table with too many splinters and not enough chairs crowds the floor. There is no colour. There is nothing soft. The room's inhabitants are young – they deserve toys and hugs and stories before bedtime. There is nothing of that here. Teddy bears and tucking in are a fast-fading memory. This is a room which struggles to meet the most basic needs.

The little girl perches quietly on her bed. All the girls sit as quietly as she does; in this room, silence is a lesson quickly learned. When it isn't, when one of them forgets and is loud and is noticed by those it is best to stay hidden from... Well there are always more children to fill up the empty places.

The little girl – who knows that she is called Renny but has brought nothing else from the outside world except her name – sits with her head down and her hands folded, and she waits. That is another important skill she has learned in the long, lost months since she arrived. Every day is filled with waiting. For food. For orders. For her mother to come back from wherever the days take her. For a snatched kiss and a hug that is never enough.

It is a strange, muffled kind of a life that she lives. It is a very different one from the colour and the chaos depicted in the books the aunties keep hidden under the floorboards. The children in those stories run around; they jump and yell and dance. They have things called adventures and no one is made frightened or angry by their never-ending questions. Renny likes it when the books appear and the aunties whisper their way through the pages, but those children may as well live on the moon for all she understands of the world they inhabit.

There have been no stories today. The aunties who look after the room haven't pulled the books or the drawing pencils out of their hiding places and they have said little to the children except 'hush'. Something is happening. The room has stayed silent but outside is all noise. Feet have been marching with a monotonous beat past the window since dawn, and the dogs Renny hates won't stop barking. Nobody asks why.

All of a sudden, as she sits watching and not watching the others, the door opens with a blast of bitter air and someone clatters across the rough floor. The feet are coming towards her. Renny makes herself smaller, just in case. There is a moment of doubt, and then the knot that is her spine relaxes. The voice that follows the footsteps is not a man's snarling shout. It is the gentle one that makes everything warmer.

'Renny, my love, it's me – I'm here.'

But something is wrong there too. The voice is the right one, but a deeper note lurks inside it today, a thrum of pain that freezes Renny through to her bones again.

She looks up; she exhales. The voice might be wrong but the face is perfect. The smile that greets her could make Renny burst into song, if she had any idea what that meant.

'Mama.'

Such a small word and yet there is so much carried in it.

Renny knows whole heaps of words – she is close to four years old; she knows more words than she has the numbers to count them – but *Mama* is the one she loves best. *Mama* is top of the list of the special ones, a list which also includes *love* and *always* and *precious*. It is the word which wraps the two of them up together – Renny and Mama, part of each other from the start and forever. *Mama* is Renny's favourite word of them all, and the meaning baked into it is her favourite story. She says it again, but then she stops. Mama is crying.

Renny instantly drops her gaze back to her toes. Crying, like asking questions, isn't allowed in the room or anywhere else in the town that surrounds it, so why is Mama doing it?

'Renny, sweetheart. Look at me.'

Renny does as she's told. Mama's cheeks are wet; her eyes are red. The aunty is frowning, shuffling her feet; glancing at the closed door and twisting her hands. When she speaks, there is nothing gentle in her voice at all.

'For God's sake, Rosa, be quick. Do you want them to come looking and take her too? If we're to have any chance of keeping her safe when you're gone, you have to get out of here now.'

They.

Renny shivers – she can't help herself. *They* is another small word which holds far more than its size. *They* are the men in uniforms, the men with the guns. The ones who control the room and everywhere else. Who march in and bark at the aunties. Who either ignore the children completely, or bend down and smile too wide and try to be friends. The ones who will scoop you up if you are naughty and stick needles in you until you go mad or send you away to be burned up in a big oven according to the night-time whispers. Renny hates those men and she doesn't want them to come in and choose her, so she really needs Mama to stop crying.

'I have to say goodbye, my darling.'

Her mother's voice has changed again: now it's fluttering up and down and won't settle on anything familiar.

'I have to go away on the train now, sweetheart, and when I do, you have to be brave.'

And there they are, falling down on her head as hard as blows. The bad words: *goodbye, go away, train.* The words that mean *not coming back*; that mean *dead.* The ones which run thick and frightening through the other whispers that emerge with the night.

Dead is a word Renny doesn't really understand, although she pretends to be as comfortable with using it as the older girls seem to be. She has seen death of course: everyone who lives in Theresienstadt has seen death, even the little children like Renny who leave the room for less than an hour a day and more often not at all. Death rides on the carts which trundle through the town's dirty streets and wriggles its way in through the window, creeping into the corners and cots. And Renny has seen what death leaves behind: bodies slumped like crumpled sacks, cold and sagging and empty. When that happens, she does what the others do and pretends not to notice, but it frightens her. She doesn't understand how a person can switch so quickly from being alive to being... not. And she doesn't want to believe what the older girls are so certain of: that dead is what happens to everyone who says goodbye.

When Mama uses the bad words, Renny doesn't want to hear them. She wants to say: *No.* She wants to say: *Don't.* She wants to scream and cry and cling to her mother. She sits still, she stays silent. She watches the aunty watching the door. And she waits for her mother to tell her this is all a mistake.

'Here. Take this. It will keep me with you whatever comes next.'

The bad words stay said. Mama bends down, drops a thin

chain over Renny's head, presses her lips to her daughter's hair and whispers, 'Be a good girl, my love; be careful, and one day all this will pass,' and then...

And then she is gone and the air and the light has gone with her.

Renny sits on her bed as the day moves on, her mind blank and her body old. As one aunty leaves the room to its own devices; as another slips in countless hours later to check on the children. Nobody bothers her. The other girls keep their distance in case the sadness that cloaks her is catching. Nobody bothers Renny at all, not until the evening's pearl barley soup and semolina dumplings arrive in an unappetising damp cloud and the room starts to swarm.

'Come on, little one. Upset or not, you have to eat.'

A swirl of pink flowers scattered across a deep red skirt dances towards her. A scent that Renny can't name but she imagines carries blue skies and sunshine within it tickles her nose. And a hand takes hers that is as soft and plump as Mama's is rough and worn. It is Galyna. The woman who comes into the room almost every day and always seeks Renny out. Who says she is an aunty and here to help with the children, but she isn't. She never goes near any of the others, and the aunties are afraid of her – they circle her as warily as if she was also dressed in a uniform. The one who calls Renny 'my pet' and 'my poppet' and fusses over her, fluffing at her hair and lamenting the state of her grimy dress and bare feet. Who whispers that 'my name is a secret; it's only for you and me to know, and good little girls never tell secrets' and is always promising to one day make things better.

Who isn't my Mama and I don't want her to be.

Renny wishes Galyna would leave her alone, but she allows herself to be led to the table. She swallows the soup Galyna tells her to swallow. She sits back on her bed and lets the woman stroke the tangles out of her dark blonde hair. But she doesn't answer as the pretend game begins yet again, the one where Galyna calls Renny her daughter and wants her to say Mama in return.

'What is this nasty thing?'

The caressing hand turns suddenly stiff. There is a tug and, before Renny can save it, the chain is lifted from her neck and sent spinning away to land in a far corner of the room where the shadows swallow it up. Its absence – Mama's absence – makes Renny's neck burn. She wants to spit and scream and scratch Galyna's wicked eyes out. She stays still; she stays silent.

A hazy sliver of moon pushes at the grime-laden window. Whatever there was of the day has gone and there are no more marching feet outside. Galyna finally leaves. The lights go out.

Renny waits for the whispers to stop, for sleep to settle across the crowded bunks. When there is nothing to be heard but deep breathing, she crawls out of her bed and creeps across the frozen floor, following the necklace's path. It is still there where it fell, coiled up in the darkness. It is safe. The small oval pendant decorated with a sparkling silver flower is unmarked by its flight. Renny's little-girl fingers can't manage the fiddly clasp, but the chain is long enough to slip over her head. She tucks the pendant inside her dress the way her mother did, slips back into a bed which is no warmer than the floor.

Be brave. Be good. Be careful.

Renny is a clever little thing, quick at learning and doing as she is told; everyone tells her that. Which means that she can be whatever Mama needs her to be. Brave and good and careful aren't frightening words – they are behaviours she has already learned. And, perhaps, if she can do them all well enough and manage not to cry or make a fuss or be noticed, then Mama will be safe and come back.

Renny closes her eyes and waits for sleep, her hand clutched tight round the last piece of her mother.

The big girls don't have to be right. Goodbye doesn't have to mean forever. Leave doesn't have to mean dead. Mama will come back one day – Renny is sure of it. As long as she remembers to be good.

CHAPTER 1

25 FEBRUARY 1950, BERLIN

'There's a queue stretching halfway down the road – we'll have to start moving people through the rooms quicker.'

'Someone had better go to the bar next door and pick up another crate of wine before we run out.'

'We need to find space for another cloakroom. None of this lot will thank us if we ruin their hats.'

Hanni stood at the centre of the scrum, listening to the gallery owner and the waiting staff trying to manage the crowds without looking as if they were doing it. She had no idea which way to turn next. The exhibition had attracted so much attention she was reeling. There were some familiar faces – the colleagues she had spent days persuading to come were all in attendance – but most of the three display rooms lined with her photographs were filled up with strangers.

Which is exactly what I wanted and worked so hard to pull off, so why am I still pinching myself?

Hanni had spent as many days running round Charlottenburg's well-heeled streets, pressing flyers on anyone who might have a passing interest in her art, as she had begging her colleagues to come to her opening night. Hoping for success did not, however, mean she'd believed it would happen. And yet the numbers thronging through the door were, as more than one visitor had commented, remarkable, especially for a debut.

'What inspires your work?'

'Where did you train? Who taught you how to take such skilful pictures?'

'Which one of these is your favourite?'

Everyone wanted to speak to her. Everyone had a question or an insight about her work that they were desperate to share. It was hard to stay poised under the avalanche of praise. It was harder still not to start clapping like a child as one photograph after another was crowned with a bright red *sold* sticker. Everything was wonderful and nothing felt real. Or not yet, not without her champion beside her.

'What are you worrying about? It'll be a triumph. You're brilliant and the location is perfect – there's as many art galleries in Charlottenburg as there are bars in the rest of the city. Win that audience over and the whole of Berlin will fall at your feet.'

Freddy had dealt with her rising panic as the show's opening drew closer by refusing to believe she could fail. Hanni had been all sleepless nights and self-doubting mornings for weeks, wishing she hadn't decided to take what suddenly felt like a wildly over-optimistic leap from portraits and press work to an actual exhibition. Freddy had been all kisses and excitement, filling her up with coffee and confidence and determinedly cheering her on.

He'll adore this. He'll be unstoppable. He'll run round greeting everyone and singing my praises and buying up all the photos himself if nobody else does.

Except he wasn't there. Chief Inspector Brack – Freddy's boss at the Kreuzberg police station where Hanni had also once worked as a crime-scene photographer – had buried him under a mountain of paperwork, delighting in the chance to spoil his subordinate's evening.

'I'll get out of here well before the end, I promise. I'll burn all of Brack's stupid forms if I have to. I've already been demoted, for the next few months at least anyway. What else can he do?'

The answer to that was quite a lot.

Freddy was still seconded to desk duties, and away from the murder team he had run for four years, as a punishment for his 'insubordination' over the previous year's Berlin Strangler case. He wasn't taking the enforced inactivity well, and Brack – who was old-school in his words and an ex-Nazi in Freddy's – was revelling in punishing him. Hanni had given Freddy as many pep talks about riding out the temporary suspension and not rising to Brack's goading as he had given her about enjoying her first show. He was almost holding steady. So Hanni hadn't got upset when he'd telephoned to say that he would be late – she had told him not to worry, that she was fine. Which she was.

But this would be twice the triumph if he was by my side to enjoy it.

The door chimed open again.

Hanni peered over the crowds, hoping that the next person to appear through it would finally be her husband, a word which still sat surprising and sweet on her tongue. It wasn't. The man removing his hat and dusting the February snow off his shoulders was another stranger. She caught his eye and smiled, assuming he would head straight to the cloakroom or pick up the list of photographs on show before making his way further in. He looked her up and down instead, with a steady and thorough appraisal that made Hanni's skin itch.

It's one of Reiner's spies come hunting me.

The thought flew in from nowhere and instantly soured all the joy in the room. Hanni gasped and stepped back, knocking an elbow and spilling a drink, covering herself in apologies and confusion. By the time she glanced across at the doorway again, the man had melted away.

It's nothing, it's nerves. I'm safe from him. My father is my past, and that part of my life is done.

Hanni wanted to believe that. She had dared to mount her exhibition, and include some of her more controversial pictures, because she had chosen to believe that. The past, however, had other ideas.

'You did it. Congratulations. You've started to tell your real story. To be honest, I was never certain that you would.'

The gallery dissolved.

Hanni stood still, locking her knees as the floor started swaying; trying to find a face or a photograph to focus on, anything that would act as an anchor.

I'm imagining things. I'm spooked. The way the man at the door looked at me was arrogant but that doesn't make him one of Reiner's men, and this one can't possibly be who I think it is either...

She swallowed hard and refused to acknowledge her racing pulse. The room was noisy; she couldn't hear anyone clearly. The voice at her elbow wasn't one from her previous life – that wasn't possible. It was surely one of her colleagues instead. Axel maybe, or Caspar. One of the editors from the glossy magazines which, rather than police work, now provided the bread and butter of her living, teasing her about the first-night nerves they had also had to put up with for weeks. It couldn't be him. Hanni knew as she turned that she was fooling herself.

'*Shadowland.* It's an excellent title; it's nicely nuanced.'

Natan Stein, the man who had given Hanni her first photography job when she'd reinvented herself at the end of the war – and the man who had fallen hopelessly in love with her despite her praying he wouldn't – was standing barely a foot away, staring at her as if he longed to wrap her up in his arms.

A serious man, and a kind one, with eyes that have seen far too much.

That had been Hanni's first impression when they had met five years earlier, and nothing about him had changed. And neither had the fact that their parting then had not been a happy one.

She opened her mouth but nothing, not even hello, came out. To his credit, Natan managed not to react to her blank expression. Hanni assumed he must have expected her to be thrown by his reappearance and she was grateful for, although not surprised by, his tact. He carried on talking, in the too-quick way she remembered, while she tried to shake off her nerves and find him the warm smile he deserved.

'And the way you've set up the three different rooms works really well – shots of the bombed-out ministries leading into the pictures of the black markets and the street kids before finishing up in the last one with the children. There's a darkness to it all – how could there not be – but you start with beauty in the buildings and there's humour in the markets, so the impact of the end is... Well, my father would have approved.'

'Thank you.'

It was hopelessly inadequate but Hanni couldn't think of anything else to say. The mention of his father, Ezra Stein – the Jewish photographer she had met as a naïve child, who had ignited her love and respect for his art and had died at the hands of the Nazis for his honesty – had left her tongue-tied. And the sudden return of his son Natan, a man she hadn't seen since she had told him the truth of her life and broken his heart, had spun the exhibition away.

He has more right than anyone to judge me, but he's come here as a friend. He hasn't lost his kindness, whatever I deserve.

Hanni's thudding heart settled a little. Perhaps he had forgiven her. Perhaps he would stick to the more solid ground that was the skill they both shared and not stray into the personal.

Her relief lasted barely a moment.

'They're from Theresienstadt, aren't they? The photographs of the children and the others in the third room? It's really daring, Hanni, the way you've mixed the official Third Reich shots of that dreadful place in with your own candid ones, sitting propaganda side by side with the truth. It's clever, and it's different – no wonder it's attracting a crowd. You should be really proud of yourself. You've put on a show that's got tongues wagging and, by displaying those images, you've tackled your past. Which I suppose means that you've also finally dealt with your father?'

Hanni stared at him, the hope in his eyes flooding tears into hers.

Proud.

It was the wrong word. It assumed there was more honesty in her work, and in her life, than she was telling. And as for his other assumption, how was she supposed to answer that? With the truth?

No, I haven't tackled it, or not how I wanted. What I've done is carried on pretending, about myself, about my life in the war. And my father is still out there, calling himself Emil Foss now, not Reiner, but nothing else about him has changed. He's as evil as he always was, and no matter how hard I tried, and I did try I swear, I never managed to fulfil my promise. I never managed to denounce him.

That was impossible, unsayable. Natan would never accept it. And if he pushed her, or was still at her side when Freddy arrived... Where that could lead was unthinkable.

A waiter passed by, a tray of drinks perched in his hand. Hanni reached out for a glass of Sekt, but her shaking fingers slid straight off the stem. She stared around, desperate to be away from Natan and his impossible question, but no one, for the first time all evening, was looking her way. Everyone was suddenly preoccupied with the art and with each other, and the only one intent on quizzing her was him.

'Hanni, are you all right? Have I upset you by mentioning Reiner? I didn't mean to, but I assumed that, if you're holding an exhibition featuring Theresienstadt, he must have been brought to justice by now. Not that I'd heard anything, but so much seems to get swept under the carpet nowadays for the sake of Germany's bright new future. Presumably his arrest and his trial were quietly done?'

Natan's voice had risen; heads eager for gossip started to turn. Hanni deliberately dropped hers almost to a whisper, although that didn't help her find the right words.

'I know what I said but it's not so straightforward as that. You have to remember that my father is clever – and ruthless. I wanted to bring him down, and I tried to do that but...'

She was still fumbling her way round a sentence she couldn't complete without far more time than she had when the door clanged open again and there, finally, was Freddy. For a moment Hanni forgot everything but him. He was on his toes, waving, pushing his way towards her, wearing a grin so wide it was a wonder his cheeks didn't split. His smile rippled across her skin, lighting her up. And then she felt the shift in the air as Natan also spotted him.

'Wait a minute, what's he doing here? And why is he looking at you like that, like he used to? Oh come on, Hanni. Surely you two aren't—'

But Freddy was already on them, reaching out for her, and Natan's sentence was left as cut short as Hanni's had been.

'I told you, didn't I, that this would be a success? I'm so proud of you, my darling. You're a star.'

Then it was Freddy's turn to spot Natan, the man who had once been his rival, although never in Hanni's eyes, and his smile disappeared.

'Look who came. Isn't it a wonderful surprise? Old friends I mean, coming to see my work, as well as all these new faces.'

She was babbling, not that either man was listening to her. They were too busy taking up their old jousting positions. It was Freddy who recovered himself first, plunging into a greeting that was far too triumphant to smooth out the meeting.

'Herr Stein, it's been a long time. How kind of you to come and celebrate my wife's exhibition.'

The stress on *wife* was too pronounced; the pause after it was too smug. Hanni winced as Natan's face hardened.

Freddy might as well have declared himself the winner and done a lap around the room. Natan won't thank him for that, whether he's got any feelings left for me or not.

She waited for the explosion to come, for Natan to act on the dislike he still appeared to be carrying for Freddy and for her world to split in two. Natan started to speak, but then he stopped at *how* and a wave of pain spread across his face. Hanni didn't know if it was for himself or for Freddy, and she didn't want to find out. Luckily Freddy had caught Natan's expression too, and the kindness she loved him for surged back.

'Why don't I have a look around and let you two catch up? There must be all kinds of technical stuff you want to discuss that I can't make sense of.'

It was a graceful retreat and it saved her. Natan waited until Freddy was out of earshot before he grabbed hold of Hanni's wrist and pulled her into an alcove that offered some semblance of privacy.

'He doesn't know, does he? He still has no idea who you are. That your name isn't Hanni Winter but Hannelore Foss. That you're the daughter of an SS officer, of a monster. I'm no fan of Freddy's but that's not how he deserves to be treated. You haven't told him, even though he's Jewish and your family ties would disgust him, and even worse than that, you've married him. How could you do it? Are you trying to break his heart?'

He didn't add 'as well as mine' but it was there in his eyes, and the accusation was no fairer now than it had been when Hanni had done everything she could to avoid causing him pain.

'Of course I'm not. I would never deliberately do that to anybody, as you should know. No, I haven't told him, and yes that is wrong and something I need to make good. But I love Freddy and, whether you think that's right or not, I'm not going to apologise for it, or for marrying him. Or for wanting to be happy.'

Natan dropped her wrist, but his stare didn't falter.

'And what makes you think you have the right to be that?'

He was angry. Hanni understood that, she sympathised with that, but she couldn't keep apologising for her choices, and she couldn't let him walk away thinking that she was a coward who had never tried to keep her word. She deserved better than that.

People were milling close to their corner; she could hear someone calling her name. Soon she would be dragged away, and the chance to defend herself would be gone, so she screwed up her courage and dived in.

'None of this has been as easy as you seem to think, Natan. I did try to do as I promised and bring Reiner down. And when I did, it was other people who paid.'

She ran through the five years of her feud with her father, and the damage which had spun out from that, as succinctly as she could. Starting with the murder of people she had cared about and the terrifying and almost successful attempt on her own life and ending with her decision to live in the present and hold some hope for the future.

'Someone said to me last year that I have choices. That the past doesn't have to rule the rest of my life. I decided to follow that advice. And maybe that was wrong, but Freddy loves me as much as I love him and I wanted to make something good out of that.'

Her words softened his anger, but the pity that flooded Natan's face instead was terrible. It made Hanni want to turn on her heel and run.

'But it's dishonest, Hanni. And after everything that Freddy's been through in the war and with the loss of his family, is it fair? Besides, how on earth will it work? Never mind the lies you must already have told him to make it this far, what about the photographs you've put on show? The ones of the children in Theresienstadt? If you haven't told him who you really are, that your father virtually ran that God-forsaken place and you lived there with him, how have you managed to explain those pictures away?'

How did you get access to Theresienstadt? How did you get so close to the little ones?

It wasn't the first time Hanni had been asked that question tonight. And tonight wasn't the first time she'd had to answer that question with a lie.

And every time I tell it, it grows.

Since she had first met Freddy in 1945, in the ruins of one of the bombed-out buildings whose photograph was also on display, Hanni had kept a curtain firmly drawn across the life she had lived before and during the war. Through all the twists and turns of their relationship, she had left Freddy to draw his own conclusions about why she had held him so often at arm's length. She had kept secrets and silences, but Natan was wrong: what she had never done was told Freddy an outright lie. It wasn't much of a distinction, Hanni knew that, but she had clung to it. Until the chance to show her work, including the pictures that truly mattered to her, had come and the step from silence to dishonesty had proved to be a shorter one than it should. Hanni hated herself for that; she imagined Natan was about to hate her too.

'Freddy hasn't seen them yet; he didn't want to see anything until the exhibition was hung and ready. But I warned him they were going to be part of it. And yes, I lied. I told him I was briefly in the town in 1944, that I went with my father who was part of the Red Cross delegation visiting that summer. I said I'd managed to snatch the photographs then. That's what I'm telling anyone else who asks me tonight. I'm not proud of that deception, but, right or wrong, that's my choice.'

She wasn't proud of herself for the deception at all, but unfortunately, Natan refused to accept that, or *my choice, right or wrong* as any kind of defence, and he was not about to absolve her.

'And it's the wrong one, but you know that so what's the point of me saying it? What I can't fathom is how you told Freddy such a far-fetched story and he believed you. What kind of a detective would choose to accept that not only would a young girl have been part of the delegation in the first place, but that she would also have been able to slip away and take such intimate pictures? I can't believe he swallowed it. You really must have him tied up and spellbound.'

Hanni chose to let him have the rage that filled his last comment.

'He did believe me, and I'm not proud of that either, but I suppose he had no reason not to. He thought it was odd that I'd stayed quiet about it, especially as he'd already told me that he'd been held prisoner in Buchenwald.' She stumbled over that name. Natan didn't help her. 'But I said I was ashamed to have been part of it. That nobody realised at the time that everything we were shown was a sham and that the SS had orchestrated the whole visit. That we were made fools of. My shame was enough for him. I hope it will be enough for anyone who asks me tonight.'

She couldn't tell if Natan's low whistle came from admiration or disgust. She didn't give him a chance to tell her.

'I didn't want to lie to him, but I had to include the photographs, don't you get that? It's only been five years since the war ended and yet no one talks about the Nazis and their crimes anymore. It's as if we're supposed to forget what they did. That's wrong. And I wanted the children who suffered and died in Theresienstadt to be seen. I wanted them to be remembered.'

That was also the truth. It made no difference.

'A new honesty about the Third Reich, how touching. And what, you're going to be the face of it?' There was no mistaking now how Natan felt – the disgust poured from him. 'Well that should be interesting. Have you thought about all the new lies you'll have to tell? Or do you really think you can become the champion of murdered children without anyone asking deeper questions? You're a fool if you do, Hanni. This will catch you out. This will uncover you.'

'Don't say that. Uncovering me would destroy him. It can't happen.'

Except Hanni had known since she had heard the first gasp at the pictures she had chosen to display that it could. A year ago she had pretended differently. She had taken the decision then to switch off all the voices in her head that said *don't*, especially when those voices talked about Freddy. *Don't love him. Don't dream of a future. Don't ever try to climb out from under your father's shadow.* She had been doing very well holding all those don'ts at bay. And now Natan had pricked the bubble where she had been hiding, and back they all rushed.

I won't listen to them, not again. I can't have this life I've built ruined. I'll make it come right – I have to.

It was one thing to think it but quite another to make it sound real. Hanni drew herself up and forced herself to sound determined.

'Why shouldn't I try to do something good, for us both? Everything that went wrong in my life, and all the misery and cruelty I was forced to stand witness to, was my father's doing. None of it was my fault. He got away with all of his crimes, so why should I be the one made to pay?'

She hated the words the moment they came out of her mouth – all she sounded was wrong. It was the coward's excuse: *it wasn't my doing; it was him, it was them; it was anyone else except me.* The defence clung to by everyone in the war who had seen and heard and done nothing. She tried to backtrack, to speak from her heart not her panic, but the damage was done.

'I'm sorry. You know I don't mean that. I know what I should have done, what I should still do.'

Her apology was pointless. Natan was already gone, and the last look he threw at her was one of utter contempt.

Hanni peeled herself off the wall she had slumped against and re-emerged into the reception hall, holding herself as carefully as if she had lost a layer of skin. The crowds showed no sign of leaving; she was engulfed the instant she reappeared.

She let herself be led back into the first exhibition room, lost herself in an explanation of why she had started the series of photographs comparing the bomb-ravaged Third Reich palaces to ruined cathedrals. She didn't look at anyone; she didn't answer anything personal. A group collected round her, brimming with questions. Hanni buried herself in their interest, pushed Natan's prophecy that she would be uncovered away. Another hour, that's all she would give them. Then she would collect up Freddy and be done. Another hour and she could be safe in his arms again, and the world could go back in its box.

'There's a right commotion going on in the back room. Someone's recognised one of the children in the photographs. They think it's one of their family, a child who was presumed dead.'

Hanni thought she had misheard but then another voice picked up the rumour and the buzz started to spread.

'What do you mean? Who's recognised who?'

No one answered her. No one was interested in her anymore. The idea that anyone could have matched up one of her pictures with a lost child sounded unbelievable to her but not, apparently, to everyone else.

Hanni stopped asking questions and let herself become part of the surge towards the exhibition's final section. That room was as busy as all the rest, but its mood was different. Whatever commotion had happened in there had calmed. A space had cleared, a hush had fallen. And there – the centre of attention and utterly oblivious to it – was Freddy. He was standing alone in front of one of the photographs, with his mouth open and tears melting over his cheeks.

Hanni began to push her way towards him, demanding that people step back and let her through. She couldn't tell if he was happy or heartbroken but, whichever it was, he was her husband and he wasn't going to go through it alone.

'It's her.'

Freddy turned towards Hanni as if he had sensed she was coming. He stared directly at her, cutting away every bystander until there was only the two of them in the room.

Hanni had never seen his face so transfigured. It was glowing, almost frightening in its intensity.

Freddy pointed at the picture, at the child whose wide eyes and bitten lip dominated the frame. Hanni stared back at the face whose haunted and haunting image told more about the truth of Theresienstadt than words could ever manage. She knew the image well; she remembered the day she had taken it clearly. The child she had snapped with more speed than the photograph's intimacy suggested was the little girl who wouldn't let herself cry. Who had held herself separate from the terrified children who flocked round their carer the moment the guards had finished their selections and marched back out of the nursery. Who had refused to look at Hanni when she stepped shaking out of the shadows she had been hiding in, with her camera raised. The girl who had held so much pain inside herself, Hanni hadn't known how she could keep breathing.

'It's my Renny.'

Freddy had her hands clasped tight inside his; the crowd gathered round them was clapping.

'It's my little sister, Renny. You've brought her back to me.'

He pulled her into an embrace that swept her off her feet, that turned the clapping into cheers. Even if Hanni could have summoned any words, he was talking so fast he wouldn't have heard them.

'I assumed she was dead. I thought she was lost at the start of 1943 when they were all taken from me, but here she is in Theresienstadt, over a year later. And that's the thing: not only was she alive more than a year after I assumed she was dead, but Renny was there, in Theresienstadt. Don't you see what that means? She wasn't in a concentration camp. It's a miracle. I know Theresienstadt was bad, but it wasn't Buchenwald, or Dachau, it wasn't the worst of places. She had survived for at least sixteen months there; she could have survived till the end. There is hope, Hanni. For the first time in years, there is hope.'

Except there wasn't. Not for a child as tiny as Renny. Not with the hatred that had ruled the ghetto town as fiercely as it had ruled the killing camps which Theresienstadt fed.

Hanni let herself melt into Freddy's arms. She desperately wanted to join in with his hopes and his laughter, but how could she? When she knew that the photograph hadn't been taken in the summer of 1944 at all, but in the October of that year. When the clearances had begun again. When the trains had started rolling out every day with their carriages bursting. Rolling out on their unstoppable way to the gas chambers and to the ovens waiting for them at Auschwitz.

CHAPTER 2

'I was losing them – my parents, my brother, my sister. It's got harder with every passing year to hold on to their faces, to stop the memories from crumbling to dust. And now Renny is returned, Renny is real again.' He stopped, shaking his head with the wonderful shock of it. 'And I'm going to find her this time, Hanni, I swear it.'

The photograph had spun Freddy out of the life he had built in the wreckage of the war and out of the man he had become. It had taken him back to his twenty-two-year-old self again. When he was still a brother and a son; when he had held a fixed place in the world. The gallery had fallen away as he stared at the picture. Its stark white walls had vanished, replaced by a hearthrug covered with his little brother's toy soldiers and the stack of mending piled beside his mother's armchair. The chattering voices and clinking wine glasses had disappeared, giving way to the hum of a nursery rhyme and the rumble of his father's deep laughter.

Hanni's skill had done that. Hanni's skill had caught the curl of Renny's hair and the curve of her rosebud mouth exactly as Freddy remembered them. And that skill had brought far more than Renny back to him: his mother was there in the almond shape of the little girl's eyes; his father was in the dark sweep of her eyebrows. She looked so real in the photo, so close; so alive. Freddy had reached out to touch her folded hands, expecting to feel their plump softness. The photograph was perfection. And yet it wasn't.

When Freddy had said 'it's her', the words hadn't come as easily or as happily as they had sounded. Pain and fear had rushed in behind them.

It was Renny, there was no doubt in his mind about that, but it wasn't the Renny whose bright smile Freddy had been desperately clinging to. The girl in the photograph was older of course, and he could accept that. It was the other changes which were harder to see.

She was far thinner than the giggling toddler he had played peek-a-boo with before his world fell apart. Hunger was there, carved into her hollow cheeks and scooped-out neck. That had been dreadful to see; the misery of it had been all too easy to imagine. Renny's pinched face had brought back the empty, stomach-twisting days Freddy had endured in Buchenwald and the knowledge of a suffering no child should ever have been exposed to. That was bad. What was worse was the desolation stamped through the little girl's eyes and bitten mouth. That had torn at Freddy's heart and kept him awake until dawn. He couldn't unsee it. And he also knew that he couldn't let himself dwell on what she had endured or the despair that that knowledge would bring. There was no place for that, not now, not after all the dead ends he had stumbled down since 1945. Not when a door was finally opening. He only wished that Hanni would make more of an effort to follow his lead. He hadn't known what to do with her reluctance.

'I know how miraculous this must seem, and I want to

believe she's alive as much as you do. But it's been a long time since the picture was taken, Freddy; almost six years. And she was a very little thing. You know how the camps worked, how brutal they were for the children put in them. And I know that Theresienstadt was a ghetto town and run in a different way to Buchenwald and the others, but it was still a hellish place. It was filled with disease and starvation. It was a deportation site. It's hard, I know, not to want this, but I'm worried that, if you get your hopes up too high, you're only going to get hurt.'

Freddy put his coffee cup down before he snapped off the handle – or threw it across the room. She might say that she wanted to believe in the miracle too, but that was the second time Hanni had tried to crush his dreams with her misery-filled warning. Freddy didn't know why she would say it at all. How was he supposed to hold himself down? He had wanted his hopes up last night when he saw the photograph and he wanted his hopes up now while he worked out a plan. He wanted them so high they were touching the clouds. Why couldn't Hanni understand that?

'And, sweetheart, you've searched so hard for them already, with no luck. The pain of that must have been terrible. Do you really want to put yourself through it for a second time?'

Why won't she stop?

Freddy got up from the table and his uneaten breakfast, biting back angrier words than he wanted to aim at her. They were a team – that was their strength. They had been a team when they worked together as detective and crime-scene photographer, solving two of Berlin's biggest murder cases, and they were a team in their marriage. So why was she pushing back at him now?

He started to pace, the way he had been pacing half the night. Unable to settle or to be still when Renny could be out there. Missing him, needing him. He didn't want to fight. He never wanted to fight; not with Hanni. His logical brain knew that she was trying to protect him, to look out for him, but he didn't want her protection. He wanted her unqualified support, not a string of *be cautious, be carefuls* that wrapped around him like chains. Maybe he hadn't tried hard enough to make her realise how he felt.

Maybe I shouldn't have to.

He pushed that disloyalty away and tried to explain himself more clearly.

'But that's the whole point: I didn't search as hard as I could've done. Okay, I did what everyone did. I combed through the displaced persons camps but I gave up too soon: when there was no immediate trace of my family in any of them, I stopped going. And I gave up going to the train stations too. When the Red Cross workers told me that picking over the noticeboards wasn't helping me, that the constant pointless searching would only prolong my loss, I listened. That's where I went wrong. I let myself get beaten down by the hopelessness of it all, and I stopped believing. And now look what's happening: there are still people finding their way home from Russian prisons and from all over Europe, and the DP camps are still running. But I didn't wait; I gave up, I stopped looking. I abandoned them.'

'No!'

Hanni was suddenly on her feet, knocking the cups over in her haste to reach out for him.

'You can't say that, Freddy; you mustn't. You searched for as long as you could bear it – I know you did. You searched in every place that would talk to you. You did everything that you could.'

Tears were thick in her voice and already falling. Freddy didn't want those any more than he wanted her warnings: her tears, whether she meant it or not, were just another way to stop him. And he didn't want to be told that he had tried his best, not when he knew the truth. That he had failed his family in February 1943 when they were caught in the round-up of Berlin's last Jews and he had escaped, and that he had failed them again when the war ended. Hanni could cry for him all she wanted, but her tears wouldn't alter the facts.

'I didn't. But now I have another chance. My sister was alive long after I thought she was dead. That changes everything. What if my parents and my brother are still alive too? What if they are lost or sick somewhere and I could find them? How can I turn my back on the possibility of that? So don't tell me not to hope or not to try again, because I won't listen. You found her and that was a miracle. If there's been one, can't I believe in another? Can't I try and catch a miracle of my own?'

He stopped, wishing he didn't have to ask the next question, that her answer to it was certain.

'And won't you help me to look?'

Hanni didn't say yes. She didn't say anything. He needed her to say yes at once, without hesitation, and she didn't. Freddy knew something was wrong. His Hanni was thoughtful and caring and kind above anyone that he knew. But she hadn't said yes, and he didn't have the time to find out why.

'I'd rather search for my family with you. I can't imagine doing it without you. But I'll do it anyway, wherever it leads me, whatever it takes. And I'm not going to waste another minute arguing about it.'

They stared at each other across the small kitchen, which now felt more like a boxing ring than the homely centre of their lives. The heart of their home, where they had poured their hearts out over candlelight and the meals they had cooked between kisses, had turned so cold he couldn't recognise it.

It's our old pattern again. Me laying myself bare, her pulling back the instant I do it.

But this time Hanni broke it. She flew into his arms, 'I'm always on your side – you know that,' tumbling from her mouth so fast the words all ran into one.

They sat down again; they held each other's hands. Freddy began to spin plans; Hanni nodded and listened. They sat shoulder resting on shoulder, and nobody mentioned being careful or cautious. And neither of them admitted what they both really felt: that the ground they had sworn that they would walk on together had suddenly started to shake.

———

'There are thousands of lost souls who we'll never find. And there are thousands more who will never stop searching.'

Freddy sat in the darkest corner of the half-empty bar, unable to swallow the beer he had ordered. He felt like a fool. He was a detective, he was meant to understand how the world worked. He hadn't the faintest idea.

'Do you know how many people the war displaced, Inspector?'

The woman from the Children's Search Service of the Red Cross – a newer organisation Freddy had decided could be his best starting point – hadn't been angry. She wasn't being difficult or trying to make him feel small when she asked. She had been weary and worn out. The only thing about her that wasn't faded were the dark circles under her eyes. When Freddy shook his head and admitted that he didn't have a clue, she had pushed a folder across her desk and gestured for him to look through its closely typed pages.

'Forty million is one of our estimates, although that's not a figure the politicians who brokered the peace like us to broadcast. I've been working here for almost four years and that's still not a number I can comprehend. Forty million people left without a family or a home or a country, some of them without even a name. Most of those, it is true, have been reconnected to at least some of their loved ones and are somewhere closer to their old lives by now, but the scale of what happened has left a legacy with a very long reach. And as for the children...'

She had taken off her glasses then and rubbed her eyes, her shoulders drooping as if even the thought of the children was too hard to carry.

'The figures – or our best guess at them, because God knows how many died unrecorded on the roads – are there, on the second page. Thirteen million in 1945, orphaned or cast adrift somehow from their parents. Another impossible number. I worked for UNRRA then, the United Nations agency set up to provide relief and rehabilitation for refugees. We were all so full of ambition, so determined to do good. And we were all totally overwhelmed by the scale of the disaster. There were a million little ones wandering around Germany alone; there were thousands abandoned just in Berlin. Every one of them lost, every one of them terrified and so many of them sick with malnutrition or any one of a dozen other diseases that we didn't have enough medical supplies to manage. But at least we could *try* to treat those. As for the rest of the damage, the scars that ran deeper... Some of the younger ones in particular were so wild, or had been so viciously treated, they preferred life in the woods to being near people.'

When Freddy had clumsily expressed his shock, and his thanks for the work she had done, she had pulled herself rapidly together.

'That was then; things have settled slightly. But we are still looking for matches, looking for families; fielding more requests for help than my office or any of the other agencies trying to unpick the mess can handle. So can I help you to find yours? To be honest, I don't know. You have more information now than you did in 1945, or on your sister at least, and we also have more resources to draw on, but even a wider search might still come to nothing.'

Freddy picked up his glass and tried a sip. The beer tasted as sour as it had half an hour ago. 'I'm Jewish. My whole family was – that's why they were taken.'

He had offered her that as if it was a door-opener, a winning ticket. All he had received in return was a sigh.

'And I am very sorry for what was done to your people. That was terrible, despicable and far more should still be done to bring its perpetrators to justice. But we don't prioritise anyone here; we can't. Everyone who comes through our hands has suffered.'

She had let him get angry at that for a moment or two, but no longer. 'I am not trying to minimise your pain or your loss, Inspector. Perhaps we should be making a special effort for Jewish families. Perhaps we are doing this all wrong and one day we will be judged badly for it, but we are doing something and that is the best we can offer. Our records are not as comprehensive as I would like them to be, and the division of Germany between East and West hasn't helped. Unfortunately, our Soviet neighbours see things very differently to us. They have always been far quicker to put children up for adoption, and after that, names change and nobody wants to disturb the new families. If your little sister ended up on their side of things, there will likely be no trail to follow. But we have a starting point in Theresienstadt, and there are arrival and deportation lists now that are relatively quick to access. As I said, we shouldn't prioritise, but...'

She hadn't finished the sentence. She had sent him away with a, 'Come back tomorrow afternoon and let me see what I can do in the meantime. I can't promise a result, but I will try to at least get things started,' that had felt like a victory. And she had been as good as her word.

Freddy stared at the sheet of paper lying next to his glass, not that he needed to read it again. He had already memorised its four printed lines.

- *Jakub Schlüsselberg, died Theresienstadt 15 November 1943*
- *Rosa Schlüsselberg, deported from Theresienstadt to Auschwitz, 22 October 1944, died the next day*
- *Leo Schlüsselberg, no records*
- *Renate Schlüsselberg, arrived Theresienstadt 2 March 1943*

The official had stayed businesslike as she handed over the information. Freddy had been very grateful for that. It had allowed him to hold on to his dignity at least until he walked out of the door.

'There is no doubt about your parents' fate. Based on what you told me about your brother's health, no records likely means that he didn't survive the journey from Berlin. As for your sister... You said you were certain that she was alive in July 1944. We have nothing to corroborate that, but the absence of her name on the list with your mother suggests that she wasn't included on that transport at least. The records up to the end of 1944 appear to have been well kept. After that, well, a lot of things were destroyed, in the last days when people feared leaving... evidence.'

'But Renny could have survived?'

Freddy had asked the question as much to wipe away the meaning of *evidence* as to gain any reassurance. The official had offered him a 'perhaps' he doubted she meant, but that had given him enough strength to stand up and shake her hand and hold back the sobs that hit him the second he stumbled into the fresh air.

Leo had been dead from the start; his parents had lasted a little longer.

And Renny wasn't on the train.

He picked up his drink and this time he drained it.

She saved her.

Freddy had known that was what had happened from the first moment he had seen his mother's and his sister's entries. Rosa had left Renny behind, which had to mean that she had found a safe place for her. It wasn't an oversight or a mistake; it was his mother's final gift to the family which was her whole life.

Freddy wiped his eyes. Drinking in a faceless bar in the back streets of Dahlem was a waste of his time, especially now that the next steps he needed to take were so clear. There were other avenues he had to check and other possible leads he would follow, but the truth was obvious: there was a trail and it started in Theresienstadt. Which meant that Theresienstadt was where he needed to be.

He gathered up his things. The journey his mind was already set on was potentially impossible – it involved entering a country which had now fallen under Communist rule. It was a journey almost everybody would tell him not to attempt. So he needed to find the one man who wouldn't.

———

Everything had spun out of control with a speed that was frightening. Freddy had changed gears so fast, Hanni could hardly keep up with him. There was no more planning, there were no more conversations about which organisation Freddy should turn to next, because Freddy had already decided what came next and it wasn't more meetings. He had met with the Red Cross, then he had disappeared for a day, and when he finally came home, he had announced that he was leaving for Theresienstadt as soon as the arrangements could be made. And now he was dragging her to Mitte and a meeting with Elias

Baar – a man who had treated her as if she was a threat to Freddy's well-being from the moment they met – to set the wheels for that unthinkable journey in motion.

'Freddy, for God's sake, will you please slow down? Never mind that this plan you're set on could be incredibly dangerous, there are so many avenues still left to explore. There are new tracing bureaus you haven't contacted. There are Jewish agencies now with more specialist expertise than the Red Cross. There are refugee camps still open that might be able to help. Why does your next move need to be as extreme as Theresienstadt?'

He hadn't listened. He wasn't interested in her fears for his safety, which were as real as her fears about what he might actually find there. He was full to the brim with arguments that were marshalled ready to knock hers down.

'Because Theresienstadt is the last place that anyone can reliably put her, and there is still a Red Cross team working there. There could be records in the town that I can't access anywhere else. And you're wrong: there aren't any other avenues in Germany left to explore. I'm a detective, aren't I? Researching all the angles is my job, so I've done it. That's what I was doing after I met with the Children's Service, making calls and asking for help, and it was all utterly pointless. Ninety per cent of the records that the International Tracing Service at Bad Arolsen have for Jewish children are marked as dead. The staff at the children's home at Aglasterhausen where orphans who survived the death camps were taken were as kind as everyone else, but they couldn't help and neither could any of the displaced persons camps I turned to. Wherever I ring, the answer is always the same: there are no unaccompanied little Jewish girls, there never have been any unaccompanied little Jewish girls. They weren't the ones who made it.'

Everything Freddy said about the steps he had taken had the policeman's logic he claimed to be working with, until the last sentence. The hopelessness in that had crushed Hanni as much as the painfully inadequate list of his family's fate he had stumbled home with. Yet Freddy was so deaf to anything but his own burning need to rescue his sister, he acted as if he hadn't heard his own words. As if the stark message in them couldn't apply to Renny. The only thing that had concerned Freddy was the amount of time Hanni's questions were wasting.

'Don't you see how urgent this is? She could have been adopted. She could have been put on a boat to America or Israel. The trail could be turning cold as we speak. Brack doesn't need me; he'd be glad if I disappeared from the office for a couple of weeks – or months for that matter. So I'm going to Theresienstadt, and I'm going to ask Elias to help me get there. Or to help us. Unless, of course, I have to do this alone.'

There had been a finality in his words when he said that. An unspoken *and if I do, that's us done for* which wasn't fair, but what else could she expect given the state he was in and her obvious reluctance to go along with his plans? She couldn't explain that to him, and it was little wonder that her stalling made no sense. She had never shied from danger, or let Freddy go into danger alone. And now he was facing the hardest challenge of his life. Where else would he expect her to be? Where else should she be but beside him?

And if I do that, if I go with him to Theresienstadt, we are done for anyway.

Hanni climbed out of the unmarked police car Freddy had borrowed to take them into the Soviet-run eastern borough of Mitte, and down the steps into a bar which never saw daylight, feeling sick through to her bones. Freddy's plan was madness; she could think of no other word for it. Even if she could put aside for a moment the sheer terror of returning to such an evil-soaked place and the all-consuming fear of being unmasked there, the journey itself was fraught with danger for both of them.

Theresienstadt was no longer part of a Germanised Bohemia the way it had been in the forties when her father had moved the Foss family there. Now it was in the newly re-established Czechoslovakia, a country which had asserted its independence after the war but had since fallen under Soviet rule. Its borders were hard, its way of life a controlled one. Getting into Czechoslovakia in the first place would involve complex arrangements she doubted even Elias could manage, and – if they made it as far as the border – the journey through it was a total unknown. It was certainly no place for a German detective.

Which means I can't let him face it alone, whatever the cost to me.

Not that Elias was impressed by her loyalty. The first words out of his mouth as he waved them to sit in the corner which served as his office were hardly welcoming ones. 'You're taking her with you? Why?'

Hanni jumped in before Freddy could attempt to offer an answer. 'Because I've been there before, during the war, and I have some idea how the town operated. And, like Freddy, I speak a reasonably competent level of Czech.'

It was a gamble, admitting anything about her past to Elias. He wouldn't believe her carefully prepared answers with the same willingness as Freddy, and he might well decide to go digging into them, but Hanni didn't have a choice. She had learned very quickly that the only way to rebuff Elias's disdain was to stand up to it.

Elias Baar – who had been a leading figure in Berlin's network of gangs before the war and had successfully reclaimed his role as soon as that ended – had been interned in Buchenwald with Freddy. They had watched out for each other there and were as close as brothers now. And Elias did not trust Hanni. He didn't like the fact that she had secrets. He sensed that the shadows she carried were threatening ones.

To his credit, he had kept that dislike between the two of them and had never betrayed his feelings to Freddy. He hadn't commented when Freddy had announced their engagement; he had stood as a witness at their wedding. He had raised a toast to the happy couple at the dinner that followed when he was asked to do it. But he had never once that day smiled directly at Hanni.

Their wedding. That was the last time Hanni and Elias had met and, despite his brooding presence, it had been a truly wonderful day.

And one I need to remember now everything is slipping.

Hanni closed her eyes, suddenly exhausted by the twists of the last few days, and let the two men talk over her. She and Freddy had been so happy then; they had been so happy since. Until the exhibition had turned their life on its head, her wedding ring had felt like a talisman.

'Marry me. Now. Or in a month if you need time to think about flowers and dresses. But let's do it; let's not wait. Life is too short for us to waste any more of it.'

Marriage had been Freddy's idea and, once he had declared how much he wanted it, the days had turned into a whirlwind. He had proposed within weeks of them finally becoming a couple. When Hanni had agreed – because there was nothing in the world she wanted more than to be his wife – his happiness had brightened the world's colours, his delight in her had made it sing. He had swept Hanni along with his dreams of the future, and Hanni had been more than happy to hold on to his hand and surrender to the ride.

In the end, the change in both their careers had made money tight, and his extravagant plans for the wedding day had remained plans.

Freddy refused to have any ties to religion so the ceremony had been held in a rather austere registry office in Graefstraβe and in the presence of a registrar who was too used to people arriving claiming that all their documents had been lost in the war to question Hanni's lack of a birth certificate. Her dress too had been a simple affair, and the bunch of lilies she had carried had barely survived the October chill. Neither of them had cared. They had floated through the day. And then they had gone home, dazzled by the gleam of their wedding rings, and closed the doors on the world for a week.

Their apartment had remained their favourite place to be, the place where they acted out the courtship that the complexities of their relationship had never allowed. Their sofa was every park bench they would have held hands on. Their kitchen table was every restaurant nook they would have curled into and unfolded each other's lives. And their bed was a treasure chest. No one had mattered but them in those first days, and that had never changed.

But it was wrong. My father should have mattered and so should all the family Freddy had lost. If I had been thinking about them and not myself, I would have let him go when he asked me to marry him. And now it's too late, and I'm going to shatter his heart.

'Are you certain you want to go with him?'

Elias's question pulled Hanni out of the sudden panic which had gripped her and back into the bar. She nodded rather than answering him. It was always easier when she kept their transactions short and without explanations.

'Very well then, but I'm not going to lie: I thought this was a mistake when you rang me and I haven't changed that opinion. To say that this won't be an easy undertaking is an understatement. Never mind that Theresienstadt is now inside the Eastern Bloc, Germans are hated in Czechoslovakia: they've never forgiven us for what was done there by the Nazis during the war. You can't afford to let anyone know where you come from. If you couldn't speak any Czech, I wouldn't be helping you to go there at all.'

He glanced over at Hanni as he said that, but she pretended not to see. Elias knew that Freddy, who had a mimic's skill when it came to languages, had developed a fluency for Czech while he was in Buchenwald. He didn't need to know that she had learned it to talk to the prisoners who had shown her the workings of Theresienstadt.

'Fine. But remember that if you are overheard speaking German or if you do anything that suggests you aren't purely Czech, the odds are you'll be arrested. Both of you need to take time to brush up your language skills and familiarise yourselves with the country's customs.'

He produced two sets of papers and gave one pack to each of them.

'You'll be travelling under new identities. Hanni as Hana Havelova and Freddy as Bedřich Havel. You're a married couple from Košice, which is a tiny town no one will have heard of and far enough away from where you are heading to explain anything odd in your accents. You'll travel from Berlin by train through East Germany as far as Dresden, or as near into the city as you can get given that the main stations there are still in chaos from the war. From Dresden you will need to go on foot to a crossing point at Eiland. The guards there are paid well enough to ignore the goods we smuggle through to also ignore you. After that...' Elias shrugged. 'I can give you a map that should help you find a safe route, but the border is the end of my reach. If you get into trouble beyond Eiland, there's nothing I can do.'

He shifted his seat so that he was turned away from Hanni and looking directly at Freddy. 'Don't think for a minute my helping you means that I want you to do this. You're a German police inspector. If that is discovered inside Czechoslovakia and you fall into secret-service hands there, you could be killed as a spy. And I'm sorry to say it but the war doesn't seem to have taught much in the way of tolerance towards Jews, especially now that Stalin's influence is spreading across Eastern Europe. There are more dangers where you're heading than you can possibly imagine, and the chances of this having a good outcome are almost non-existent. So I'll ask you again: do you really want to make this journey?'

'I don't have a choice.'

Freddy's voice was the only sound in the room.

'You know how it was for us, Elias. You know how we came out of Buchenwald burdened by ghosts. You know how hard it was to keep going on the outside when everything that mattered was lost. And you also know what it felt like when some of your missing ones finally came home again, after all the years you'd spent mourning them. I want that feeling. I have a chance of that feeling. And here's the thing, I know that you don't care for Hanni...'

He shook his head as Elias started to speak. 'It doesn't matter – I don't need to know why. What you don't see is the light and the colour and the love that she has brought back to my life. And now she has also brought me hope. Her photograph could mean that one of my family is still alive. I could have them both, Elias: I could have my wife and my sister. I could have more than I ever dreamed could be mine in those days we spent fighting to keep our minds and our bodies together. So I don't care if this trip is dangerous or makes no sense. I have no choice: I'm going. And so, thank God, is she.'

The look Freddy gave her as he said that was so pure, so filled with love that the pain and the fear gripping Hanni's heart melted away. He loved her. He was part of her. What did it matter what came next, if this was what she had now?

Natan was right: he deserves honesty; he deserves the best life he can have. So I'll tell him. As soon as we have some news of Renny, for good or bad, as soon as I know he is strong enough to bear it, I will tell him the truth about me. And if there is any forgiveness to be found, I'll do everything in my power to earn it.

Hanni slipped her hand through Freddy's as they made their way out of the bar. She took him to bed as soon as they returned to the flat. And she lay awake as the morning light filtered around the edge of the curtains, watching his sleeping and finally calm face and hoping against hope for the moon.

CHAPTER 3

APRIL 1945, THERESIENSTADT

'Be a good girl. Don't wriggle when I lift you. Don't make a sound.'

The hand across her mouth was soft and sweet-smelling. But it was still a hand rammed hard across her mouth. Renny kept her eyes squeezed shut. She knew the whispering voice was Galyna's. That didn't stop *it's my turn, they've picked me* roaring like thunder through her head.

'Well done. Stay quiet now.'

The hand moved; Renny didn't. She kept her eyes closed and her body still as she was scooped up and out of her bed, as the door opened with a soft creak and the night air hit her.

'Get a move on. There'll be a patrol coming soon, and the new inmates can't be trusted to stay where they're meant to be.'

The second voice was guttural and harsh and not one Renny knew. She eased her eyes open until she was peering through tiny slits. She was outside, inside Galyna's embrace, balanced beneath a sky which was far too big. Without the window bars criss-crossing it, the moon hung heavy and full and low enough to drop onto her head. She shrank back, and the arms around her tightened.

'Don't worry. You're safe. It's me. It's your mama.'

The last words bit worse than a bed bug. Renny couldn't control herself any longer. She bucked and began kicking, jerking her body away from the one that was holding hers far too close. 'No.'

She never used that word, and the voice didn't sound like her own. The sharp snap belonged to a dog. A dog that could bite and snarl. Its growl wiped away the ever-present *be good*. It made Renny kick harder. If this was a new version of Galyna's night-time 'let's pretend you're my daughter' game, she had no intention of playing it.

'No.'

The word cracked through the cold air a second time. This time the hand that covered her mouth wasn't soft or sweet-smelling. It was sour and meaty, and it slapped.

'Shut her up or leave her behind. I'm not taking a bullet because you're obsessed with a child.'

The rough hand clamped round her face, squashing her mouth, pinching her nose. Then it was gone with one final slap she didn't dare react to, leaving Renny gulping for a breath that was clean. Galyna's head dipped as Renny spluttered, and she whispered into Renny's ear.

'Herr Friedel doesn't mean what he said. He won't leave you here and neither will I, but you have to be quiet, little one, or we will all get into serious trouble.'

Galyna's voice was gentle; she was trying to be kind. Renny could hear that. Now that her eyes were wide open and adjusted to the dark, she could also see that the woman was wearing a smile that was meant to be comforting. It wasn't. The smile hadn't made it to her eyes. It had got stuck at Galyna's lips in exactly the same way as the aunties' mouths froze when the men in uniform told them to cheer up and be thankful.

She's scared. She's as scared as me.

That realisation stilled Renny's kicking feet and silenced her cough.

Galyna's body immediately sagged. 'That's better. Not a sound now, do you promise?'

Renny didn't promise – her skin was still smarting from *it's your mama* – but she didn't say *no* again. She let herself be carried down the deserted streets until the room which had been her home for longer than she could remember vanished. She didn't protest again – or not until the truth of what was happening suddenly hit her.

'But you can't take me away, or how will she know where to find me?'

There was no hand to hush her this time, no panicked command to be quiet. They hadn't heard her. Renny could barely hear herself. Her voice was too light. The wind whipped her words out of her mouth and away. Then suddenly she was in the back of a car, bundled beneath a blanket that smelled of cobwebs and dust, and there wasn't any room for her voice at all.

Renny curled up in the dark and sucked hard on her thumb. The car's bouncing and swaying made her feel sick. Its roar made her head hurt. And every grind of the engine was taking her further away from the one place her mother knew to come back to.

'If we get caught, they'll shoot...'

The rest of the words fell away, muffled by the blanket and the engine. Renny was glad; she didn't want to hear them. She knew what shoot meant. She knew that the man snarling in the front seat was angry and that she didn't like him. She was fairly certain that he didn't like her, or Galyna.

Be a good girl and all this will pass.

She whispered the words over and over until they drowned out *shoot* and began to weave their soothing magic. Her eyelids grew heavy as the car settled into a steadier rhythm. Maybe this was an adventure, like the ones in the stories the aunties told. Maybe Mama would be waiting at the end of it, to be reunited with her necklace like the way the prince with the gold slipper had finally found Aschenputtel.

Renny squeezed her eyes tight until the darkness filled up with colours, crimson and blue and splodges of purple. She concentrated until a picture book opened its pages in her head. She made herself dance across the first page, her arms flung out, her face spilt by a grin.

The image grew bigger than the smelly blanket and the car and the horrible man. It led on to another, with a green hill at the centre and a yellow bird perched on a tree.

Renny grabbed on to the pretty images and began to tell herself a story. About a little girl with dark blonde hair setting out on a journey, who had to face... challenges, that was it, that was the adventure word. And who would find a happy ending when she'd solved all the waiting clues, because there was always a happy ending to be found. She fell fast asleep while she was waiting for the next page to flick over.

'You'll have to carry her if she can't walk. And if you can't manage that, don't go looking to me to help you. We should never have done this; I should never have listened to you. Leaving my post, running away before the conflict is done – where's the honour in that? If Foss hadn't already been called back to Berlin, I'd never have gone along with it. And now the car's a useless lump and there's no chance of fixing it out here. I told you Prague was a stupid choice. Any relatives I still had there will be long gone anyway, given all the Germans fleeing this way. We should have taken our chances and headed for Germany. Foss would have helped me there, he promised me as much.'

On and on the angry voice went. Renny could barely hear it

anymore. Every bit of her body hurt; her feet were on fire. She was so tired she couldn't walk any further; she never wanted to walk anywhere again.

'Maybe that's true, or maybe Foss would have done what he always did: looked out for his own skin and left you to do all the real work. All right, I'm sorry, I shouldn't have said that. I know how much you admire him. We're exhausted, that's all. We need to stop, to eat and rest. She'll be fine in the morning, she's a brave little soul. And Berlin was too far to go, you know that, and too dangerous. Prague's the best choice. We're nearly there, Hauke, we must be. And there will be someone there to help us, you'll see – they won't all have fled. Your family are Czech as much as German; they won't have been harmed.'

Galyna was doing what she always did: talking without taking a breath, calming things down, soothing her bad-tempered husband. All Renny cared about was that she had said stop and sleep. Sleep sounded wonderful; sleep sounded like heaven. But Renny didn't understand where it could happen. They had passed buildings whose square shape should have meant they were houses, but nothing else about them was right. They didn't have roofs or windows, and the walls were battered and black. The smoke-filled stink of the last one had made Renny feel sick. And even if they had wanted to go inside, so would everyone else, and there were far too many other people on the road to fit them all in.

'Don't look at anyone. Don't go near anyone and don't speak to them, even if they speak to you first. We don't know who they are or what their sympathies might be. Do you understand me?'

Renny didn't but she said yes anyway. She had learned very quickly that it was best to do and say what he wanted. Herr Friedel was nothing like his wife. He didn't call Renny 'pet' or 'poppet'. He barely looked at her, and when he spoke, it was only to bark orders. And, although he was dressed in the same tatty old clothes as every other man on the road, Renny instinctively knew that he was one of *them*.

'Over here – come on, sweetheart. And let me take those off. The grass will be kinder to your feet than the stones.'

Galyna had found shoes for her. Proper ones with laces that Renny couldn't do up and soles without holes in them. They were supposed to be life-savers, but they pinched her toes and rubbed her heels. Not that Renny was allowed to complain; she was supposed to be grateful. For the shoes and for everything else, according to Herr Friedel.

She sank down on the grass and stretched out her legs, but the pain didn't stop, and when Galyna pulled the thin leather away, it got worse. Her feet were a mangled mess, covered in blood and burst blisters. She had to stuff both fists in her mouth not to cry.

'I'll carry you tomorrow, poppet. It will be better then, you'll see.'

Renny couldn't imagine a tomorrow, not if it was as endless as today. She burrowed into the nest of coats Herr Friedel had grudgingly built for her under a tree and tried to shape the soft sides into walls. The world outside the room was too wide and too open and too full of people who didn't seem to know about not arguing and not crying and not making a fuss. The wood they had made camp in was as choked as the roads. Fights kept breaking out. There had been more than one heart-stopping scream.

Renny rolled onto her back and put her hands over her ears. The sky's thick black was covered with tiny pinpricks of light. Stars. That was what Galyna had called them. It was a pretty word and a beautiful sight. If Renny stared hard enough she could see them... twinkling. That was it. Sending light down from the heavens to say hello.

Maybe Mama can see the same stars as me.

The idea of sharing the starlight with her mother brought

more tears to Renny's eyes. She blinked them away and switched her attention to the tree arching above her instead. She had thought trees were still and solid things the way that they appeared in books, but the leaves on this one twisted and fluttered, and the branches kept shivering.

'We're going to a beautiful city. We're going to build a home there for the three of us. We're going to be happy, I promise.'

Renny shut her eyes as Galyna fluttered towards her. She didn't want any more games. She didn't want any more promises. She didn't know what a city was, and happiness wasn't Galyna's to give. And she didn't want to hear her say 'call me Mama, please, sweetie; it's best if you learn to sooner rather than later' one more time.

Renny rolled onto her stomach and ignored the hand that patted her shoulder. Galyna could promise whatever she liked; it would never make her into Mama. Renny wished she knew how to make the woman learn that.

Prague wasn't beautiful. Prague was full of spiky towers which reared up as if they were trying to scratch holes in the sky, and it was dirty and ugly and broken. Renny hated it, and she was afraid of it. She wanted to be inside the safe walls of the room again. The roads had been too wide and the woods had been too open, but the city was worse: that was a beast she was certain would swallow her.

Thick grey clouds glowered over the buildings, and the burned smell that had hung over the houses on the journey was worse here. It got into her nose and settled there. The streets crunched with rubble that bit through her shoes. One of the bridges spanning the river was cracked open and gaping. And there were soldiers everywhere, their guns permanently pointing round corners and down alleyways, or at anyone who was brave or foolish enough to look at them. Every time Renny saw one she expected to be shot at – or chosen. It was little wonder that so many people were pouring out of the city, moving in endless columns with their belongings strapped to their backs as if they had all transformed into giant snails.

Renny wanted to run away with them. She didn't want to stay in the damp-smelling cellar that Galyna kept pretending was home. She didn't want to play the hiding game Herr Friedel said made him feel sick and ashamed. And she didn't want to be Renáta Novotná, which was apparently her name now. She couldn't be; she didn't know who that girl was. For the first few days they spent huddled in the cellar, she didn't answer to it on the second or even the third go. Not because she was being wilful and disobedient as Herr Friedel, or *pane* Novotný or whatever he was called now, insisted but because she simply didn't recognise it as hers.

'Can't we just call her Renny, like she's used to? Can't that name do for a little Czech girl as easily as it did for a German? She's a child, Hauke, trying to adjust to a whole new life. Can't you at least try to help her out?'

That plea had led to another argument and another storming away which made the cellar's cracked walls tremble. To another night when Galyna, or *pani* Jana Novotná, sobbed for hours and held on to Renny far too tight.

'We can't upset him, pet. If he leaves, what will we do? I got everything wrong – that's what's makes him so mad, not you. The people we had here are gone and Germans are hated, which will only get worse when the end comes. There's no one to help us, and he blames me for that. And I'm not sure he'll keep believing the story I told him about you, so you have to learn to make him smile, sweetheart. You have to be—'

'Good.'

Renny finished the sentence without thinking. Galyna's tears instantly dried up. Renny stopped being a problem. All at once she was an *angel*, she was *God-given*, she was a *gift*.

Renny listened; she let herself be petted. She added the new words to her list. None of them were true. Renny knew the word that fitted her best – it was the one the children used in the stories when an adventure went wrong. She wasn't an angel, she wasn't a gift.

She was lost.

CHAPTER 4

20–24 MARCH 1950, DRESDEN

'I shouldn't have made you come; I shouldn't have put you in danger. This is my responsibility, not yours. You could turn back at Dresden, Hanni. You could go home to Berlin and wait for us there.'

The way Freddy said *us* made a happy ending to their quest sound like a certainty, but Hanni knew that the word was a bluff, one of the tools he used to convince himself that failure was impossible. There were more and more tools like that.

Once the euphoria of recognising Renny in the photograph had worn off and all the arrangements for the journey were in place – once there was nothing else to do but set out on it – Freddy's faith in the search had started to crack. He was too proud to admit that he was wavering; Hanni was too careful of his emotional state to comment. The visit to Elias, and more specifically the way Freddy had looked at her in the bar and the night that had followed, had made her remember the basis of their bond.

His happiness matters more to me than mine; mine matters more to him than his.

So when Freddy's hopes started to fly, she didn't pull them

down again: she encouraged them to soar. And when they crashed, she didn't beg him to listen to the voice of reason in his head, or in hers, and stop. It was a change he was grateful for, a shift in mood that pulled them back together. It didn't mean Hanni was blind. She saw the doubts clouding his eyes when he thought she wasn't looking. And she had seen the tremor in his hand when they were finally travelling through the German Democratic Republic and the GDR train guard spent too long scrutinising their papers.

'It's unusual to see a police inspector from the West venturing into the East. This conference in Dresden must be an important one.'

Freddy had agreed, very seriously, that it was. Then he had launched into a speech about shared investigative processes still being a focus despite Germany's political divisions, which was horribly flimsy but bored the train guard away.

The instant the man was gone, Freddy's façade collapsed. He crumpled back into his seat and immediately started to fret over Hanni's safety.

'That was rough. That was harder than I expected and those are our legitimate papers. If the Czech ones are subjected to the same level of interest...' Freddy left 'which they will be' unsaid, but it still hung there between them. 'Well, you heard what Elias warned us could happen. I won't blame you if you want to call it quits, Hanni. And I won't hold it against you, no matter how hard I came down on you before.'

It wasn't exactly an apology, and Hanni wasn't looking for one of those – she understood why he had felt let down – but it was good enough, it came from the heart. They had always had a language of their own. They had learned to say 'I love you' and 'I need you' in a myriad different ways while they navigated who they were going to be to each other. They might forget how to use it at times, but, so far, that language had always come back.

Hanni slipped her hand into his, grateful beyond anything for that. 'And since when did I give up on things, or sit waiting at home like a good little wife? It's not your responsibility to find her, my love – it's ours.'

Ours sounded good; it sounded as certain as *us*. Hanni wanted to believe it; she wanted Freddy to believe it. She had filled her voice with all the confidence Freddy had been trying to pour into her for the last three weeks. They had learned how to wrap that – or the imitation of that – around each other as well.

He smiled and pulled her closer. Hanni nestled into his side and took refuge in a silence she hoped Freddy would decide was a companionable one. The last thing her nerves needed was questions. Unfortunately, his senses were still on alert.

'I really needed to hear you say that. You've been so on edge since we left Berlin, I thought you were regretting coming with me.'

Hanni shifted away from him before her stiffening body betrayed her. She thought he had been too busy to notice her fears, or that she had been successfully hiding them.

Tell him who you saw on the platform at Berlin. Tell him why that scared you. Don't hide the truth again, or lie like you did with the Theresienstadt photographs.

It was the right impulse, but Hanni couldn't act on it. The truth – 'there was a man I recognised at the station. He was at my exhibition, behaving oddly, and I think he might be following us' – opened up a minefield. They were about to illegally enter a country where – or so rumour had it – Soviet-backed secret agents were as completely embedded as they were in the GDR. Hanni didn't need Freddy to have even the slightest suspicion that there were eyes already on them. That would only convince him that he was right to be cautious, that he should go on without her.

Which might be the best thing; it would at least get me out of this.

As much as Hanni wanted to support Freddy, she also desperately wanted to turn round and go home. She wanted Theresienstadt to disappear back into history and for Freddy to give up. Except he would never do that, so she couldn't either. Never mind that he might discover secrets in the town which she wouldn't be there to explain, his quest could very easily end in heartache. How could she abandon him to face that pain alone? So she couldn't turn back and she couldn't tell him that they might be being followed, either by a secret agent or by her father. Admitting the possibility of that was unthinkable. It would involve spilling the whole story of Reiner and his web of spies, and it wasn't the time for that yet. Besides, she could be wrong. Hanni wasn't certain that the man she had seen boarding the Dresden train at Berlin's Ostbahnhof was the one who had thrown her off balance at the gallery. His height was similar, and so was the dark hair combed neatly under his hat. But it had been a moment's glimpse in a crowded station. He hadn't turned; she hadn't seen his face.

And why would Reiner set a tail on me when I am so clearly not following him?

Freddy had noticed her nerves but that was all he had noticed, and telling him the truth was too dangerous. So, despite what she had promised herself, it had to be another lie. But a small one; a deflection.

'Of course I'm not regretting it. And yes, I've been a little on edge but it's nothing to worry about.'

Hanni kissed Freddy's cheek and smiled into his eyes, hating how easy it was for her to convince him she was never anything but honest.

'I'm nervous about my language skills, that's all. If I've been quiet it's because I've been running all the phrases and grammar I learned years ago back through my head and testing my fluency. I'm not sure it's as good as it could be.'

That too was a minefield. Hanni had told Freddy that she had learned Czech but she hadn't told him why, and he had been too caught up with Elias's complicated chain of arrangements to ask her. Now that his detective's brain was re-engaged and he was weighing up the journey's dangers, she could see the questions forming. She kissed him again, on the mouth this time, offering a silent thanks for the luxury of an empty carriage.

'So maybe we should take the time now to practise. Run over our cover stories in Czech rather than German and quiz each other about them.'

It was a good suggestion, it did what was required and diverted him. They spent the rest of the journey turning their identity papers into fully fledged characters and helping each other iron out their accents. By the time the train pulled into the tiny suburban station on the edges of the city, which was as close as the rail line still went, Freddy's nerves had vanished and his enthusiasm was racing.

He helped her down the steep step and onto the platform, holding on to her hand as they weaved their way through the press of people and bags. Hanni knew how they appeared to the world, there were enough admiring glances to tell her: like a couple perfectly in step and in tune with each other. It was what she wanted them to be, and she knew Freddy would have agreed with that assessment if anybody had asked him.

What would he do if he knew the truth? If he knew what a good actress I've become? How devastated would he be then?

The thought of that was as bad as the lying.

The war's bombs and street battles had hit Berlin hard; parts of the city still bore the scars five years later. Hanni and Freddy were used to the sight of broken, half-restored buildings and streets suddenly turning into rubble-strewn wastelands, but nothing had prepared them for the old town of Dresden. That was a horror show, a shock to their souls.

They stumbled through what was left of its centre, trying to square the city's nickname – Florence on the Elbe – and the stories of its magnificent architecture with the carnage around them. It couldn't be done. Dresden's once fabled beauty had been reduced to a myth, its splendour smashed to pieces by a series of devastating bombing raids in February 1945. And the ruins of that carnage were still everywhere. They were impossible to look at and impossible to move around.

Elias's map had taken them into the city, and it showed them the exit but didn't offer any clues beyond broad strokes on how to navigate their way through. Some streets had vanished. Others had their names roughly painted onto cracked walls or wooden signs in lettering which was too haphazard to read. The roads and pavements were choked with rubble, the paths cut into the toppled masonry as hard to steer through as the twists of a maze. Churches and palaces whose walls and arches had been reduced to a memory shivered above them as if the bricks no longer had the strength to hold on.

'I knew it was fire-bombed and turned into an inferno. My father was—'

Hanni stopped herself before she could describe Reiner's fury over the hell that had been unleashed on the city by the RAF bombers.

'Well everyone who knew what had happened was horrified. But this? It's been five years. How can buildings reduced to this state still be standing? How haven't they all fallen down?'

Hanni's fingers itched to scoop up the camera hidden in the bottom of her bag and start snapping. The destruction around her was imprinted with agony. It was far worse than she had expected, far worse than the blurred images she had seen in the days after the raid took place. It needed to be captured and shown. She managed to rein the impulse in, although Freddy had apparently forgotten the need for discretion.

'*Why* are they still standing would be a better question to ask than how. To make some political point about the cruelty of the Allied bombers? To remind everyone how bad the West is and make them toe their new Soviet masters' line?' He dropped his voice as Hanni glared at him. 'I don't see why it hasn't been cleared away, that's all. It's a constant reminder of devastation and death. How does that help anyone?'

Hanni followed him down another twisting, torn-up street, sneaking a glance over her shoulder as he stomped on ahead. She hadn't seen the man from the platform since they had left Berlin, but that didn't mean she'd imagined him. They hadn't left their carriage on the train, and the hiding places offered by the ruins were endless.

'Perhaps the people who live here can't, or don't want to, forget what was done to them. The damage inflicted on Berlin was bad, but this...'

She stared up at another roof whose few remaining wooden beams were blackened and fossilised, her head filling with the details from the classified reports Reiner had forced her to read, 'because you don't seem to know who the enemy is'. The fires that had flared so hot they were white and so strong they melted iron and steel and turned stone to dust. The roads in flames, their tarmac bubbling. The people suffocated by the scorched air and burned up in their thousands. They were standing in the middle of what had become a monument to the savagery men could inflict on each other, and it was unbearable.

'Hatred did this, and hatred has kept it all standing. That was what the war was soaked in. And where we're going, the things that were done in the places we will pass through, never mind in Theresienstadt, they will be soaked through with the same hatred too.'

Hanni stopped. She had never been the type of person who latched on to echoes, pretending that they spoke to her in a way that they couldn't – she had witnessed too much real horror to indulge that. But these broken buildings still pulsed, and she couldn't get a breath. Her chest was tight, the flimsy walls and shattered roofs pushing down, crowding in. Her throat was as dry as if the smoke that had once eaten up the city had come pouring back. Her ears throbbed as if they were filled with the screaming. And the skin on her arms itched and smarted so badly she was terrified that, if she glanced down at her hands, they would be glowing red, or melting.

'Hanni. Hanni, look at me. Come back.'

Freddy was at her side, kneeling by the tumble of stones she had sunk down onto, holding tight to her shoulders as if she was swaying.

'I was there, for a moment. I could smell it; I could taste the smoke in my mouth.' She shuddered and pulled herself upright. 'I'm sorry – I'm being ridiculous.'

Freddy pressed his lips to her hair and helped her back to her feet.

'It's all right. You haven't eaten for hours and this place...' He shook his head. 'It would make even the hardest heart fanciful. Come on. We need to find a room well away from here. We need food and sleep. We've got a very long walk ahead of us.'

He picked up her bag, ignoring her protests that she was fine, and set off at a pace that quickly took them out of the worst of the bomb sites and into a newly rebuilt and far blander setting. The landlady who took them in charged an extortionate rate and cooked them an indifferent meal, but the bed was soft and wide, and they were both very happy to be in it.

His arms helped. Sleep helped. The spring-scented air that greeted them the next morning helped. They agreed to look forward and to put Dresden and its horrors behind them. They set out for the border holding tightly on to each other, one repeating that everything would be fine if the other fell suddenly silent, Freddy insisting that Elias wouldn't fail them. And that the war and its horrors was a very long way away.

That was a fiction Freddy clung to far longer than Hanni was able to. She could only pay lip service to the idea that everything really would be fine, but he was determined to believe it, and anything that wasn't a setback soon became a success.

'He'd never forgive me for saying it, especially if any of his men overheard me, but I swear Elias is my guardian angel. Whenever I need him, he's there – sporting a knuckleduster maybe, rather than a set of feathery wings, but still. Perhaps we should have brought him along with us for luck.'

Luckily Freddy wasn't expecting an answer, or looking at Hanni when he spoke. The thought of Elias let loose to dig around in Theresienstadt, or watching her trying to pretend that she wasn't sickened to be there, flipped her stomach. Not that she could argue with Freddy's assessment. Elias had made their journey – Dresden notwithstanding – a far smoother undertaking than either of them had expected it to be.

Once Freddy had handed over the letter he had been instructed to give to the Czechoslovakian border guards, they were waved past with barely a glance at their papers, and their luck had continued to hold. The guards were uninterested, the route Elias had pointed them towards was deserted and the finely detailed map he had provided them with was a godsend. Elias had warned them that the first part of their journey – through a range of rocky mountains and thick forests – would be a scramble. They had come prepared, but it was the map with its carefully located landmarks more than their boots and warm jackets which got them from one side of the rough terrain to the other. And the village they came to as they dropped into the first valley was as secluded and silently welcoming as he had promised it would be. It was clear that Elias's reach extended far further beyond the border than he had admitted.

'The road he's got us on is a longer smuggling route than I thought he controlled, and I don't want to know what goods he brings down it. But it's served its purpose – it leads almost as far as we need to go.'

Freddy squinted at the map's contours and symbols and held it closer to the candle, which was the only light source in the barn they were housed in.

'See.' He held it across to her. 'The final landmark he's highlighted is only a handful of kilometres from Terezin. A town called Litoměřice. Maybe it'll have a hotel. Maybe we could stop there and use it as a base while we see how Terezin operates.'

'No, not a chance! I'm not going there!'

It took Hanni a moment to match up the Czech names Freddy was determined to practise with the German ones – Leitmeritz and Theresienstadt – she was used to. The instant she did, she panicked, she couldn't help herself, and she batted the paper away.

'Why? What on earth is the problem with Litoměřice? I've never even heard of it.'

Freddy picked the map up out of the straw where it had landed and started smoothing out its creased corners. Hanni struggled to get her face and her voice under control, thankful that he was focused on Elias's directions and not on her. She couldn't think of an explanation for her outburst that she could use. That wouldn't require her admitting that Litoměřice was where she had lived, in a palatial villa requisitioned for SS use, for almost two years during the war. Until she caught sight of the way the towns and hamlets had been marked on the map and a lifeline appeared.

'It's too big.'

Once the idea came, she ran with it.

'Litoměřice is too big. Elias kept everything to scale and look at the way he's drawn the town. Where we are now – a tiny cut-off village that doesn't seem to have changed for decades – is one thing, but it will be very different there. This area we're in is the part of Czechoslovakia that was once called Bohemia. Don't you remember what Elias told us about that? It was a protectorate. It wasn't only under German control, it was Germanised. Czech culture was banned, as well as their language. The swastika replaced their flag. And Litoměřice was at the centre of all the repression so life in the town must have been drastically changed. There'll be scars there still.'

Hanni stopped. She couldn't remember how much of that was what Elias had told them and how much had come from her own memories. And she couldn't allow Freddy enough time to start wondering.

'The point I'm trying to make is that Litoměřice is surely going to be one of those places he warned us about. Where anything and everything German is hated and even people who could claim Czech as well as German heritage have been thrown out. A hotel is impossible; going there at all is impossible. We'd be sure to attract more interest and questions there than we have here, and I'm not confident that we've got a strong-enough grip on our stories. I'd really rather not be tested yet, if it can be avoided.'

That much was true. Hanni didn't want them to be tested at all, never mind yet: she didn't think they would pass. From the comments she had overheard about the two of them in the village, their knowledge of Czech words would hold steady, but their accents still hit the stresses in all the wrong places.

What Hanni actually wanted was for the two of them to stay hidden and quiet the rest of the way to Theresienstadt. Once they got that far, there wouldn't be any need to keep up the pretence that they were Czech and not German. And they had agreed – or Freddy had proposed and Hanni had had no choice but to go along with it – that they would go back to their real identities when they got to the town itself. He was convinced that the Red Cross would be able to offer them some protection against local hostility and, as he had quite logically pointed out, 'What's to be gained by me hiding who I am? All that will do is get in the way of the search.' As to the need for having more confidence with their new identities after that...

Unlike Freddy, Hanni had no real belief that there would be an after that, beyond a return home which she hoped Freddy would be able to make in one piece. She couldn't believe it because she knew all too well how Theresienstadt had worked. Every instinct told her there was little chance that the trail would end in anything but the tragedy of Renny's deportation, or her death. Or, more likely, a disappearance that, like so many others, could never be explained. That outcome would be terrible. It would break him. Even the warning of it could break him. So Hanni stayed silent and prepared herself instead for the grieving she knew would have to be done in Theresienstadt, the last place where Freddy could place his family. She had convinced herself that remaining inside its walls and staying steady while he faced his pain was something she could do. That if her secret held for one day in the town then it would stay hidden. She was trying harder to believe that. And then, when he was ready, she would take him home to Berlin and...

When he's through the worst of it. When he's safe again and I think his heart can bear it, then I'll do what I have to and tell him who I really am.

She pushed *but what if your switch from Hannelore to Hanni doesn't hold up in Theresienstadt?* away. She refused to hear *but what if the first person you meet recognises you? Or wouldn't telling him now be the most honest thing to do, when he's still got hope for his sister and isn't already broken?* She told herself instead that the truth was too big a step in this place, with so much still at stake. She decided to trust that some of the luck Elias had sprinkled over the journey would rub off on her. That waiting was the kindest thing. That was something else she was determined to believe.

'You're right.'

Hanni was so absorbed in her own thoughts, she had forgotten what they'd been talking about. When she gazed at Freddy blankly, he waved at the map again.

'Spending time in Litoměřice isn't a risk worth taking. There'll be another road, another way round. I'll find us a safer route, even if it takes longer. And we can go straight to Terezin rather than hanging about trying to find out how it works from the outside. Why build in delays?'

He smiled at her with the boyish smile that was only ever hers; the open one filled with love that always made Hanni's heart leap.

'We're so close. Another day or two and we'll be there. To a place which took my parents' lives but where my sister could have survived the end of the war, and that's what I need to focus on. I do know how crazy this is, even if I pretend not to. And I'm not the kind of man who believes in signs or good omens, but don't you see? All we've had so far is luck, and that's going to continue. I'm certain of it. We're going to find her, Hanni. I truly believe that we are going to find Renny.'

It wasn't bluff this time. Freddy's eyes were too bright and too clear for any doubt to be lurking. Hanni had to look away from him before he could see the tears welling in hers.

There's nothing coming for him, and for me, but pain.

She shook herself. The *me* didn't matter; how could it? The pain coming for Freddy was none of his doing; the pain coming for her was what she deserved.

She reached out for him and matched his smile with all the warmth left in her body. And she spent the rest of the candle-light hours making sure his hopes flew.

CHAPTER 5

25–26 MARCH 1950, THERESIENSTADT

'The Red Cross? You're too late, they shipped out a couple of weeks ago. If it's them you're after, you're best going back where you came from.'

The man wasn't hostile; he was matter of fact. And he wasn't interested in answering any more questions. He walked away, leaving Freddy's confidence in tatters.

'They can't have gone. I was relying on them to be here, to have answers. What am I supposed to do now, if everyone else is as unhelpful as him?' He stared at the square buildings lining what was clearly a recently swept street. 'There's order here, you can see it, so there has to be someone in charge. There has to be someone I can speak to.'

There has to be someone I can speak to? Why would he choose those words?

The moment they had stepped through Theresienstadt's black-and-white arch, Hanni's grip on the present had started to loosen. She had fought that, trying to focus on why they were there, breathing deeply, refusing to let her hands shake or the shadows thicken. She had tried to walk under the grass-covered ramparts and along the town's wide streets as if they didn't hold any significance for her. As if she couldn't see the ghost of her younger self wherever she looked. It hadn't worked; there were too many echoes. But she had been clinging on, trying to be a support not a weight. Until Freddy's choice of words tripped her.

There has to be someone I can speak to.

With that one simple phrase, the memories surged back. First the smells that had once layered over Theresienstadt as thickly as mud: dirt and neglect and fear. Then the sounds that still plagued her dreams: the marching feet, the bark of an order; the quiet, hopeless sobs that had once filled the attics. And finally a ghost who was more than a shape, who had a face and a name. A desperate pleading ghost who came to her now as he had done then: trailing the fate of so many others. He had spoken those exact words to her, almost in this exact spot.

Hanni shook her head, but she couldn't dislodge him. She could hear Freddy's distress as his plans fell apart. She could hear his voice rising. She knew that he was in the grip of the kind of raw panic that hadn't struck him for years. It was horrible to hear him in so much pain and to be so utterly powerless to help him, but Hanni's brain was clouded, the years all colliding. She wasn't sure that, if she reached out, it would actually be Freddy standing there.

Hanni was inside Theresienstadt, she knew that. She was standing on the edge of the bleak space which had once been laughably known as the Market Square, opposite the hospital where she had taken some of her most distressing pictures. She knew that too. But as for the rest... The rest was shifting until she wasn't in March 1950 anymore. She was in September 1944 and the man begging her for help wasn't Freddy, but he was also white-faced and shaking.

·   ·   ·

'Why aren't the cameras rolling? What's the delay this time? Didn't I make it clear that this has got to be finished by the end of the week?'

Hannelore flinched as her father stormed round the corner, his whip held high and cracking.

'Where's that idiot Gerron?'

There was a snort of laughter from one of the guards as Reiner caught sight of the empty chair emblazoned with *Director* and sent it flying. A second later, the dazed guard who had laughed was wiping blood from his cheek.

'He either appears by the time I'm done counting or I start shooting his precious extras.'

Reiner tucked his whip into his belt loop. His hand moved to his holster. The guards dropped their cigarettes and straightened up. The hundreds of prisoners who had been gathered and scrubbed and pressed into startlingly clean clothes froze into one solid mass. Nobody spoke. Nobody was foolish enough to look directly at Reiner, including Hannelore.

'I'm sorry, Herr Gerron, I really am. I want to help you, but whatever it is you need has got to wait. You have to go out where he can see you. You have to restart. He's not bluffing: you know as well as I do that's something my father never does.'

Kurt Gerron, the director – and prisoner – whose chair was now upended and broken, took a step forward at Hanni's frantic urging, and then he turned back instead and grabbed at her arm again.

'You don't understand, Fräulein Foss – there's no time for waiting. There has to be someone I can speak to. This was supposed to save them; it was supposed to save us all. That's why so many people agreed to take part in it. But...'

His *but* disappeared as Reiner raised his pistol and began counting, jumping far too quickly down the numbers from ten. A whimper broke free from the crowd, pushing Gerron out of the shadows and into a place where Reiner could see him.

'I'm here, I'm here. There's no need for anyone to get hurt. A small script issue, that's all. The deadline is in hand; everything required will be done.'

Gerron – whose once heavy body was now all pouches and folds – bundled back to where his cast was waiting, his voice booming as if he was addressing a Hollywood film set, not a man holding the power of life and death over everyone currently shrinking away from him. Hanni saw Reiner twitch at the director's overfamiliar greeting. For a moment she was certain that Gerron would be the one who met with a bullet. There was a collective sigh of relief as Reiner holstered his gun.

Gerron – who was no fool despite all his bluster – began to reassemble his scene as the camera rolled into position. Everyone was instructed to 'ramp up their energy'. Hanni had no idea how the prisoners – some of whom were visibly shaking – were supposed to manage that. It was the third week of filming and not even being clean and, on some days, decently fed could outweigh their fear. The documentary Gerron was shooting, at the insistence of the SS, was intended to show the world how kindly the 'residents' of Theresienstadt were treated, but the production was no more kindly than the world its actors actually lived in. It had become a monster of long hours and bad tempers and threats.

The film's working title was *The Führer Gives a City to the Jews*. Its set was all the areas which had been beautified a few weeks earlier for the Red Cross visit. And its cast was the town's exhausted and hungry inhabitants, or a version of them in which they were well fed and well housed and grateful. It was a sham, another orchestrated spectacle Hannelore was desperate to capture and to unmask.

She had failed with the Red Cross delegation: they had taken no notice of her at all, and the photographs she had been so certain she could get them to carry out into the world had remained in the bottom of her bag. Hannelore was determined to do better this time. She made friends with the cameramen who had been sent from Prague to shoot the footage and made herself useful to them. She took pains to praise their skill and not to rail against what they were doing. She took the same care with her father, focusing on the technical aspects of the filming, rather than the lies the cameras would capture. She forced herself to be impressed. She doubted Reiner was fooled for a moment, but he had been amused enough to let her walk relatively freely around all the sets. So Hannelore came into the town every day that the film was under production, waiting for no one to care where she was. Whenever that moment came, she prowled behind each staging area, taking more candid shots than the film itself would ever contain.

Shots of the children who had been left behind, hungry and neglected in the overcrowded nurseries. Who didn't look Jewish enough to play on the swing boats or the rocking horses which had been specially brought in, or eat the slices of thickly buttered bread which had to be nibbled by the cast as if hunger was an unknown in Theresienstadt. Shots of the men who had been starved so long and worked so hard that their chests were sunken and spindly. Who weren't considered fit enough to be put on parade shirtless, pulling vegetable-laden wagons and swinging their scythes in the fields like the ones who had more recently arrived. And of the thin women who were riddled with consumption and couldn't stop coughing, whose hollowed-out bodies couldn't be concealed by a pretty dress.

Those weren't easy pictures to take – they demanded a speed and a secrecy which wasn't always possible. When those conditions couldn't be guaranteed, Hannelore prowled among the actors, angling her camera so that it focused on their faces, the blank spaces where the real story of Hitler's gift was being told.

'It won't work; it can't. I can direct their bodies, but I can't do a thing with their eyes and their souls. And when Foss sees that, when he sees how their emptiness makes a lie of the film...'

Hanni had overheard Gerron whisper that to his wife, on a long night when the director was exhausted by the insults the guards continually rained on him as he tried to turn hell into a flower-filled playground. It was the first time Hanni had seen or heard anything more from the man than a pompous show. She knew that Gerron – who had been an actor in the outside world – had been forced into the director's chair, but she had presumed it was a role he relished. He certainly carried himself round the sets like a king. And then he had sought her out when no one was looking, 'because you are a fellow artist and you have your father's ear', and the only thing he was carrying was fear.

Which means I need to try and quickly find out what 'this was supposed to save them' means, and how he thinks I can help.

Hannelore watched Gerron pick up his chair and reset the scene – families strolling through the gleaming Market Square as if wandering there was an everyday activity, pointing with delight at shops which were empty façades – as Reiner stood with his fists on his hips by the camera and glowered.

'Where will the film be seen when it's finished?'

She turned to a young guard as she spoke. He immediately squared his shoulders and tried to look older.

'In Germany of course. And in Italy and Switzerland. After that, or so those of us trusted to work on it have been told, copies will be distributed to America and Britain, to show them how decent Germans really are.'

Hanni smiled at him and pretended not to notice his deepening blush. It was a risk asking the guard anything more, but she sensed that she had to try and find out what the intentions behind the documentary really were if she was going to be of any use to Gerron.

'Well didn't I pick the right man to talk to.'

She leaned in closer so that their heads were almost touching and he could smell the perfume in her hair. The boy's eyes misted; a sheen appeared across his top lip.

'And it's all very clever what's been done here, but, between you and me, isn't it a bit of a risk? Isn't anyone even the slightest bit worried that someone who shouldn't will tell the... well, that one of the cameramen might perhaps let slip that the town isn't always as clean and tidy and well provisioned as this? Or one of the prisoners who appears in the film might be moved to a different camp and spread rumours?'

The effect of her words was instant. The guard's face hardened.

Hanni stepped back as he frowned, horribly aware that, once again, she might have misjudged the situation and caused more harm by interfering than good.

'Forget it – I shouldn't have said anything so foolish.'

But he wasn't listening. He was looking out over the cameras and the crowds scurrying into position with a smile that should never have appeared on such a young boy's face.

'How would that happen? The cameramen are all loyal servants of the Reich, and as for the prisoners... Why do you think that they'll be a problem? There won't be another camp for them: once the filming is finished, everyone who was in it will be cleared.'

Cleared.

It was yet another bland word the regime used to hide its murders and its hatreds and its lies behind. Another that rinsed away the venom and the suffering.

Hanni stared across the square, seeing it as it had been within days of the film production's ending. Neglected again. Forbidden again. Hearing the streets round it filled with the sound of tramping feet as its cast was herded onto the trains which would take them to Auschwitz. The guard had told her the truth: they had all been taken away. All the children who had been forced to laugh and the women who had been forced to smile. All the couples who had posed hand in hand for the camera, including Gerron and his wife. Thousands of them, anyone who the film had touched, packed onto the trains and murdered.

As for the film itself...

Hanni had no idea what had happened to that. There had been one showing, a specially invited evening put on by Reiner for the camp personnel and the SS officers from the Jewish Affairs Department in Prague who had commissioned it. Hanni had invented a migraine to miss that: she didn't want to sit in an audience mocking the naivety of the dead. And she had too vivid a memory of Gerron turning towards her during the last days of filming, telling her to relax, to link arms with her father and his second-in-command and smile.

Hanni had left Theresienstadt and wiped the film from her mind. She didn't know where the copies that were presumably made of it went; she doubted anyone but a handful of men did. None of the reports or the trials at the end of the war had mentioned it; no pictures of its lies had surfaced.

But I have the photos I took behind the scenes. So the film must be the subject of the next exhibition I do. It must be the next story I tell.

The few undeveloped photographs she had taken weren't anywhere close to enough, but they were real, they were something. And if showing them stacked the deck against Reiner...

'Hanni. For God's sake, will you stop daydreaming and listen to me. The Red Cross have left, didn't you hear? I don't know what to do. I don't know how this place worked when Renny was here or...' Freddy stared at the knots of people gathering outside buildings which were badly run-down but clearly inhabited. 'Or what on earth it's become now. Is there anything you can remember? Is there anything that could help?'

Is there anything you can remember?

The sudden jolt out of memories that were so vast and so damning made the question impossible, laughable even. Hanni swallowed hard before the panicked impulse to do that turned into tears. She needed to pull herself together and be the reliable partner he thought he'd brought with him.

Focus on Freddy. Helping him is what you can do now. The rest of it has to wait.

That was an easier prospect. She took his hands and waited till his breathing, and hers, slowed.

'I'm sorry, I got lost in the past, but I'm back with you now. Maybe there is something, yes. The way this place was organised was very different to the way you described how Buchenwald worked. The SS gave the orders and the guards kept discipline, but there was a Jewish Council which was responsible for the day-to-day running. I don't know what records they kept, but they did have an administration building, I remember that much. If that's still here, it could be a start.'

That lifted his mood. His face unclenched, he followed her with a more determined step through a grid of streets Hanni pretended to get confused by. The sense of being watched was worse here than when she had convinced herself they were being followed. She grew more certain with every step that she would be recognised. She pulled her hat down and kept her face averted as the curious and potentially dangerous inhabitants of Theresienstadt – if, although Hanni found it hard to believe, that's who the watchers were – began to emerge from the town's doorways to stare.

Keep your contacts to a minimum; stay hidden.

She hung on to that mantra as if it was a lucky charm. But

Theresienstadt had changed in the years since she had left it. It was no longer a place that tolerated secrets, and pulled-down hats and turned-away faces only ignited its interest.

Hanni hurried on, holding on to Freddy's hand so tight he had to ask her to loosen her grip. Aware that they were being scrutinised and weighed up, feeling her skin getting thinner. The further away they got from the entrance, the more panicked she grew until her feet stopped obeying and she came to an abrupt halt.

'Maybe this isn't such a good idea. Maybe we need to prepare more; maybe we should go away and rethink.'

But Freddy wasn't listening. He was staring ahead at a building which still bore a Red Cross flag, and where a reception committee was waiting.

'I remember her.'

Her. Not the hammer blow of *you*. The relief was so overwhelming, it was a moment before Hanni realised the true meaning of what had just been said. Freddy had understood it immediately: he was half out of his chair.

'You saw Renny in here? You saw my sister?'

Once Freddy had raced through their reason for coming, the reception committee had turned from silent and watchful to welcoming, and they had found the person they needed. Irene Eichwald was as German as they were and, if the title the other residents had bestowed on her was anything to go by, she was clearly at the centre of the town's affairs. The Record Keeper. Freddy had started to breathe far more easily when he heard the certainty in that name. Hanni had almost choked at the thought of what those records might hold.

Now, Irene studied the photograph again and nodded, while Freddy stared at her as if she had been cast out of gold.

'But that's incredible; that's the best news. When was it?

This picture was taken in the summer of 1944. Was it then that you saw her?'

Irene shook her head. 'No, I remember seeing her, but it was much later than that. I wasn't sent here until February 1945, until the last Jews who were still holding out in mixed marriages were finally swept up. That was my husband's doing – he did everything he could to keep me safe. He refused to divorce me, even when he lost his job and was beaten senseless for the sin of not handing me over himself. We left Berlin after that happened and moved to a small village. Lived the quietest of quiet lives. But then, in 1945 when the war was as good as done, they came for me. And they shot Erich as they marched me away.'

She paused, blinked, straightened.

'Which is my story and not the one you need. I came here and here I still am. And I remember your sister, Inspector Schlüssel. I can tell you that, in February 1945 at least, she was alive.'

Freddy's mouth was open but his voice was gone. Hanni – who hadn't spoken since they were ushered into the building, who had barely breathed until *remember* was followed by *her* – realised that the news could be the holy grail they had been hoping for and finally found hers.

'But that's wonderful, that's exactly what we wanted, as long as you're sure it was Renny. Can you be, sure I mean? Weren't there thousands of other children here then?'

Irene's eyes were pale and watchful. Hanni suddenly realised how well The Record Keeper fitted her: she looked like a woman for whom details were food.

'No, there weren't. Thousands did pass through here it's true, but very few survived to the end. By the time I arrived, the number of little ones who had been spared sickness or, for most of them, the trains, was down to a few hundred.'

The trains. Hanni had seen those go out, crammed with

terrified people cowering from Reiner's whip. The thought of Renny being pushed onto one of those was unbearable. She willed herself not to crumble as Irene picked the photograph up again, tracing a finger across it as if to absorb its story.

'There were a lot more people here when I arrived, and in the weeks after, than when the town started. The deportations had stopped the November before I came, because the Russians were advancing and the Nazis were afraid that the soldiers might get too close to the trains, or to the ovens which were their final destination. And then in the April so many more prisoners descended. They were in an unbearable state, even worse than anyone here. Wrapped in rags, bone-thin, barely clinging to life. They'd been uprooted from the camps Hitler didn't want found, crammed into trains or marched here, most of them only days out from death. There wasn't enough food. There wasn't enough space. The new inmates had to be herded behind barbed wire to stop the infections they carried from killing the rest of us. There was a madness soaked into this place in those days that ran so thick even hell isn't the right word for it. There was talk of gas chambers being built; the building work had started...'

Irene paused again and did the blink and straighten Hanni could now see was a reset, a pushing away of the past. She gave the photograph back to Freddy, who clutched it so hard the corners curled, and reverted to a less emotional retelling.

'Then it was over, the last of the SS and the guards finally fled, and the Red Cross came and brought us some semblance of order. But that was April. In February, there was still some of what passed for normality here. That picture was taken in the Ward for Motherless Children; I recognise the beds. Your sister must have been put there after your mother was...' Irene shrugged. 'The point is that I used to help out there now and again as one of the aunties, the women whose job it was to...

well, look after the children implies more care than we had the time or permission to give. An aunty went to the ward for a few hours a day. To keep the children disease-free and quiet. To make sure the littlest ones got a share of the food. And I remember your sister because she was...'

The pause that followed wasn't a reset. For the first time since Irene had taken charge of answering Freddy's questions, the pause was a stumble. And the silence that followed it was too long.

Someone had to ask what *she was* should have ended in. Hanni was about to jump in, to save Freddy having to do it. When Irene had said that out of the thousands of children who had arrived, only hundreds had survived, he had looked so sick Hanni didn't think he was capable of pushing on. But Freddy had recovered himself. He was no longer grey. He had slipped back inside his calm detective's skin. He leaned forward before Hanni could intervene.

'Tell me, Irene, what you were going to say. Whatever else she was, Renny was alive. Two years after I thought she was dead, eight months after what I thought was the last sighting of her, she was alive. I came here with hope, and you have given me more of it. So whatever word it is that stopped you, use it.'

Hanni sat in silence, her fingers clenched as Irene looked as intently at Freddy as he was looking at her.

'I was going to say chosen, Inspector. But I felt that, like selected, that word comes now with too many of the wrong connotations. So perhaps the right word is special.'

'Special to who?'

It was such a small question, said in such a quiet way. It shouldn't have had the power to shift the air, to make the floor shiver. But it did.

Hanni turned to Freddy, but he was oblivious to anyone but Irene. The two of them had moved into a place of their own where Hanni knew she had no right to be. She sat back, willing whatever was said next to be good news.

When Irene started speaking again, her voice was as quiet as Freddy's had been.

'There was a woman who came to the ward, almost every day. She called herself an aunty and demanded that everyone else call her that too. But she wasn't one of us. She wasn't a prisoner; she was a wife. And the only child she was interested in was your Renny. She had... I don't really know how to describe it except to say it was some kind of a fixation on the girl. She played a game where she pretended Renny was her daughter. It was strange; it made the other children uncomfortable. But she was a wife, so there was nothing to be done.'

'Did you know her name?'

Hanni didn't know how Freddy could hold himself so calmly together, but he did.

Irene shook her head. 'No. I was told not to ask and I knew better than to disobey orders. This was a place that ran on punishment and I wanted to survive. She was pretty, I do remember that. Big green eyes and honey-blonde hair. But she was also one of them: she could turn from a smile to a snarl in a heartbeat.'

A wife. One of them. With her hands on Renny.

Hanni could see the same thought flashing across Freddy's face. And quickly turning into horror.

She reached for his hand, held tight to it. *A wife.* She racked her brains but she couldn't think of anyone who matched the green-eyed description. Not that she had met many of the officers' wives. Her mother's fragile health meant that there were fewer entertainments hosted at the family house than Reiner would have liked, and the wives tended to live in Prague rather than in the 'provincial backwater' she had once heard Leitmeritz described as.

When they were herded into the garrison – to attend one of

the entertainments the prisoners were encouraged to put on for the SS to mock – they clustered together in a tight-knit group, desperately pretending that they were somewhere far grander. Attracting the attention of a wife wasn't good. That one of them would visit the nursery in the first place was odd. But what Hanni really couldn't understand was why any of them would single out a little Jewish girl for attention.

Freddy voiced the same question, but Irene had no clear answer to offer.

'I can't tell you. Maybe the woman was a fantasist. Maybe she wanted a child of her own and it hadn't happened for her. Your sister didn't look Jewish – or not in the way that the Nazis pictured us; she could have passed for a little Aryan girl. And she wasn't only pretty herself, she was a calm and self-contained little thing. She didn't make a fuss when the woman petted her, which isn't as straightforward as it sounds. By that stage, some of the little ones who had been here too long would have screamed and bitten her hand.'

There was a silence while both Hanni and Freddy tried to digest the implications of that and couldn't bear the picture of neglect and deprivation the image conjured up. And were left with only one question to ask.

'Do you know what happened to Renny – or to the wife? Are either of them listed in your records?'

Freddy couldn't keep the hope from his voice this time. Hanni's heart ached as she waited for Irene to dash it.

'I don't personally know what happened to either of them, I'm afraid. Once the refugees started flooding in, I was rarely with the children. And I didn't see Renny or the woman again once the Red Cross came, which – given the muddle we were in by then – could mean something or nothing. As for the records...'

She got up and crossed to the bank of filing cabinets which covered the back wall.

'The Record Keeper is a very grand title for the little I manage to do here. Almost everything is gone.'

She pulled open one of the lower drawers, which they could see was half-empty. 'When I first came here, these were crammed full. Every prisoner and every staff member was recorded. But then the Russians drew closer, the refugees overwhelmed us and the Nazis scrambled to destroy anything that would give away the scale of their crimes. They burned almost everything, including the majority of the staff records. Some of us tried to hide what documents we could... some of us paid dearly for that. We tried to register all the new transports, but it was overwhelming. So what I have now is scraps and memories. That's why the Red Cross left – they couldn't help the people like you who come searching. And it's why I can't leave, because somebody has to keep trying.'

Irene began opening the rest of the drawers and pulling folders out.

'I'm not the only one who has made a strange kind of home in this place; you've seen that for yourself. People have stayed, or drifted back, because there is nothing for them in the world outside anymore. We have rebuilt what we could; we have learned the skills we need to put food on our tables. We have made a community here – one that is wary of strangers perhaps, but you have to allow us that – and the new regime, for now, leaves us alone. But none of us have escaped the past. We have all suffered loss; we all want others to find what we can't.'

She handed one pile of files to Freddy and another to Hanni and carried on pulling out more.

'These are what the Red Cross left behind, because they were too incomplete to be of much use to them. That doesn't mean that we shouldn't try. And people will come and help. If your sister – or the woman who potentially kept Renny alive, at least until the last days of the war – is in here, we will find them.

We all want a success story, Inspector. We all need that. Let's hope that it's you and your sister.'

It wasn't.

Nobody they needed was there, although the group of volunteers Irene gathered together combed through every piece of paper the room contained. Nobody but Irene had ever worked on the Motherless Children's Ward so Renny's photograph was admired, but it was of no practical use. Freddy was left with nothing when dawn broke except another dead end and the suspicion that a woman whose every belief he loathed could have somehow saved his sister. He didn't know whether to be grateful for that or terrified. And he wasn't prepared to give up.

'Do you think Prague is a possibility?'

Hanni stretched her neck and shoulders, wincing with the effort, as they emerged from the administration building. She was stiff and sore from the long hours spent hunched over the records, trying to find clues in a jumble of paperwork which had produced more holes than help. That Renny could have ended up in Prague had been Irene's suggestion. She had offered the city as a potential destination for a Nazi officer and his wife fleeing from the war's brutal end with a child in tow. Whether it was a real possibility or a lifeline produced to pull Freddy out of his midnight despair, Hanni couldn't tell. Although she knew how Freddy was determined to take it.

'I don't know. I can see the logic. Any attempt to return from here to Germany in the war's last days without...'

She stopped herself before she slipped into *the protection of a car and a driver which at least my father provided.*

'Well it would have been very dangerous, especially for an SS officer, given all the armies and refugees who were on the move. But Prague is close enough to be manageable even on foot. So I suppose that, yes, it's a possibility that this woman and her husband fled that way. But, Freddy, I'm sorry but I don't know if we should dare to believe it. Given the state of Bohemia at the time, with the Russians advancing and everyone running, never mind the chaos Irene described here – what are the chances of them getting there in one piece, if at all?'

Freddy wasn't listening. Or he was listening only to what he wanted to hear. To *possibility* and *manageable* and *chance*.

'You've just said it yourself: Prague is nearby, and it would have been a safer bet than trying to make it back to Germany. And the city being so close also works for us. Irene said she could find us a guide, and we have the money to pay. We could manage the walk there in a day if we tried, two at most.'

Hanni sank onto one of the benches that the town's new craftsmen had carved. The air was cold enough to make her shiver, but at least its bite would keep her sleep-deprived brain sharp. There was so much she needed to say to him, and so much that she couldn't bear to.

We don't know the wife's name. We don't know that she took Renny. Or if she went to Prague, or made it out of here at all. And we don't know the city – asking around for a lead there could expose us to serious danger.

Freddy already knew all that. Hanni saying it would only put her back into the enemy camp, where she so desperately didn't want to be. So she didn't say it. She chose instead to answer with, 'If that's what you want to do, I don't want to get in the way,' which brought a tired smile back to his face.

'I know this is crazy, Hanni. I know chasing a trail as cold as this is a risky and stupid and probably pointless thing to do. Brack would laugh himself sick if he heard what I was proposing.'

He was on the bench beside her, his hands cupped round hers. For the first time since they had entered Theresienstadt, Hanni finally felt at one with him. So she didn't agree out loud with his assessment, although it was accurate; she didn't say anything. She waited for him to explain himself.

'But none of that matters, or at least I'm not going to let it. I honestly think Renny got out of here. And I think the wife, and presumably her husband, took her when the guards fled, before the Russians arrived. All my instincts are pointing that way. Perhaps I'm wrong and Renny is in Germany now – or in America. Or perhaps she is in Prague, only hours away from us. And if she is there and with them, then she is in a Nazi's house. Think about what that means. Think about the filth they could be filling her with. I have to rescue her from that, don't you see? If Renny is out there, living her life with the worst kind of people, then I have to save her. I don't have a choice in that.'

Hanni didn't need to think about what that meant: she had grown up in the same kind of home and it wasn't any place for a vulnerable child. And she could see that in his head he was donning armour, saddling his horse, getting ready to ride out on a quest that couldn't fail this time.

Which is exactly what he should be doing, and I should be by his side.

'No, you don't. And you're right: we have to go to Prague.'

His arms swaddled her so tight she could feel his heart beating. She didn't say anything else. There was no point in thinking beyond Prague. There was nothing for her to do but keep his hopes flying.

'It's hard to believe so much horror happened here. It's not like Buchenwald. When the sun hits the buildings like this, they look rather beautiful.'

What is he talking about? What beauty is here?

Hanni wriggled out of his embrace and followed Freddy's gaze. The sun was rising, sending pink and pale lemon light dancing across the ochre walls and red roofs, softening the cracks and blurring the peeling plaster. Behind them, the ramparts rose thick with grass, silvery with dew. At the other end of the street, pale green buds dotted the trees edging the Market Square. Dawn had turned the town into a storybook village, ripe to be filled with milkmaids and minstrels and a golden carriage carrying a princess. It was beautiful; he was right, and that was the last thing Hanni wanted it to be. She forgot that Freddy meant nothing more by his comments than to acknowledge a lovely morning. Her nerves were strained almost to snapping, and Theresienstadt was still Theresienstadt, the place where countless lives had been ruined; it could never be beautiful.

She leaped to her feet, her stomach lurching, determined to make him see it in its true light. 'No, it's not – you can't say that. This isn't beauty; it's an illusion. Don't you see? That's all this place has ever been – a web of lies and false images. It's never been anything but a trick. Meant to make you forget or not care about the dying and the dead who once filled its streets and its attics. About the old people who were conned out of their life savings and promised a riverside villa if they came here but were left to starve to death in squalor instead. About the trains that pulled out of its station packed with passengers on their way to be murdered. We can't fall for it again. This is a hateful, hate-filled place and no amount of sunshine will ever change it.'

She was shaking, shouting, delivering a lecture he hadn't asked for or deserved. Filled with disgust for the town and herself.

'Hanni, sweetheart, please. Calm down. You're exhausted. You've bad memories of a day here that you were too young to understand. A day that's gone, that no amount of reliving can make better.'

Freddy was on his feet beside her, ready to wipe her misery away. Hanni stared at him, at the love freely offered in his outstretched arms, and suddenly everything became clear.

Don't let him turn the past into nothing to make you feel better. It's a new day; it could be a new beginning. Tell him what really happened here – face up to yourself and who you were, and trust him to love you enough when you're done.

It was the right thing to do. It was the right place to do it. Hanni took a deep breath and looked into Freddy's eyes.

'But that's not true, Freddy. I did understand.'

If there were people around them waking up and starting their day, Hanni could no longer hear them. If there were birds stirring in the trees, they were doing it silently. There was nothing in Theresienstadt anymore except her and him and a chance to start making the world right again.

'I need to tell you what it was really like here the day the Red Cross came. The town they were presented with was a lie. I knew that from the start. I knew that the shops and the cafés were empty behind their painted windows. That the people were famished, not eating freshly baked bread every day. That even the cemetery was an elaborate hoax, that there was nothing beneath the grass except concrete, that the headstones were made out of cardboard. What else could they have been but fakes? Who needs a cemetery when the bodies have all been burned? Who got a headstone in Auschwitz?'

She stopped before she started another lecture. Freddy had taken a step back. His hands were raised. He was shaking his head as if flies buzzed around it. She sensed with every inch of her body that he wanted her to leave the whole subject alone. She couldn't.

'And I knew that because—'

'You were clever. You knew it because you were too bright to be fooled. Then, later, when you really had time to think, you pieced the stories together with the scared faces in the photographs that you took and the guilt overwhelmed you. It's still overwhelming you.'

She stared at him, her mouth empty. Her head filled with *he knows.* For a wild moment that thought was dislodged by *because Natan told him.* Hanni couldn't believe that: such a damning revelation about her past from Natan would have led to fights and fury at the exhibition, not this determination to stop her talking. *He knows* slipped away; *he suspects something he hasn't made sense of or doesn't want to* crept in instead. And it wouldn't do.

'No, that's not it. You need to listen to me, Freddy. There are things—'

But he was too quick for her again.

'Not now, Hanni, please.' His voice cracked but he kept on going. 'I know you've got secrets; they've overshadowed us for years. But I also know you, and I cannot, I will not, believe they are bad ones. So not now. Let me find Renny. Let me fix that hole in our family and then we can deal with whatever the rest is. We can do that, can't we? With all the love we have for each other, can't we fix anything?'

'I have found a guide who will take you to Prague, if that's still what you both want to do.'

Neither of them had heard Irene coming; both of them jumped at her voice. Freddy was immediately lost to Hanni, caught up in 'thank you' and 'how soon can we leave?' and clearly relieved to be freed from a difficult conversation. Hanni let the two of them return to the administration building to sort out arrangements and sat back down on the bench. The sun was higher now; the roof tiles were sparkling.

Can't we fix anything?

She wanted to believe it. Whatever the truth of her surroundings, the morning really was a pretty one. It was hard to sit in the sunshine and believe that anything could happen but good. Except another chance to tell the truth had slipped away from her, because she hadn't fought hard enough to make it stay.

Not because I was a coward but because I love him and I listened to what he wanted, and he has enough to contend with without adding me.

That was true. It was also an easy way out.

Hanni closed her eyes to stop the dawn's tricks. What she had said to Freddy was right. This wasn't the place to believe in miracles. This was Theresienstadt with its lies and delusions, and she carried Theresienstadt with her wherever she went.

CHAPTER 6

MAY 1945–MARCH 1950, PRAGUE

Renny Novotná didn't like jigsaws.

As soon as she attempted to put one together, her normally careful fingers turned fat and fumbled. The shapes that wouldn't fit made her uneasy. The gaps she couldn't fill, which left holes in the pictures of kittens or cottages or Alpine villages, made her pulse race. It wouldn't have mattered if her failure hadn't mattered so much to her father.

Renny's father prized concentration and discipline above everything. Acquiring those attributes, or so he told her, was the most important lesson she would learn. So he allotted her a strict amount of time to complete a puzzle in, and then he tapped his watch when she couldn't complete it and sighed when she couldn't work out which pieces matched. He said that she failed because she was stupid.

Renny knew that wasn't true. Renny knew why she couldn't do jigsaws, even if she didn't completely understand it and couldn't articulate it, or certainly not to him. Jigsaws reminded her of the way her mind behaved when she was alone or tired, or on the nights when sleep wouldn't come. There were gaps in there too, and sometimes there were images – of women whose faces kept changing and sharp-voiced men and a crowded room and a sky with a moon that was far too big – which flared up all broken and disjointed. So Renny was certain that she wasn't stupid – how could she be, if she could make the connection between the puzzles and why they unnerved her – but she didn't point that out to her father. And she didn't say that she didn't want to do them. Nice children didn't complain like that; they were glad for what they got. She tried. She listened to him tut and sigh and shout, until he finally gave up that battle and her ninth birthday arrived without the stomach-churning square box. She knew there would be other battles to come.

Renny wasn't a difficult girl; no one could ever call her that. She did as she was told. There were lots of things in her life that she liked.

She liked to lose herself in a book, especially her favourite, *Peter Pan,* which she had read so many times she had memorised it. She really liked to draw. She had filled as many notebooks as her mother would buy her with sketches of the Lost Boys packed tightly into their jammed-together beds and Wendy's worried face leaning over them. She had come to like Prague, far more than her parents did. She liked the spires that filled its centre, now that she had accepted that they would stay standing and weren't trying to rip holes in the sky. She liked the wide sweep of the Vltava River which cut the city in two and the way it swirled under the arches of the Charles Bridge as if no one could ever tame it. And she liked the necklace with the silver flower that never left her neck. No, she loved that. Even if she could no longer remember anything about who had given it to her, except that their name was Mama, and that word was theirs alone. Removing the necklace was the only thing Renny had ever openly refused to do. The beating she had received before her mother intervened had been worth it.

Unfortunately, for all the things Renny liked, there were as many things in her life that she hated and could do nothing to change.

School was one. Renny was clever and quick to learn, but that didn't matter. She was different, and that was a sin. She was marked out by an accent that didn't fit and a family that was too small to match the surfeit of grandparents and aunts and uncles the other children paraded, who had all been heroes of something called 'the resistance' during the war. Renny couldn't provide the pedigree her classmates demanded and that led to whispers, which led to taunts filled with phrases she didn't understand. *You've got no family, what are you then, a dirty little Jew?* And *How did you get away? Wasn't the plan to wipe you all out?* Phrases which, when she repeated them at home, made her mother panic and her father rage and ask questions which made her mother panic even more. So Renny stopped repeating them.

Her size was another problem, another excuse to torment her. Renny was small, slight for her age even in a world where everyone had spent years living on rations, and she had a cough which came back every winter and left her smothered in blankets and steam. She also hated that her house had secrets. Especially that her parents spoke a language to each other when they thought she wasn't listening which wasn't the Czech everyone else spoke. A language whose words she somehow knew but was forbidden – under the threat of punishments that would definitely be delivered – to use.

Secrets and her size and her miserable life at school: it was a lot for a nine-year-old to manage. It was little wonder Renny ran for her books and her pencils whenever she could. But it could all be borne, Renny was certain of that: she had a sense from somewhere she couldn't fathom that all of it, one day, would pass. What couldn't be borne was her father. Renny hated him more than she hated anything.

Her mother – who Renny couldn't call Mama no matter

how much Jana begged; the word kept getting stuck in her throat – was a gentle soul. All she wanted was for Renny to be happy, although she could never explain what that meant. Or why, whatever Renny pretended to keep life steady, deep-down Renny wasn't happy at all. Perhaps if it had just been the two of them, the Novotný household would have been a less complicated place. *If only he wasn't here* was a wish Renny made every day. It showed no sign of coming true, no matter how many times he swore he would leave.

Her father, who now called himself František Novotný, was an angry man. He was angry at his wife. He was angry at Renny. He was angry at the communists who ran Czechoslovakia. There was rarely a week that went by without a lecture on how the world should be run and the better kind of men who should be running it. Or about the Jews, who he loathed as if they had caused him some kind of personal pain.

Renny had stopped listening to his ranting long ago; she played stories in her head while he droned on and on. None of that was pleasant – and the threat of another beating was frightening – but none of that was why Renny hated him. Renny hated her father because he hated her. He flinched when she came near him, which she did as little as possible. He blamed her and her mother for all the bad decisions which had led him to a city he detested and a job that was far beneath him. When he was really mad, when he came home late at night stinking of beer and spoiling for someone to fight, he yelled at Jana that they should have *left the brat there*, wherever *there* was, and gone back to their *own people* while they still could. Renny didn't ask what he meant. Part of her was afraid he might say.

So many things to hate and not one she could admit to. Good girls apparently didn't use such a nasty word as hate, and Renny was nothing if not a very good girl, even if she was no longer sure why that mattered. So many things to swallow and not speak about.

Sometimes Renny lay curled up in her bed at night, crammed to bursting with everything she couldn't say. Certain that she wasn't where she was meant to be in the world. Certain that if she opened her mouth and started to roar, the roar would never stop.

CHAPTER 7

30 MARCH 1950, PRAGUE

It wasn't as simple as leaving at once, no matter how much Freddy wanted it to be. There were papers to be checked and a fee to be negotiated which wouldn't use up all their money. And there was a timescale to be followed when they got there, although Freddy fought hard against that.

'I don't care how much time you think you need, what you've got is five weeks. That's how long the apartment I've found for you will be empty. If you go beyond that, the price of helping you rises and so does the danger, and you'd better hope your cover stories hold. Prague is a tightly wound place these days. No one likes strangers, especially ones whose accents don't fit.'

Marek, the guide Irene had found for them, was sour-faced and suspicious and had no love for Germans. He made it clear from the start that their relationship was a purely financial one. He had no interest or stake in their search.

'He's not the friendliest of men, I'll grant you, and his view of the world is a bleak one. He has his reasons for that. But he's Czech, which matters, and he knows the back roads and Prague better than anyone else here. He also has a network of associates who will assist with the search, *if* he asks them to. You don't have to like him, and I wouldn't suggest that you question anything about his business, but you can trust him. In your situation that surely counts for a lot.'

Freddy chafed against Marek's open hostility: Hanni was glad to take Irene's advice. Three days in Theresienstadt, surrounded by memories of the dead and fearful of the living, had whittled her nerves to shreds. She had spent the waiting time hidden in the room Irene had cleared for her and Freddy, laid low by a bout of sickness which she suspected had a different explanation to the food poisoning she blamed it on.

Pregnancy. It still wasn't a word she could associate with herself; she had only begun to consider it as a possibility in the last few days. And it was a shock, but she was starting to think she might like the sound of it. If they had been anywhere else she might have shared her suspicions with Freddy, but Theresienstadt wasn't the place for that kind of news. Freddy was far too on edge to listen to anything that wasn't directly related to his little sister; he couldn't settle and couldn't sleep. He scoured the town instead, searching for anyone whose memories he hadn't already picked clean and obsessively hunting back through the records. By the time they finally set off on the next stage of their journey, on a cold grey morning when nothing about Theresienstadt looked beautiful at all, it was all Hanni could do to keep up.

'If we meet a patrol, you are my cousins visiting the area on a walking holiday. I do the talking; you do whatever you are told. And if that doesn't work...' Marek shrugged. 'I won't be waiting around to see what else you come up with.'

His mood remained sullen, but the day eventually brightened and their route was at least a pleasant one. They walked past gently rolling fields which were gradually coming into spring and through forests whose floors were so thickly overgrown they could have stood untouched for centuries. And they walked in a silence that Marek had imposed, which continued even when they made camp in a deserted barn as darkness fell.

He shared out the food Irene had packed but refused any attempt to engage him in conversation beyond the basics of where the road would take them the next day. Hanni's tentative 'So were you a prisoner for long?' was met with silence and a scowl. Freddy observed that exchange and he left Marek alone. But by the time the three of them crawled stiff and cold into the next morning, he was seething.

'So you hate Germans, fine. But why does that have to include us? We didn't fight in the war. And I am a Jew – I lost my whole family, and I was held prisoner too, in a far worse place than Theresienstadt. I've as much reason to hate the Nazis as you have, maybe more. Is a little civility too much to ask?'

Marek stopped, his shoulders twitching. When he turned, Hanni wished that he hadn't. His face carried a lifetime's worth of bitterness.

'Forgive me, Inspector, for my woeful lack of manners. I wasn't aware that, because we have both suffered, although clearly in your mind to different degrees, we had a duty to be friends.'

He snorted at Freddy's 'Why not? Doesn't it give us some kind of a bond?'

'What a simplistic view of the world you must have. No, it doesn't give us a *bond*. We're not the same. You lost your family and I'm sorry for that, but you continue to call yourself German. That is your choice. And you continue to live in Berlin. That is your choice too, as was your German wife, who I doubt has ever seen the inside of a synagogue. And that's where I'm struggling, where our *bond* breaks down. How do you do that, Inspector? How do you live with yourself, when you still live hand in glove with your enemies?'

Marek spat in the dust and strode off again, at a pace which was clearly intended to keep Hanni and Freddy at a distance. It didn't work – or not on Freddy at least.

'I know he's a nightmare but Irene said that he has his reasons for acting this way. Can't you let his hostility go for the sake of the next few days?'

It was too late to calm him: Freddy was spoiling for a fight.

'But it's not hostility though, is it? It's contempt. And no I can't let it go, not if his reasons lump me in with the Nazis. He doesn't have the right to judge me, whatever he's been through. Being German doesn't make me a part of the Third Reich's crimes. Everything about that is ridiculous.'

He shook off Hanni's restraining hand and stormed away, leaving her to sprint after him. She caught the two men up as Freddy was repeating *ridiculous*, fully expecting Marek's response to start with his fists. It didn't. Instead of fighting, he wrong-footed them both.

'Look out there. What do you see?'

Marek pointed to the fields stretched out in front of them which were as empty of people and buildings as the dozens of others they had passed. The only obvious things in their eyeline were a row of stunted trees and a distant meandering river.

Freddy frowned. 'Nothing.' He squinted and peered again. 'I don't know, some ropes maybe, and what could be a trench marked out over there, but nothing of meaning.'

'Nothing of meaning. That's the right answer.'

Marek swept his hand across the view as if he was holding a paintbrush. 'If you had come here seven years ago, you would have seen a very different sight. You would have seen my birthplace, the town of Lidice. A bustling community with a church steeple that wouldn't have looked out of place in Prague, and rows of neat, well-cared-for houses. Over there, farmers would have been working the fields. Over there, women would have been hanging out their washing. And coming down the road that you can't see anymore because every stone of it has been lifted, miners would have been returning from their shifts.' He stopped, cleared his throat, carried on. 'In other words, you would have seen families quietly getting on with their lives.'

When he stopped the second time, tears sprang into his eyes and his face switched from hardened to human. The change was too naked to look at. Hanni turned her gaze back to the grassy plain, although she didn't want to look at that either. There wasn't a ruin to be seen. No remains of a house or a road or any mark that suggested a settlement had ever been built there. Not that Hanni expected one, not now that Marek had explained where they were.

'What happened?'

She asked only because someone had to and Freddy was struggling. She didn't need or want to. Unlike Freddy, Hanni already knew what had happened. The story of the little town of Lidice and its destruction in 1942 following the assassination in Prague of Reinhard Heydrich, the Reichsprotektor of Bohemia, was one Reiner had returned to time and again. Along with his regret that he hadn't been assigned to the region to play a part when the murderous punishment that was visited on Lidice had been meted out. His vicious words had sickened her then, and the memory of them sickened her now, although not as much as the loss clearly still impacted on Marek. His voice when he answered was as empty as Reiner's had been joyful.

'It was wiped from the face of the earth because someone needed to pay for Reinhard Heydrich's assassination, and Hitler decided that Lidice would do. Every building was burned to the ground. Every last timber and pebble and handful of ash was buried so that not a trace of its existence could ever be found.'

'And the people? What happened to them'

Freddy had recovered his voice and there was nothing belligerent in his tone anymore. His words were shorn of anything but pity.

'They were wiped away too, so that not even a memory of

the place would remain. One hundred and seventy-three men were shot. Eighty-two children were sent to the ovens. Its women were sent to the camps. My family and my friends among them.'

'And you were in Theresienstadt when this happened?'

Marek nodded at Freddy's quiet question. 'Yes. I'd been caught in Prague committing what the Germans called anti-social activities and I would call legitimately fighting the enemy. I was tortured; I was sick for a long time. I knew nothing about what had happened until the war ended and I went racing home. I stood on this spot that day and I thought I'd lost my mind. A whole town vanished, and the grass grown up as if it had never been.' He stared into the far distance, to where Freddy had spotted the ropes. 'And now they are planning to rebuild it, marking out a new Lidice, as if that is some kind of compensation for the old.'

'And every morning you wake up and you remind yourself of the hate that you carry. And you embrace the despair and the fury that comes with the pain.'

Both Hanni and Marek turned towards Freddy at the same time. His face was white; his eyes were red-rimmed.

'I did the same thing, Marek. You talked about my choices, well I made that same one. For a year, for longer if I'm honest, the first thing I did every day was to replay the sight of my mother and my baby sister being marched away from me by armed guards. Not to do that felt like a sin, so I recalled every sight and every sound of it. The shouting; the dogs; the boots clashing over the cobbles. The last brief glimpse of my mother's face as she silently begged me not to step forward and be taken along with them. Every detail, every morning; memorised and relived. I drank it like fuel.'

Marek was no longer looking at the place where his heart had been broken. He was staring directly at Freddy, his eyes filled with a hunger he didn't have the words to express.

'You said "did" and "was". So you stopped?'

Freddy nodded and spread his hands as Hanni asked, 'How?' and Marek asked, 'Why?'

'I had to, or I would have gone mad. *You have a duty to the dead to carry on living.* That was what I was told, after I survived the round-up that took them but not me. It took me a long time to do more than go through the motions of that, but, eventually, I managed it. And I didn't want to leave – what do I know about life in America or Israel? All I knew was how to be German so that was what I stayed.'

He shook his head as Marek frowned and tried to butt in. 'That was my path, Marek and there are still too many days when it isn't an easy one. I can share it and I can hope you will listen, but I wouldn't insult you by telling you what your path should be.'

There was a moment of stillness. Then Marek stuck out his hand and Freddy shook it, and the two men nodded. Hanni fell into step as they continued down the road. There was a bond between him and Freddy now, and the silence between them was no longer a fraught one. It contained a deeper under-standing both of each other and of the pain Czechoslovakia and its people were still in. Hanni wanted to acknowledge that, to tell them that she shared it. She didn't feel worthy. She dropped slightly back as the men began talking, not wanting to eavesdrop on a conversation that was so personal.

He chooses this way of being in the world. Letting go of hate, living with hope. Please God that continues, whatever we find. Whatever I have to do.

Freddy turned to her and smiled as if he knew he was in her thoughts. He held out his hand again, waiting until Hanni took it. She returned the squeeze she knew was meant to mean *I am here; I am with you.* And wondered how he could feel so close to her when the reality was that they were falling apart.

. . .

'I'll come back in a few days, when I've had time to put some of my people on this. Don't go out while you're waiting – there's food in the kitchen; there's nothing you need. Practise your Czech, and your stories.'

Marek was out of the door almost as soon as he had ushered Hanni and Freddy inside the cramped and dark apartment that was to be their home for the next few weeks. And then he turned round on the doorstep.

'If this goes well, you'll need new papers for the child to get her out of the country. You won't get those done in Prague but there is a man in Jirny, a village not far from here who can organise those, if I ask him to. If you get that far, leave a message for me at the Tygra bar on Husova Street. And if anything goes wrong, leave a message there too.'

He didn't wish them good luck. He was gone before either of them could thank him.

'He could be a stand-in for Elias. Another gruff guardian angel with a heart he's determined to hide.'

Freddy's smile was too bright, his laugh louder than the comparison deserved. He was on edge, a ball of nervous energy whose face had fallen when Marek had ordered them not to go outside.

He sat down on one of the faded chairs and sprang immediately up again, prowled round the room, opening cupboards and barely looking inside. The apartment, with its overstuffed living and bedroom and shabby narrow kitchen, was already too small to contain him. Hanni's heart had sunk when they followed Marek into it. Despite her determined chatter about the very few touches the place needed to make it more homely, she couldn't imagine what would make it rise again, inside the flat or out.

The Old Town area of Prague where their lodgings were located was no Dresden – the streets were passable, the buildings were solid and what war damage remained had been at least partly patched over. That did not mean the city had moved on. If anything, since its new Communist regime had arrived two years earlier, Prague had gone backwards, and the timeslip that presented was hard to adjust to.

A month ago, Hanni had been holding a cocktail in an elegant art gallery and running in and out of the colourful magazine offices which had sprung into life in West Berlin. The women she photographed had nipped in their waists and wore skirts that swung out like a bell – 1950 had thrown itself at their side of the city full of youth and promise and fun. There was nothing of that in Prague. Hanni had entered a place which had dropped her back into 1945. A place where she had to keep a wary eye on the gangs of ragged and rough-looking boys hanging around the street corners. Where she had to weave her way around the queues that circled the empty shop windows and avoid eye contact with the grey-clad and grey-faced pedestrians who were avoiding eye contact with her. And where she was surrounded by soldiers whose uniforms looked Soviet and walls bearing giant portraits of Stalin. It was a jolt. A tipping back into an alien landscape Hanni only saw now in flashes, as she was driven in a comfortable car through the eastern neighbourhoods of Berlin.

The sullen, suspicious atmosphere they had encountered as they moved through the city and the disorientation that came with it was like a magnet sucking up memories, some buried deeper than others. The older ones came first. The last few hate-filled weeks of the war and the constant fear of the Soviet troops who were determined to prove to the German people that they no longer had any rights in the world. The reinventions that had come after that, both hers and her father's, and the threat that Reiner would always be watching whatever she did to try and expose him, or to shake off his shadow. She and Freddy, stalking the murderers they had eventually brought to justice while wondering if the two of them had turned into prey. And then the newer ones, the horror of Dresden and a face at a gallery and then again at a train station which was too interested in hers.

By the time they had reached Michalská Street and its crammed-in apartment buildings, Hanni's neck was prickling and the sense that someone was keeping a far-too-close eye on her – a feeling which had fallen away in the fields and the forests – had flooded back. And now Freddy was coiled and pacing and the walls weren't just listening, they were closing in.

'There's no cigarettes. There's plenty of food but there's nothing to smoke.'

It was the first thing that came into her head, a reason to get out and find a green space to calm down in.

'And there's no wine either. We've made it this far, which is surely something to celebrate, and we can't do that without wine.'

Hanni moved in a whirlwind she knew would distract Freddy, wrapping herself back into her headscarf and rebuttoning her old tweed coat as she spoke.

'And I know what Marek said about lying low, but my Czech is better than yours and I won't stand out, not in this outfit anyway. I won't go far and I'll stay close; I'll be no more than an hour, quicker if I can. Why don't you find some glasses, cut up some cheese and some sausage, get a fire lit?'

She was out of the door before he could speak. But there was no green space to be found – there was no space at all.

Hanni emerged out of the dank stairwell into a labyrinth of alleyways lined with cobbles that caught at her feet and overhanging, uneven buildings which swallowed the daylight. She wound her way on, looking up despite the stones that were eager to trip her, trying to catch a glimpse of the spires which would point her back to the Old Town's central square.

It soon proved to be a hopeless task. What Hanni hadn't realised was that Prague was a city covered in spires: twenty minutes of craning her neck and twisting this way and that trying to find a landmark simply led her further into the jumble of alleys. Ten minutes became twenty became thirty. The streets narrowed. The jutting houses above her head reached out for each other and blocked out more of the sky. When another corner led her back to a window whose sagging blind Hanni recognised, she made herself stop and stand still.

I'm lost.

Panic pushed in behind that.

She closed her eyes, refused to give in to her shuddering pulse. Trying to find her way by the city's sights hadn't worked, but using its sounds might. She took a deep breath and began to listen for something besides her racing heartbeat.

It took a moment, but then it came. A rumble which was surely a tram. A bell that had to be a bicycle. The floating chimes of a clock.

Hanni opened her eyes, trusted her instincts; let her feet follow them. Until with a rush, there she was: out of the maze and into the wider expanse of a square tucked below another tower and a clock whose once ornate face was blackened and smoke-damaged.

The centre was still drab. The thin sprinkling of shops and cafés edging the first piazza and the larger one it opened onto were still neglected. Hanni didn't care. She was worn out and hungry and she needed to regroup.

One of the cafés had a table outside which – although there was a cold snap in the air – seemed a safer option than trying to broach its invisible and steamed-up interior, particularly as she didn't know the city's customs when it came to women entering cafés alone.

She sat down and ordered tea from a disinterested waiter. All of a sudden, the afternoon changed from a fright to an adventure, a tale to entertain Freddy with.

The tea was weak and the cup was none too clean, and

none of that mattered. Hanni drained the pot and contemplated a refill although what she really wanted was a cigarette. She scrabbled through her bag, completely forgetting that buying cigarettes was the reason why she had come out in the first place. She was still preoccupied with her rummaging when a shadow fell across the table.

Hanni looked up, assuming it was the waiter come to clear away her things, but the face looking down at her was a younger and more attractive one than the taciturn man who had thumped down her tea. It was also familiar, although it took her a moment to place him. And then she did and everything around her stopped moving.

The man smiled as recognition dawned. He sat down and held out a foil-topped packet. 'Have one of mine, Fräulein Foss. I believe these are your usual brand.'

It was him. The watcher from the gallery; the man from the train station.

Hanni's brain registered all that, but she couldn't do anything with it. She couldn't take the cigarette; she couldn't challenge him. Hanni had frozen at *Foss*.

CHAPTER 8

30 MARCH 1950, PRAGUE

Whatever his intent was in following her, he was a professional, that much was clear. He sat down in the chair opposite Hanni looking perfectly at ease, but he scanned the entire area around them at speed as he did so.

He's mapped it out. He could tell me exactly who is present and what they're doing here, the same way that Freddy could.

Which meant that there was no point in denying the name he had called her. What she had to do was meet him head-on.

'So are you with the Czech police or the secret service?'

His answering smile suggested an admiration Hanni hoped she could play to. Nothing about their exchange so far had set them as equals, but she couldn't afford to crumple at that.

He took his time answering, pausing far more between each sentence than was needed. 'No attempt to pretend I've mistaken you, that's brave. And an interesting question to open with. I'll need my wits about me with you, won't I? Well, firstly, I'm no more Czech than you are, although we both seem to have developed an ear for the accent. As for the rest, am I with the police or the security services? Well I suppose the most accurate response to that is that I've been one and now I'm the other.'

He was playing with her. And the way he commanded the space around them and the condescending way that he spoke told Hanni that he was arrogant. The first was a problem – it suggested that he was a man perfectly capable of cruelty. The second could be an advantage. Hanni had dealt with arrogant men before, and she had used their arrogance against them. Cruelty was dangerous, but arrogance was a weakness, and she very much needed one of those. She waited, letting him fill the silence, not her.

His smile widened. 'You're good. I assumed you would be a tough nut to crack and you haven't let me down. That's fine, or it is for now anyway. All right, why don't I elaborate a little, get the cards out on the table so to speak? Have you ever heard of the Stasi, Fräulein Foss?'

Hanni shook her head. The movement was a reflex rather than a thought-out response. She was more focused on not letting him see how much his continued use of *Foss* sickened her than listening to what he had asked.

Her interrogator raised an eyebrow. 'Really? Elias Baar never warned you about us? That's good to know, given that he's on our payroll.'

Of all the things she had expected him to say, that was not on her list. Hanni's involuntary jump sent her handbag flying. The man waited while she stuffed its contents back together, making a joke about his girlfriend's clumsiness when the waiter reappeared at the clatter.

'I don't believe you. Elias is his own man – he wouldn't be in your pay or anyone's.'

The man snorted. 'Really? You're surprised? Oh come on, work with me here. I know he and your husband share a special bond, but how connected do you honestly think Elias is beyond his little bar? Enough to engineer it so that you crossed the border without any difficulty? Or never met a patrol? Or found a farmer so relaxed about taking you in, given what you presumably know about how tightly Czechoslovakia is run? Did you really think a two-bit gangster from Berlin could have arranged all that on his own?'

He'd moved beyond playing; his claws were flashing. Hanni refused to be ruffled by that, or to let him see she was ruffled at all.

'I still don't believe you. You're implying that he sold Freddy out. Elias wouldn't do that for any amount of money, he's a better man than that.'

The sigh and the hand to his heart was worse than the mocking grin. 'Is that the best that you've got? Really, Hannelore? Let's overlook the fact that you can't stand him and he can't stand you, so *better man* is a bit hard to swallow. Haven't you learned by now that nobody is better than that? That anyone will betray anyone if the price, or the pressure, is right?'

There are more dangers where you're heading than you can possibly imagine.

Hanni stiffened as Elias's very deliberate choice of words at their last meeting came back. At the realisation that they might have been his only way of offering Freddy a warning.

The man, who was observing her far too closely, sat back and crossed his legs as if they were discussing the weather and he had all the time in the world.

'And there's the doubt. You don't really know Herr Baar, do you? I bet, for example, that you have no idea that he has a girl-friend, the rather beautiful Marianna. Or that they are expecting a child. No? I'm not surprised. He holds his secrets even tighter than you do. Every man has his weakness, but you know that – you've been watching me and trying to work out mine the whole time we've been talking. Well Marianna is Elias's. All it took was a couple of nights holding her in one of our prisons and your Elias Baar was totally ours.'

Nothing he was saying made sense, and this insinuation

that he knew more about her life than she did, that he was somehow in control of it, was too much.

'That's enough. I don't care who you are, or what you think you know about me, or what you want – I'm not going to sit here and listen to this nonsense.'

Hanni was half out of her chair when his hand shot across the table and grabbed her wrist. His grip was like iron; there was no smile anymore.

'Sit down. Draw attention to us again and I'll hurt you.'

He was already hurting her, and she couldn't take the risk of anything worse, not now when it wasn't only herself who was at risk. His grip twisted. Hanni's knees buckled and dropped her back into her chair.

He sat back again, although this time his body stayed coiled. 'That's more like it. I thought we were having a nice conversation. I was going to explain who I was. You were going to be honest about yourself. We were going to strike a little deal. It was going to be such a civilised exchange.' He leaned forward. 'Which it doesn't have to be. I could walk you out of this square in a moment to a place where things wouldn't be civilised at all. So what will it be? Shall we start again?'

Hanni nodded. There was nothing else she could do. The area around them had cleared. Even if she screamed, nobody would come.

'A wise choice. Then let me drop Hannelore and Foss – it clearly makes you uncomfortable. Let us be Hanni and' – he paused so that she would understand that the name he was about to give her was as false as hers – 'Luca, from now on. And let me tell you who I am so there'll be no more mistakes in the way that you treat me. I am a detective, like your husband. Or I was. Now my interests lie more with... let's call it security. I'm from Berlin, the same as you are, although I belong to the GDR, not to your west. And my job is maintaining the safety of our new state and its citizens. Managing people who don't share our ideals or who might seek to threaten them. Managing people with secrets.'

The Stasi.

Hanni had indicated that she didn't recognise that name when he first said it, but she realised as she listened that she did. Freddy had brought home stories about a new Ministry for State Security which had been set up in East Germany, under the control and direction of Moscow, and was rattling nerves in the West. She had been too caught up in preparations for the exhibition to take much notice, but she remembered now some of what he had said. A hidden prison that wasn't on any maps, into which people vanished, and a hidden police force who were already spreading a climate of fear.

She glanced at the red mark round her wrist and tried not to think about Marianna. When she looked back at Luca, he was watching her as if she was a specimen, waiting to see what damage the word *secrets* had caused. As if all of hers were already laid bare.

He's another bully. Stand up to him. Don't let him believe he holds all the power.

Which would have been a good strategy if her voice hadn't cracked as she spoke and betrayed her.

'What has any of this got to do with me? I'm not one of your citizens; I don't come under your authority.'

She thought for a moment that he was going to applaud her, but he lit another cigarette instead.

'Oh, Hanni, you are quite the treat. I'm starting to enjoy it when you decide to be fierce. But don't be such an innocent: this has everything to do with you. You've been in my sights for quite a while now, from before my new role with the Stasi was established. Don't you know how much interest the young photographer who helped crack the SS Killer case whipped up? Never mind that debacle last year with the Berlin Strangler and all the upset you caused the Americans. There isn't a policeman in Berlin, east or west, who hasn't heard of you. All of that was fascinating stuff, but then, when I started to properly dig and to follow you? That's when the fun really started. Do you know where I was when I first began to piece together who you really are?'

Hanni didn't but she wouldn't give him the satisfaction of answering. Luca carried on anyway.

'In Wannsee. Outside a school set up to teach a new generation of children how to be Nazis.' His voice suddenly hardened. 'What was it your father threatened you with? A web of spies watching your every move? Did it never occur to you that if there could be one network on your tail, there could be another?'

It hadn't occurred to her at all, and now the possibility was both terrifying and horribly real. Hanni gave up any pretence that she didn't believe him. The only thing that would help her now was learning, and telling, the truth.

'Who else was in your pay?'

Luca began counting names off his fingers with an ease that made Hanni want to cry.

'Your landlady, Frau Greber. She was pretty good: she told us about the roses and the postcard your father sent you. Two of the street kids, although not Oli; he really was devoted to you. One of the murder team from the Kreuzberg police station. A clerk in the American press office last year, an assistant to the captain you took your suspicions about your father to. It wasn't hard for us to find willing recruits; it never is. Anyone who's tired of struggling on low pay or low rations, or sick of seeing men whose pasts should have put them in prison getting promoted instead, is easily persuaded to slip us the odd word. Although there were a couple of others in your circle who wouldn't. Your Herr Stein for one. He made his feelings about our methods very clear. And there was no point in approaching your miserable guide from Theresienstadt, but that didn't matter. We have close contacts with the security forces here – whichever country agents like me work in, the GDR or Czechoslovakia or anywhere else in the Eastern Bloc, we all follow Moscow's bidding, we're all Stalin's men in the end. And our network has had eyes on you the whole way from Berlin.'

'Why?'

It was all Hanni could manage. The list of people who she had trusted and who had betrayed her had drained all her fight. And the moment she asked, and saw the delight on his face, everything he had said fell into place and she knew.

'It's not me you want, is it? It's my father.'

Which made sense until she paused and considered where they were sitting.

'But why follow me to Prague if it's Reiner you're after? Why didn't you do all this in Berlin?'

Luca shifted on the hard metal seat. For the first time since he had sat down, Hanni caught a flicker of doubt in his eyes. It vanished as fast as it had come, but it felt like a glimmer of hope. If there was doubt, perhaps she could pull back at least a thread of the power.

She pulled herself straighter, sat up taller and looked him in the eye. 'You made a mistake, didn't you? You thought me going to Theresienstadt had something to do with my father. That's why you followed us: you thought I was here to uncover a secret or another crime to use against him.'

She had overplayed what had been a tiny moment. She shouldn't have sounded so confident; she shouldn't have goaded him. The second the words came out of her mouth, his hand was back round her wrist, but this time his fingernails were turned in.

'I don't make mistakes. That's your area. Do you still not get how much of a blackmailer's dream you are? You're married to a man who knows nothing of your past, who will hate you when he does. You're on the trail of a child who could have been taken by Nazis. Don't look so surprised that I know that now, even if I didn't at the start. I told you, we have eyes everywhere.' His hold on her wrist tightened, his nails tearing her skin. 'What will you do if you get that far, Hanni? If your hunch is right and the Nazis have her but they recognise you? How will that work out, if you find the girl but the man playing the role of *her* father turns out to know *yours?*'

The pain where his nails had ripped into her stung like a burn. She couldn't pull away. She couldn't think how to fight him. Her head was too full of *he's right.*

'Why do you want him?'

The words came out smothered in a sob.

Luca let her hand drop. 'That's better – a bit of contrition. I don't want to have to keep reminding you who is in charge here, though I will. But yes, why not give you the little victory you've been angling for. I'll concede that we initially thought it was business with Reiner that brought you here. We wondered if, perhaps, you were finally going to make good on that old promise of yours to unmask him.'

He gave her a moment to appreciate how intimately he knew her before he went on.

'What we got wrong doesn't matter. This quest of yours, and this ongoing charade with your poor deluded husband, works better for us than for you.'

That made no sense to her, but Hanni was in too much pain to form a new question.

'But I still don't understand why you want Reiner.'

She slipped her wrist under the table where she could more easily cradle it without Luca seeing. He was the one in control, there was no point in pretending that he wasn't, but she wouldn't give him the satisfaction of falling apart.

Luca signalled to the waiter to bring them both coffee. He didn't wait for the man to move out of earshot while he answered. Hanni suspected he wanted the whole square to hear the lecture he launched into.

'Because we are not the West. Your side has been turning a blind eye to Nazis since the end of the war, no matter what atrocities they committed. We've got higher standards in the East: we've never tolerated them and we never will. Denazification was a joke to you, but our purges meant something; our institutions are free of their influence. Your new chancellor's suggestion that it's time to let bygones be bygones might have won him cheers on your side of Berlin, but we would have thrown him in prison on ours. Which means that the search for the ones who got away has never stopped. We're still hunting the men whose existence shames us as Germans and we always will.'

He's as much of a zealot as my father. He just cloaks his hatred under a different set of beliefs.

The thought was chilling. Hanni resisted the urge to pull her coat tighter. She needed to be as still and as measured as he was.

'I understand that you hate Reiner. I'm glad that you do. What I don't understand is why you would call him a threat to your country.'

Luca took a sip of his coffee and immediately pushed it away again with a grimace at its unrelieved bitterness. 'Because he is working to destabilise it.'

He sighed as she frowned. 'Of course that's a surprise: you only know what goes on in the West. Why would bombings and sabotage in Magdeburg and Dessau be of any interest to you? Well they should be, because your father – possibly with the co-operation of the American intelligence services, possibly with his own people – is behind them.'

He dismissed her 'That doesn't make sense' with a flick of his hand. 'It does and we can prove it. The trouble might be happening in the GDR, but the targets are within easy reach of his Harz Mountains' base. One of the boys responsible for disrupting a factory line who wasn't quick enough to get away gave us his name.'

His explanation didn't make what he said any easier to accept: Reiner was many things, but a covert saboteur wasn't one of them.

Luca shook his head as she frowned. 'What, don't you think that scenario is possible? Do you think men like your father only hate Jews? Do you think they were big fans of the Communist party and cheered when Germany was split into two? Well I'm sorry to disappoint you if you do. Your father and all the others who have clung so tenaciously to their fascist beliefs loathe the GDR. They want Germany reunited, preferably under the control of some new kind of Third Reich. That's why he's exactly the kind of man who would order our farm machinery sabotaged or our production lines blown up. Or at least a plausible culprit, which works just as well.'

Now Hanni really didn't understand, and she hated Luca's delight when she said so.

'Oh come on, Hanni, try harder. The GDR is the perfect country. Surely you know that? We proclaim it often enough. No one is unhappy under Communism – how can they be when the State supplies all that they need? When everyone is equal so jealousy is pointless? And if no one is unhappy, then there can be no crime, because crime is a Western sickness.'

He paused briefly as he caught Hanni's frown. 'I know how that sounds and, as much as I love my country, I also know that some of the claims we're making are going to come back and bite us. Obviously we have crime, quite a lot of it if I'm honest, which I shouldn't be. But we're not going to admit it, so we—'

'Need men like my father, Nazis and capitalists, to be the bogeymen and the criminals. Even if, in reality, they have done nothing at all.'

This time he did applaud. 'Clever girl. And nicely put: the

jury – if we had a jury, which we most certainly wouldn't – would be out on whether Reiner is actually involved in the attacks, but that doesn't matter – we can very easily make him fit. And that's what's going to happen here: every so often we need to catch one of our *bogeymen* as you put it. To parade their wickedness publicly so our good citizens can sleep safe and smug in their beds. Now do you see where your father comes in? Reiner Foss's war crimes are well known to the American and the British intelligence services; they have been for years, but they've never challenged the fiction of his reinvention as Emil and they won't. Doing that doesn't fit with West Germany's determination to stride into the future without the burden of its past. And your father's current plans might unsettle anyone who's looking closely at them, but they won't be challenged either. I don't imagine that's good news for you.'

It wasn't, but it wasn't a surprise either. Hanni had been telling the truth when she had explained to Natan Stein how she had already tried and failed to bring Reiner to justice. Less than a year ago she had been told a similar story to Luca's by an American captain she had gone to for help. He hadn't exactly said, 'You're the only one who cares anymore,' but he had come close.

Luca saw her face fall and his brightened. 'Exactly. The West won't bring him down, but we will, and that should be very good news for you. An ex-Nazi who has already tried to set up a Hitler School is bad enough, but we believe he's in the process of setting up more. And he lives in the middle of the American-occupied sector of Germany, which could suggest – or could be made to suggest – that he is operating his new venture with their co-operation. You didn't know that, did you? Well it's true. So now can you imagine the delight when I bring this prize home?'

Hanni could but she didn't like the wild light in his eyes. The one that whispered fanatic. Even if what Luca was promising – the destruction of her father – was what she so desperately wanted, she knew all too well that no good ever came from dealing with a man as zealous as him. She forced herself not to give him the thanks or the admiration he so clearly expected. To focus instead on how she could best get away from him.

'I do, yes, and I understand about the GDR's need for an enemy, and why Reiner so perfectly fits the mould. I can also imagine that there are plenty of your citizens who have suffered at his hands and who would be happy to see him suffer in return and get what's coming to him. So I sympathise, I do. And if there's anything I can do to help track him down when we get back to Berlin, I won't hesitate to contact you, I promise.'

'That's very kind of you.'

There was a new menace in Luca's voice which made Hanni's skin tighten.

'But that's not how this plays out. We've already tried to pick him up in Germany and he's too well protected, which is where you come in. You're going to bring Reiner to Prague. On his own, without his henchmen. Away from all his networks and help. You're going to deliver him here, to me.'

Hanni stared at him, wondering if he knew how crazed his plan sounded; doubting that he cared. She bit her lip and tried to hold in the panic. It didn't work: her words fell out all over each other.

'How on earth am I meant to do that? To get a message to him in the first place, never mind one he would listen to. To convince him it isn't a trap? And how could he even make the journey here, when we apparently only managed it with your help?'

Luca packed his cigarettes and matches away and shrugged. 'We can get a message to him – all you have to do is provide the touches that prove it's from you. We can make border guards look the other way. As to what you say to him, that's not my concern. This isn't a negotiation, Hanni. You are in a city where you shouldn't be, on a fool's errand I could end in an instant. Your name is a lie; your marriage is a lie. There are a dozen ways I could rip your life up. So you need to stop asking questions and start focusing on answers.'

His smile this time was intended to frighten her and it worked. 'After all, you have a whole life to lose if you don't.'

CHAPTER 9

2–5 APRIL 1950, PRAGUE

The more Hanni tried to manage her secrets, the bigger they grew. They filled her, and they filled the flat. Her skin no longer felt strong enough to contain all the parts of her that Freddy didn't know. The ones which would turn her from the love of his life into a monster. And now Luca. Another layer of lies, another stumbling block.

'I'll give you a few days to work out a plan. Then I'll be back for you. Don't let me down, there's a good girl.'

Luca hadn't embroidered his parting shot with any more threats; he hadn't needed to. Just as he hadn't needed to warn her not to tell Freddy: he knew as well as she did that she wouldn't say a word.

Hanni had stumbled back into the flat, pretending that her shaking hands and washed-out face were the result of getting hopelessly lost in a jumble of dark alleyways. She had let Freddy wrap her in a blanket and fuss with tea and had used the excuse of that and the forgotten cigarettes to burst into a flood of tears which were a shock to both of them. Since then, they had been circling around each other, using soft words and awkward apologies to hide their confusion. Hanni was too quiet; Freddy was too fidgety. They occupied the flat's cramped spaces like strangers, barely speaking beyond the most basic information.

When the doorbell finally rang on their third morning of hiding and waiting, Hanni almost jumped out of her skin.

'Don't answer it!'

It was Luca, she was certain of it, and the only plan in her head so far was *get out of here.*

'Or at least let me explain first, or try to.'

But Freddy had already run to the door and flung it wide open. 'What's wrong with you? It's Marek – it has to be. No one else knows that we're here.'

'I thought you were a policeman, so why are you behaving like a complete idiot?'

Marek barrelled into the flat at a speed which silenced them both, his face contorted with fury.

'What the hell do you think you're doing? Shouting my name down the corridor, announcing our business to the world. Do I honestly have to explain to a detective how things have to be done here? That you edge open the door – you don't fling it and offer yourself up as a target. That you ask for identification, rather than hearing a Czech accent and assuming it's me.'

Freddy was immediately all shame-faced apologies, and Hanni's outburst was forgotten. Marek waved away their offer of tea and refused to sit down.

'It was easier than I expected to gather the information, although that doesn't guarantee anything else will be as smooth.' He dropped an envelope onto the table and gestured to Freddy to open it. 'Luckily for you there aren't many families in Prague who meet the profile I used as the basis for the search.'

'And that stayed exactly as we agreed?'

Marek frowned as Freddy extracted the thin sheaf of notes. 'Yes, of course it did. A couple with a daughter aged around nine who might display the physical consequences of being held prisoner when she was a baby and who have no other children. A couple without wider family or obvious roots in the city, who are loners; whose accents or manner don't fit. I didn't add Nazi into the mix, I'm not that much of an idiot, but the rest was what you wanted.'

Freddy said nothing this time, although his whole body stiffened. Marek nodded to the papers Freddy was holding.

'There are five possibilities listed there. The names and addresses are included, plus the schools the girls attend. Your safest option would be to start with those. Maybe it will go smoothly and you'll recognise her.'

Freddy was turning the papers over and over, as if that would make the meagre pile magically expand.

'We're grateful, obviously we are, but it's not many names. We hoped there'd be more. What happens if it turns out to be none of the ones you've given us?'

Marek already had his hand on the door. He shrugged at Hanni's question.

'Then you go home. If the people in my network can only find five matches, then there are only five matches to find. Pretending any different is a fool's game.'

Freddy managed to rein himself in until the sound of Marek's footsteps disappeared, then he stuffed the notes in his pocket and grabbed for his coat.

'Where are you going?'

Freddy looked at her as if she was speaking an unknown language.

'To use the information and find Renny of course. Are you coming?'

He was so brittle, Hanni had a sudden vision of him crashing into the first address on the list and running out again with a screaming child flung over his shoulder. Or losing his temper if she pointed that madness out. She put a hand on his sleeve, which at least stopped him tearing at his coat buttons.

'Sweetheart, please, can you take a breath? It's Sunday. I know how desperate you are to find her, how close this list must make her feel, but is this the right way? Marek suggested that we start with the schools and we can't do that on a Sunday. So don't we need to wait until tomorrow?'

Wait took the air out of him. He sank down on one of the overstuffed armchairs and pulled the notes out again, clinging on to them as if they might vanish. Hanni sat down next to him and gently eased the papers away.

'It's not a bad thing to have this day, to think about the next steps. I don't blame you for wanting to hurl yourself into this, but wouldn't it be better to make a plan? One that won't put you in danger – or frighten her? Renny knows none of this, so she's going to need careful handling. All of this is going to need careful handling. You have to stand back from your feelings, my love. You have to be a detective.'

Hanni wasn't certain that Freddy would listen; his body was tensed again, ready to spring, and his face was a closed book to her. So it was a relief when he nodded. It was a relief when he got up far more calmly than when he had sat down and went to look through the cupboards for a city map to mark the schools onto. And it felt like a miracle when they managed to get through the rest of the day without him asking what it was she had been so desperate to explain in the seconds after the door-bell rang.

———

You have to be a detective.

Freddy had done that; he had done everything Hanni had asked him to do. He had put his emotions aside. He hadn't rushed out of the flat and gone roaring round to the addresses Marek had given them, yelling for whoever had stolen Renny to give his little sister back. He had paused. He had found a map, he had located the schools, which were all within a reasonable walking distance of their apartment. He had devised a plan where he and Hanni would walk past each one at opening or closing time, as the children were filing in and out. He had promised not to speak to anyone unless they were spoken to first and to stick to their cover story, posing as a couple interested in enrolling their young daughter if anybody asked. He had done everything that Hanni had persuaded him would lead them to the best possible conclusion, and he had done it all calmly. And now they had failed at the first hurdle and all he wanted to do was to grab her by the shoulders and yell.

They were at the first school but there wasn't a child to be seen: all the pupils were already inside. According to the message displayed on its noticeboard, the classes operated in two shifts, one in the morning and one in the afternoon, and the first session had begun at 7 a.m. Which left Freddy and Hanni standing alone opposite its closed doors half an hour late and without a single face to scrutinise.

'We couldn't have known that the timings are different here. We couldn't have...'

Hanni's voice trailed on with all the things that they couldn't have known and weren't their fault, but Freddy wasn't listening. She was trying to soothe him and he hated it. Managing each other was what other couples did, not them, or at least not until they had left Berlin. And now here they were again, where they had been for days – dealing in platitudes, tiptoeing over hot coals, not having one single meaningful conversation. It was false and uncomfortable, and Freddy had no idea why they were doing it. He was also too frightened to ask. So many things were wrong about Hanni, he was afraid where the wrong question might lead.

The Theresienstadt photographs – or, more precisely, her explanation of how she had come to take them – had unsettled him far more than he had admitted at the time. It hadn't seemed right that such a young girl would have been included in the Red Cross delegation, but Freddy had decided that must have been a factor of her father's job and not a decision under Hanni's control, and he had accepted it. What he couldn't understand was why she had never mentioned being in the ghetto town before, particularly given that he had shared his experiences of being held prisoner in Buchenwald. The story she had given him, about her shame and her guilt, had felt too rehearsed. He had decided, however, to accept that as well. But then, when they had actually got to Theresienstadt...

She was terrified.

It was a strong word but he couldn't think of another to describe Hanni's behaviour. She had hidden herself away. She had recoiled every time they met someone new. She had handled her share of the records as if they would burn her and had jumped like a deer spotting a hunter whenever one of the volunteers declared they had found something. And the way she had reacted to his casual comment about a pretty spring morning had been... The only word he could think of to describe that was *extreme*.

This isn't beauty; it's an illusion. That's all this place has ever been.

Freddy knew she hated the place. He had tried to recast her fury over a harmless sunrise as coming from a photographer's need to cut through to the truth. That explanation, like all the oddities he had made his peace with before, was the one he wanted to believe. But it wasn't just that outburst: everything else Hanni had said had been too specific, too personal. It had spoken of a far deeper knowledge of Theresienstadt and its workings than a one-day visit could claim. That had disturbed him. That and all the other disjointed things she had said – or started to say and he had refused to let her finish – since they had stood in the hollowed-out centre of Dresden.

It was fire-bombed and turned into an inferno. My father

was... The town was a lie and I knew that because... Don't answer it... let me explain...

There was a dark road leading from all those broken sentences, Freddy could feel it. Darker than the stories he had concocted for himself over the years to fill in the gaps Hanni had left in her life, and to explain her closely held secrets. Those were pressing even harder on him in Prague than they had done in the past. And Hanni was no better: she was a bag of nerves, looking over her shoulder every few minutes the way she had also done in Dresden. Acting like someone who wasn't his Hanni. In the middle of the previous night she had woken up weeping, insisting that their marriage was a mistake, that it had been done without her thinking it through, that tricking him into wanting to marry her had been wrong, and his heart had felt clamped in a vice as she said it. When he had, tentatively, asked her in the morning what had happened, she had acted as if she didn't know what he was talking about. Neither had mentioned it since. It had become one more unspoken fear in a far too long list.

'I know this is a blow but I don't think we should stay here. We'll draw attention to ourselves.'

She was right. Freddy pulled himself back. The maxim that no one in the street didn't mean no one was watching should have been second nature to him.

Hanni was still talking. 'Why don't we come back when the first group of children are due to leave, and wait while the sessions swap over? There'll be too many parents milling around then for us to stand out, and we might be able to see the whole intake.'

Her smile was too bright and it didn't reach her eyes the way Hanni's smiles usually did. It was fake; it wasn't her.

'Is that what you would like us to do, Freddy? To come back?'

Her too-cheery voice grated over his skin as roughly as her

false smile. She was trying to pretend that they were a team when he knew that they were currently anything but. He agreed anyway, if only to soften the tight lines of her face.

They returned as the pupils swapped over, but there was no match to be found there, no matter how hard he looked. They went home. They repeated the same desperate exercise the next day, running between two more schools.

What happens if it turns out to be none of them? lodged itself in his head, jostling for space with his deeper fear: *What if one of them is her but I don't know it.*

By the third afternoon and the fifth school, Freddy had lost any sense of himself. He stood on another pavement watching another troop of children wearing red scarves knotted at their necks march two by two into another drab building and wasn't sure if he was really there. The task was, once again, an impossible one. There were so many little girls, all with their neatly wound plaits and their tightly buttoned coats. How was he supposed to know if one of them had once been a two-year-old with an infectious smile and a laugh that tumbled in ripples from her lips? How was he supposed to turn fading memories and a black-and-white photograph into the colours and the warmth of a child?

'I'm so sorry, Freddy. I know how much hope you had.'

He hadn't spoken but his silence had told her all that she needed to know. The last pair of girls had walked past and neither of them was Renny.

Hanni was apologising again. Freddy didn't want to hear it. He didn't want Hanni telling him that it was time to give up, to go home, to accept that his family really was lost to him. He didn't want Hanni telling him anything at all. He wanted to scream and rail at the universe for sending him this one last soul-crushing chance that had never been a chance at all. And he was done with platitudes and nice. What he needed was someone to blame.

He wrenched his arm out of Hanni's with a force that made her gasp. He decided, this time, to let all the anger and the unanswered questions come, and to hell with the consequences. He got as far as, 'For God's sake will you stop,' and then all his words got stuck in his throat. There was a woman coming towards them who was obviously late and was caught up in the worry of that, oblivious to anything except the closing school gate. A woman with a girl at her side, who was small and slight and...

'Mouse.'

Freddy was vaguely aware of Hanni's 'What did you say?' He didn't respond to it. Hanni and all the confusion that went with her was gone; the only thing Freddy could see was the child.

The world faded out as she came into focus. Her dark blonde hair pulled back in a braid and clipped so that it tucked behind her rounded ears. The slight point that finished her nose. The eyes that were a little too large for a nine-year-old girl but that one day would be breathtaking.

'My baby mouse.'

A nickname from years ago, and how it still suited her.

Freddy could have laughed. He could have cheered. He had never had anything to fear. Not one inch of his sister had left him. He knew her face as well as he knew his own. There on the pavement, not a dozen yards from him, accepting but not returning the flustered woman's kiss, was his Renny.

CHAPTER 10

5 APRIL 1950, PRAGUE

'I have to save her. Why can't you get that into your head? She's Renny, I know she is – she's even called Renate for God's sake. And she's been with the Novotnýs for five years. How much poison could they have filled her with in five years? I listened to you on the street, I've listened to you all along, but I'm done with listening now. I have to go to their house. I have to get her back.'

The fight flared the instant they returned to the flat and it stripped the skins off both of them.

Hanni had forced Freddy away from the mother and away from the school, and he had hated her for doing it. That was the first thing he said when they closed their front door, followed by 'I didn't ask you to do that; I don't want it' when she protested that she had only been trying to protect him and stop him making a mistake they might not be able to recover from. Everything had escalated, badly, from there.

Whatever the gaps that ran underneath it, theirs was a relationship built on mutual respect and taking care of each other. Neither of them had the tools required for a row which would leave them both in one piece. Both were stubborn and convinced they were right. Neither had the armour to with-stand a deliberate attack from the other. And – in the frustra-tion of the distance and the tension which had grown up between them, and the pressure of secrets that had been held for too long – neither of them knew how to back down or stop.

Hanni's well-meant but badly put, 'What if we're wrong? What if the Novotnýs aren't the guard and his wife; what if she's with new parents now who are different people entirely?' was met with an eye-roll. And her 'You need to take a breath: okay so they match the profile but that isn't the proof we need. It could be a coincidence; her parents could be perfectly reason-able people' was met with a 'Don't be so stupid' which made her finally see red.

'I'm the one being stupid? You want to snatch a child from her family like some third-rate kidnapper, in a city you've no right to be in, and I'm the one who's stupid? Have you forgotten what happened the last time you saw a little girl who you thought was your sister? Dear God, wasn't that a success. You frightened the poor thing half out of her wits and then you collapsed in the street and couldn't get up again. Is that the strategy you're going with this time, or are you going to break in and grab her out of her bed?'

Hanni hated herself the minute she stormed through the last sentence, but it was too late to wish the words never said or solve them with the 'I'm sorry' she immediately blundered into. Her fury had opened doors that shouldn't have been opened, and Freddy was staring back at her through an equally angry mist.

'That's a brave move, bringing up the past. Is that really where you want to go right now?'

He had never looked at her with such fury. Hanni started desperately trying to backtrack, but he was too far gone in his rage to let her.

'Where would we start if we did? With the photograph?

With Theresienstadt, where you said you'd been for a day? Except that's not true, is it? You knew it too well. You were too afraid of it, and everyone in it, to have only ever been there for one day. Or should we go further back again? To why Natan Stein looked at me in such utter disbelief when I called you my wife? Or to why Elias doesn't trust you? Or to why there's been nothing in your background since we met but holes?'

'Stop it.'

Hanni didn't know if the snarl was for herself or for him, but it worked. Freddy instantly fell silent and so did the voice in her head screaming, *Rip off the plaster and tell him.* It couldn't be done. Not with him so enraged.

With an anger that's not meant for me. That's meant for the life Renny's been living, and the part he stupidly thinks he's played in creating that.

She knew on some level he was also aware of that fact, but it didn't matter; his fury would still turn its full force on her. So Hanni jumped into the gap Freddy's stunned silence had gifted her, before he could round on her again.

'I'm sorry, I really am. I didn't mean to sound so harsh. But is this the time or the place to be picking our lives over? Don't we need to focus on Renny? To be certain before we do anything that the parents are who we think they are and the child really is her?'

If she had stopped at *Renny*, there was a chance that Freddy would have listened and calmed down. *We* had managed to soften the taut lines round his mouth. But she hadn't stopped: by counselling caution so clumsily, she had voiced the doubt he didn't want to hear and flared him back up instead.

'What do you mean, *certain?* Do you think I don't know my own sister?'

He was saddled and ready; he needed to charge. All the fight suddenly drained out of her. Freddy was filled with a madness only he could let go of. Hanni's head ached, and so did her heart. She couldn't stop him. He had to realise on his own that they needed a plan that kept all three of them safe rather than plunging everyone into chaos. And the only way to end this endless argument that was hurting them both was to push him away and force him to work that out for himself. She turned her voice so cold she hated the sound of it as much as he did.

'I think it's possible that you may be deluding yourself, yes. You were desperate and that girl was the last one. Perhaps that made her into who you wanted her to be.'

He exploded, as Hanni knew he would. He accused her of never having wanted to find Renny, of wanting him all to herself. He accused her of a lot of nonsensical things Hanni refused to react to. Then he stormed out, slamming the door with a force Marek would have had him strung up for.

The silence was instant. Hanni sank down into it and onto the floor. She was too shocked to cry. All she could hope was that he would go away and nurse his wounds and finally hear what she needed him to hear: that they had no concrete proof yet that the child was Renny and no sensible plan to safely take her back if she was.

Part of her wanted to pack. To take her own chances at the border. To go back to Berlin and disappear and let Freddy and Renny – because whatever she had said to wake him up, Hanni had seen Freddy's face when he looked at the girl and she desperately wanted him to be right – move on with their lives. Until she thought about the child who had stood there so quiet and so self-contained while her mother had fussed, who had no idea of what was about to break over her. And about Freddy, whose hopes and heart would be shredded if his sister didn't want him the way he so desperately wanted her. Leaving him alone to face even the possibility of that couldn't be done. So Hanni didn't pack. She got up, found herself a blanket, curled up on the sagging sofa and did the only thing left for her to do. She waited for Freddy to come home.

The tap on the door woke her from a heavy sleep. Hanni came to slowly, her neck stiff from the sofa's lumpy contours. The clock on the sideboard said nine thirty, which meant Freddy had been gone for hours.

The tap came again, more insistent this time. Hanni got up, presuming it was him without his key, trying to be more discreet with his return than he had been with his leaving. She didn't have to pretend to be glad that he was back. She had missed him horribly within minutes of his going.

'I'm so sorry. I'm so glad you're home.'

Her delight died on her lips as Luca not Freddy pushed his way into the flat.

'Well that's all very lovely to hear, I'm sure. But the object of your affections is still in the pub, scowling into his beer. But hey, you're a pretty girl; I'd be happy to stand in for whatever welcome you were planning.'

He dropped onto the sofa and grinned. 'No, did I misread things? Never mind. Well he found her, which even to my good communist eyes must be some kind of a miracle. And yet here you are, and there he is. What happened? Don't you believe that the kid is her?'

He knew there was a rift between them, there was no point in denying that, but Hanni wasn't going to let him widen it any further.

'Freddy believes it. He's seen some traits in her that he remembers. That's good enough for me.'

'What a good wife you are. And presumably you'd never seen the girl's "mother" before or you'd already be running for the hills.'

His mocking tone was unbearable, too like the one favoured

by Reiner. *Same man, different system* slipped into Hanni's head and she had to hold down a shiver. She hadn't recognised the woman with Renny but she wasn't going to share the overwhelming relief of that, or anything else about finding the child, with Luca.

'What do you want?'

Luca brushed a piece of imaginary dirt from his knee and sighed. 'Really, you're going to take that tone with me? Fine, play the plucky heroine as much you like; it doesn't mean you're going to be the winner here. The web is tightening – don't pretend you can't feel it. So you didn't know the wife, that was a bit of luck, but the husband? That could be a very different matter. And how are you going to avoid meeting him when this thing progresses? I was there – I saw the touching scene. The Novotnýs – that's them, isn't it? My contacts got that right? Jana and František, and their delightful daughter, Renate. Residents of Prague since some not quite certain date in 1945. Their backgrounds on the surface a rather too familiar tale of lost homes and families and that ever so useful post-war muddle. I've got my eyes on them now. I imagine that if and when I choose to send someone to do some real digging, there will be another fake identity and a story that takes us back to Theresienstadt. Such parallels, and such irony. Everything found, everything potentially lost. It's no wonder you're keeping such a tight grip on yourself. Admit it, Hanni. For all your brave face, inside you're shaking'

He wanted her to know that he was matching her step for step and that his contacts were wide ones, and his manner wasn't mocking anymore. It was hard and cold, and capable of anything.

'You won't hurt her, will you?'

Luca knew she was afraid of him. There was no point in pretending otherwise. There was no point in trying to outwit him, and there was no time for games. The only vague comfort was that he frowned at the question.

'Hurt a child? No, of course not. I'm not the monster here. But I can make the family disappear to a place where you'll never find them. Or I can have her removed from their care and placed in one of our frankly rather disturbing orphanages. I can do far more interesting things than hurt her.'

And that was when Hanni finally saw where his cruelty and his power really lay. In making Freddy's life never his own again.

'And you'd let Freddy know what you'd done, wouldn't you? You would put Renny out of his reach, but not out of his hope. He'd never be done searching.'

'And...' Luca's handroll was deliberately theatrical.

'If...' She corrected herself as he shook his head. 'When I hand over Reiner, you'll leave her alone.'

'There we have it. You are finally taking me seriously.'

He got up and straightened his dark overcoat. 'The clock is ticking, my dear, and not only with me. "That's a brave move, bringing up the past." Wasn't that Freddy's starting volley when your fight really got serious?'

What in God's name doesn't *he know about me?*

Hanni fumbled her way to a chair.

Luca's mocking tone returned. 'You're not so brave now, are you? And that question that's written all over your face but you don't want to ask me? The answer is nothing. The walls are thin here. Your next-door neighbour has been in my pay since the day you moved in. And your husband is getting suspicious. He's starting to look at you with fresh eyes. It wouldn't take much more than a nudge before he believed every nasty thing I could tell him. Which I would be happy to do, long before you get a chance to spin a better version.'

'I'll get my father here. I'll do what you want.'

There was no life in her voice and no plan in her head. There was also no alternative.

'I know you will; I've just been waiting for you to catch up. And you'll thank me when he's in custody and I've done the job you always promised you would do. He's up to his old tricks again, Hanni; more people are going to suffer at his hands. Take a look at these if you need a reminder.'

He dropped a packet on the table and left the flat with a smile she wanted to rip from his face. As if she needed a reminder of what Reiner was capable of, or a reminder of how she had failed.

She dragged herself up and tore the packet open anyway. It was a set of photographs which her professional eye told her had been taken from a distance. They were all in a similar vein. A group of young men marching in a mountain setting, swastika-embossed bands tied round their arms. Another group lying on the ground and loading up rifles. A building set behind a pair of high gates which looked not unlike the Wannsee villa, although better protected. A fleet of limousines making their way along its immaculate drive and a woman in a fur coat standing on the building's curved steps. There was no accompanying note, but the meaning behind the images was clear. Reiner had set up another school exactly as Luca had said, perhaps a whole chain of them, and the boys attending it had parents who were powerful and rich. Being told it was one thing; seeing the evidence was another. Hanni had seen the textbooks and the teaching materials Reiner had filled the classrooms with in Wannsee. They had been filthy, poisonous things, and now that poison was spreading. Which meant that he had to be stopped.

Which Luca can do, if I help him, but won't that simply replace one man who could ruin my life with another?

Hanni ran to the kitchen and drank a glass of water so quickly her already queasy stomach turned over.

Freddy can't come home and find me like this. I can't come up with any more stories.

She rinsed the sourness out of her mouth, washed her clammy hands and face, and held on to the sink until her head stopped spinning. When she looked into the mirror propped up on the shelf, all she could see was Luca's self-satisfied grin.

You'll thank me when I've done the job you always promised you would do.

On one level, what he had said was true: there was nothing she wanted more than her father finally facing justice. But Luca also had her past in his hands, and she knew with absolute certainty that he would never be done with her. He would keep coming back. Whatever she did, she was in his net now and he would never let her get free of it. Even if she could somehow reel Reiner in, that wouldn't be enough. Next it would be her press connections and her camera he was after. And if she somehow managed to hang on to Freddy, Luca would drag him in too. There would be a whole lifetime of secrets and lies, a lifetime lived under another twisted man's control. She couldn't allow that, not for herself and not for Freddy and not for the child she was carrying whose life would be blighted.

So I have to take a leaf out of their book and beat Luca first – or find a way to play them off against each other.

Hanni went back to the living room. She had very little experience of Freddy drunk – she had no idea whether he would come home wanting sleep or another round of their fight. The sensible thing to do would be to go to bed, curl up with her eyes closed and pretend not to hear whatever mood he was in. Except the thought of lying down was impossible; her brain was spinning with ideas that wouldn't turn into anything concrete. She knew she had to focus on Reiner, and she tried. She could imagine a message reaching his hands – she presumed Luca had foolproof methods – but as to what that message would say?

Hanni was no closer to puzzling that out than she had been in the café.

Because he isn't the threat anymore.

She had to co-operate. She had to work out how to entice her father to Prague and she had no idea how to do it, but that wasn't the problem that was dragging her nails down the arms of the couch.

The real problem that needed solving was Luca.

CHAPTER 11

10 – 11 APRIL 1950, PRAGUE

'I'm so sorry, for lashing out and for leaving, but I can't do this. I can't fight you at the same time as doing everything I need to do to prove who Renny is and get her safely home. I'll crack in two if I try. So can we do what you suggested and not talk about our stuff? Can we let all of that wait?'

When Freddy finally stumbled home, he was no longer angry and intent on a fight. He was as drained as she was. The relief that he didn't want to scratch over the past again, or not yet anyway, was the best kind of reprieve. When she nodded, he collapsed onto the sofa and fell straight asleep. And when he woke, far sooner than she expected him to, he was back to being a detective again.

'We know who the family is, now we need to establish their patterns and find a way to insert ourselves into their lives. It's a simple surveillance task, something we're both good at. And we have to get started on it right now.'

'Okay, but if we do that, do you promise not to dive in and do something rash?' Freddy nodded. 'Then you take him, and I'll take her.' Hanni shook her head as he started to argue. 'I know you want to be near the girl but there were hardly any fathers outside the schools, so this is the only way we'll both blend in.'

Hanni didn't add that, whatever he might promise, she didn't trust Freddy to follow the child and not get carried away by his longing, not without her there to restrain him. And she couldn't add that just because her luck had held with the wife, that didn't mean it would with the husband.

Freddy didn't like it, but her logic didn't leave him any choice. He headed for the brickworks in Lesser Town across the Charles River where František Novotný was employed as a foreman. Hanni's patch spread between the school and the family's apartment on Šafaříkova Street. The area to be covered by them both was a small one. The brickworks were a twenty-minute walk away from Hanni and Freddy's lodgings. The Novotnýs home in Vinohrady wasn't much more. Hanni traced the streets separating Renny from them on the map and wished there were more: she didn't believe Freddy's patience ran any further than skin deep. When they came together again in the evening to compare notes, he was so calm as he reported František's movements, it was unnerving. Until he asked his first question and his hunger spilled.

'What's she like?'

It was the question Hanni had been dreading. She knew what he wanted to hear – a description of a lively, laughing child who ran into school surrounded by an equally exuberant group of friends and ran out again holding her arms wide for her mother. That, or at least so far, wasn't Renny. The only honest words Hanni could offer him were 'quiet' and 'reticent' and 'shy'.

'She watches everything, and yet she doesn't. I don't know how to explain it. She checks who and what is around her – I've seen her do it – but she doesn't make eye contact with anyone, and she holds herself separate even from her... from the wife, who gushed all over her again today.'

It took Freddy a moment to respond, and his voice was thick when he did.

'If that's not proof that she's Renny, I don't know what is. She's learned to behave like that – we all did. In Buchenwald, we used to call it watching without watching. You stay perfectly still and you catalogue everything around you. You read faces and mark threats, but you don't react to anyone or look directly at them. It's a survival skill that, if you're lucky and you've been taught it well, turns into an instinct. It had to. The ones who couldn't do it, who didn't get it right—' He stopped and couldn't find the rest of the sentence.

Hanni laid a consoling hand on his arm. 'Having that knack must be why you're such a good policeman now.'

It was an attempt to lighten his mood that came out far more clumsily than she intended. Unsurprisingly, it didn't work.

Freddy blinked and shook his arm free. 'Don't, Hanni. Don't try to make this better. My baby sister learned how to stay safe in a prison when she should have been learning how to play, and she clearly still carries the scars. Nothing can soften that.'

They had spent the rest of the night in a silence which continued until they left the house the next morning. Freddy was desperate to be gone. Hanni was far more apprehensive: every moment she was outside, she expected Luca to pounce again.

The hours stretched out as she shadowed Jana between the flat and the school and the café which was their afternoon stopping point without her knowing quite who to watch out for. She came back to the apartment with nothing new to add to her previous report, to find Freddy how she had expected him to be from the start. Prowling round the living room and incapable of even pretending to be patient.

'It's easy. He goes to his job. He goes to the same pub when he's done there, and no one goes with him. She takes Renny to the same café after school every day. That's enough, that will do. The café and the pub are where we will meet them and strike up a friendship. Then we'll dig into their back stories and work out how to get her free.'

Even though Hanni had expected his calm façade to vanish, the speed of the switch still horrified her.

'Freddy, no. It's only been two days – how is that every day? How is that a pattern? You know better than anyone how this works – you taught me. There has to be at least a week of watching them, and there has to be a better way in than a pretend chance meeting, particularly here where no one is trusted. We've nothing concrete on either the husband or the wife that matches them to Theresienstadt. What if we make them suspicious – or we scare them, and they run?'

But his mind was made up, and he flicked her panic away.

'Which may be true, but I don't have a week of this in me. And we don't have any other strategy except a chance meeting, unless you want us to take on waiting jobs and get to know them by serving their drinks? Monday, Hanni. You go to the café, I go to the pub. But we do it on Monday, and once that's done, we move as fast as we can on to the next stage. She's not slipping past me this time.'

The next stage.

Hanni knew Freddy hadn't a clue what that was. She stopped herself pointing that out. The cracks in their relationship were too thinly covered to risk another fight, and Freddy was too close to an act that was reckless. Besides, Hanni could hardly admit her real reason for stalling: that she needed more time to conjure up a plan that would summon her father to Prague and stop Luca, not the girl's parents, whisking Renny away. So there was no point in arguing with him. It was Monday.

She loves her.

Jana Novotná's heart wasn't only visible on her sleeve, the love it bore was written in her face and her hands and soaked into her being. And it wasn't just on show; it was raw and it was vulnerable. She couldn't keep her eyes off Renny – it was as if no one else existed in the café but the child. And she couldn't keep her hands away from petting and straightening and touching the little girl.

I had that directed at me once. That all-consuming kind of love.

The memory hit Hanni like a hammer blow. She never let herself think about her own mother; there was too much grief tied up in that, but now Talie was here, pushing up through all the layers Hanni had packed her in.

The image in Hanni's head was so vivid and so real it could have lit up a movie screen. The two of them together on a summer's afternoon in the Adlon Hotel. Sunshine dancing through the coloured lozenges set into the windows, wrapping blue and green ribbons round the lobby's marble pillars. Water gurgling from the famous elephant fountain. A slice of choco-late-glazed *Baumkuchen* waiting to melt all over Hanni's fingers. And her mother a vision in apricot chiffon, the prettiest woman in the hotel. Smiling at the waiters and at the day and at the daughter she adored. Because she had adored Hanni, and she had also adored the baby who came next – Luise, whose heartbreaking death had meant there would be no more good memories to be made.

Luise's death broke my mother. And losing Renny will break Jana, and neither of us have given a single moment's thought to what that might make her do.

Jana hadn't been real. She had been *the wife*. She had been a Nazi and a problem to be shoved out of the way. She was still all these things, but she was also a woman tied tightly to a girl who was, in her mind at least, her daughter.

We have never acknowledged her as what she is now, as Renny's mother. And if we don't, if we don't plan how to deal with her, she could turn into a far bigger problem.

Hanni put down the yeast-heavy bun she had been pretending to eat. Jana would fight tooth and nail for her child, Hanni was in no doubt about that. As for how Renny would react if she was taken...

The little girl was unreadable. She was as self-contained sitting in the café as she had been when they had first seen her outside the school. As she had been all those years ago in the ward after the guards had taken away the children who had been selected for the next deportation, on the day Hanni had taken her picture.

Oh dear God, Jana isn't the danger to me here: Renny is.

It was all Hanni could do not to leap out of her chair and run. She had been so relieved that Jana was a stranger, she had forgotten how close she had already come to the child. How could she explain herself if Renny recognised her from Theresienstadt? If she remembered Hanni as the girl whose camera she had once shied away from? If she screamed? Hanni could hardly pretend she had been a prisoner there too; Jana would surely bolt.

She won't know me. She can't know me. It was half her lifetime ago; she barely saw me that day. And what would I say to Freddy if I ran? I'm not the important one here, she is.

Hanni sat very still, forcing Luca's too-accurate comment about the tightening web out of her head. Trying to focus on now, not on then; to read the story in front of her.

Jana loved Renny, that wasn't in question, but that was only part of the picture. There was a disconnect between mother and child which grew more apparent the more Hanni watched them. Jana was fussing. Asking Renny about her day, worrying that the tea which the girl hadn't touched was too hot or too cold, that the pastry she had chosen for her was the wrong one.

Renny was unmoved by it all. She was absorbed in the paper and pencils she had produced from her bag the moment she sat down, offering only the briefest of answers to Jana's stream of questions. It was impossible to tell whether the child was simply withdrawn, or if there was some kind of gulf in the family that all Jana's best efforts couldn't fix. But then, as Renny finished with one colour and moved on to the next without looking up, Jana began staring around her, trying to catch someone's eye in a direct way even Hanni knew was alien to Prague and the truth was as clearly written as her love.

She's lonely. She's pouring everything she is into Renny and it isn't returned. She comes here because going home with such a silent, distant child must be too much for her.

If it had been any other mother and daughter, the truth of the relationship would have been tragic to see. In this situation, it was a gift. Danger or not, Hanni grabbed it.

'You have quite the little artist there.'

She was only a table away; she didn't need to raise her voice. From Jana's overeager answering smile, it was clear that Hanni could have said anything.

'She really is, isn't she? I know that every mother thinks that her child is special, but my Renny truly is.'

My Renny. They had kept the diminutive. Hanni's mind went blank at the ease with which Jana said a name that, until today, had felt like such a private thing. Not that the woman noticed. She was too intent on holding on to her moment of pride.

'Show her, sweetheart. Show the nice lady your drawing.'

Renny didn't want to. Her hand was rigid as she inched the paper around and her head stayed down, but she did as she was asked at once and without question. Hanni would have preferred a more normal reaction. For the girl to be excited at the opportunity to show off her work, or for her to say no and to have to be coaxed into it. There was something odd in the child's stiff and silent compliance. It wasn't, however, the moment to unpick that. Hanni glanced at the girl's notebook, already conjuring up a suitably gushing compliment, and then the skill on show caught her eye and she looked properly at it.

'It's really good. It's a good deal better than I would have expected from someone so young.'

Hanni's reaction was genuine. The drawing was of Peter Pan and Wendy flying over a line of moonlit rooftops and the perspective was perfect. Her reaction also brought Renny's head up, forcing Hanni to grab for a handkerchief and turn her startled gasp into a cough. Renny didn't appear to know her, but she knew Renny. The eyes staring up at her were Freddy's. She grappled round for something else that would stop the girl retreating back into her shell.

'You really do have the makings of an artist, and I should know, because I'm one of those too.'

Jana was crowing with delight but Hanni could barely hear her. The café had shrunk down to her and the child.

She reached into her bag, no longer caring if she tipped the girl into a dangerous set of memories or drew unwanted attention to herself. All that mattered now was forging a connection.

When she pulled out her camera, Renny's eyes widened. The resemblance to Freddy then was so vivid that Hanni brought the camera down far too heavily onto the table. The clatter turned heads which – when the watchers saw what Hanni was holding – turned immediately away.

Hanni spotted the furtive looks passing round the café and instantly raised her voice – she had to establish a set of credentials quickly; she didn't need some concerned, or spying, citizen calling a policeman. 'Do you know what this is?'

'Yes.' Renny nodded, her paper and pencils forgotten. 'But I've never seen a real one before.'

'I've been taking photographs with it for the city council. Of popular landmarks like the Town Hall and the Powder Tower, for a book which will show the rest of the country what a beautiful place Prague is. That's my job.'

Shoulders loosened at the tables around her; the chatter picked up a normal hum again.

Hanni dropped her voice and made it solely for Renny. 'I do what you do. I make pictures that will bring people pleasure.'

'And you get to do that every day, for work?'

Renny was leaning so far out of her chair, it was natural to beckon her over and let her handle the camera and the other pieces of equipment Hanni pulled out of her bag. When she finally remembered Jana and looked up at her, the woman was beaming.

'I hope you don't mind me being so forward but she has a very good eye – I could see that from the drawing. Maybe I could—'

Hanni stopped. It was too quick. She signalled for her bill and began packing up the spare lens and the film cannister.

'Could what?'

The girl and her mother both said the words at the same time in the same eager way, and suddenly Renny laughed like the child she was meant to be. The sound of it was exactly as Freddy had described it, a gurgle that lapped around the room like ripples breaking. It was impossible to resist.

Maybe I can do this as fast as Freddy wants. Maybe I can make a friend of Jana.

She smiled at Renny. 'I was going to say that perhaps I could give you a lesson, if you would like that. Show you how to properly take a photograph.'

Renny's immediate 'Say yes, Mother, please' ran straight

into Jana's 'Oh how wonderful' and left the little girl almost bouncing with excitement.

'Tomorrow – can we do it tomorrow?'

The offer couldn't have gone better; Freddy would be delighted. And then Hanni had a sudden vision of him using the opportunity to snatch Renny away and nothing resulting but chaos. She instantly changed her mind and shook her head.

Jana muttered something about good girls not being so eager. Renny's face returned to the blankness she had worn earlier, which was worse now Hanni had seen how happy she could be.

'I'm sorry, Mother. I shouldn't have been so loud and insistent. It wasn't polite of me.'

She sounded robotic and far too old for her years. Hanni couldn't bear it. She pushed Freddy from her mind and backtracked. 'No, it's fine, you didn't do anything wrong. I'm busy tomorrow, that's all. But I could come here on Wednesday. Wednesday would be wonderful, if you can do that too.'

Renny's face relaxed; Wednesday was agreed. Hanni gathered up her belongings and left, unsure whether she had done the right thing and unsure how to manage Freddy when she told him. The switch in the child's mood from excitement to a flat obedience had been disconcerting, but something else about the way the child had spoken was niggling at Hanni more. It wasn't until she walked underneath a tree newly coming into blossom, whose pale petals reminded her of Talia's apricot dress, that she realised what was bothering her. It was Renny's hollow and far too formal use of *Mother* rather than the more usual *Mama* Hanni would have expected from a nine-year-old girl. It suggested that, for all Jana's devotion, Renny might not be such a hard prize to pull free.

———

He hates her.

The knowledge of that was a horrible thing. Freddy had no choice except to swallow it, but then he let it burn through him, feeding his determination to rescue Renny at the first possible opportunity.

I hate him more.

There was no doubt in Freddy's mind about what kind of a man František Novotný was. He was a Nazi – Freddy could smell it on him. When Freddy had walked into the bar, Novotný had been sat alone, a large beer and a full ashtray in front of him. His suit was the shabby and shapeless serge uniform worn by foremen all over the Eastern Bloc. He should have been another faceless, worn-out man blotting his day out with drink; the kind Freddy had seen walking head down on every street in the city's centre. He wasn't. František Novotný may have been dressed the part, but he was different. He was still wearing his old life.

He carried an air of authority that went far past a foreman's badge. It was there in the tilt of his chin and the straight line of his shoulders, and in the way he sized up strangers, quickly and efficiently, assessing and dismissing their threat. He didn't watch without watching, he stared. It was the reason why nobody was near him. That and the menace Freddy's acutely tuned senses had spotted in his tightly drawn mouth.

Novotný was a Buchenwald man, an Auschwitz man. Used to total obedience, trained to be ruthless; merciless and quick to strike. Everything about him made Freddy long for the gun he had carried when he was part of the murder team. The only saving grace had been that he was also far more drinks down than Freddy was and clearly nowhere near ready to stop. That was a godsend. Freddy had seen plenty of men like him; he had used plenty of them as his sources. A drinker like Novotný – who drank from anger, not from pleasure or defeat – always, eventually, accepted the offer of a beer or a schnapps and

always craved an audience to throw his world view at. So
Freddy had sat and sipped his beer slowly, and he had waited
patiently while the bar thinned out.

'You're not a regular here.'

And there it was, the opening gambit he had been waiting
for. Offered in whatever way Freddy chose to take it – as an
invitation or a warning or a challenge.

Freddy landed with a half-smile on the first. 'I could be.
The beer's not bad. I'm new to the area, trying a few places out.'

Novotný's appraising stare was a longer one this time and
intended to be disconcerting. It made no impression on Freddy:
he had become impervious to men like Novotný calculating his
worth a very long time ago.

'From?'

One word, rudely put; intended to establish who was in
charge. Freddy let that go too.

'Košice, in Slovakia. Miles and what feels like centuries
away from here. I've come with my wife to make a fresh start.'

Novotný's lip curled. He took a gulp from his glass that half
emptied it. 'With your wife? What's fresh about anything if
you've brought her along?'

It wasn't said to be amusing. It wasn't intended to form a
connection between two men who were happily ruled by their
women. It was said with a malice that made Freddy want to
pick up the beer glass and hit him with it. And it also gave him a
way in. He picked up his own drink, nodded at the vacant chair
at Novotný's table and sat down when the request wasn't
denied.

'What could I do? She got wind of my plans before I could
get out of there and she's got no one else. And of course she
started begging so I could hardly abandon her. Don't tell me a
man like you is in the same boat?'

Novotný was just drunk enough for the flattery to work.

By the time they were two glasses into the bottle of

schnapps Freddy called to be sent over, he was drunk enough to lay what he described as his miserable marriage bare. It was a muddled tale which would have been of no interest to anyone except someone searching for clues the way that Freddy was. It was full of complaints about a wife who hadn't fulfilled the role she was meant to and a child who was a noose round his neck. When Freddy pushed him carefully on that, manufacturing some fears of his own about being trapped by a baby, Novotný got as far as 'and she's not even—' before he pulled himself up and settled on 'she's a brat'.

Freddy didn't probe any deeper; it was clear that, even when he was full of schnapps, the man had some level of control – or something he was determined to hide. He let Novotný ramble on from the disappointment that was his family to the disappointment that was his life in an endless diatribe which centred around one repeated phrase: 'Men like me, who've been leaders, who know how the world should be run, shouldn't be reduced the way I've been.' It went nowhere, but the bitterness gave Freddy everything he needed to know about Novotný's past, and his present. By the time they parted on the pub's steps – with Novotný stumbling and Freddy pretending to – they were the best of friends, with Freddy declared as a 'fellow soldier' even though he had barely said a word about his own life.

It took Freddy a while to steady himself once Novotný had wobbled away around the corner. His stomach wasn't sour from the effects of the alcohol – he had barely drunk half of what he'd poured into his own glass. It was sour from the poison he had been forced to listen to. From knowing what Novotný would happily have done to him if they had met only a handful of years earlier. And from knowing that this man, who evidently from his ramblings still believed in some form of a master race, who had no doubt once sent wagonloads of Jews to the ovens and clapped them on their way, had the care of his precious little sister. And once Novotný discovered that his secret was out or, worse, discovered that the cuckoo in his nest was a Jewish one...

It was the cold-water shock of that which pulled Freddy off the wall and spurred him home. He had to see Hanni, to tell her that things needed to move even faster. That he was going to confront Novotný sooner rather than later. And that Renny wasn't coming home on some far-away, still crept-around date. She was coming home to him now.

CHAPTER 12

12 APRIL 1950, PRAGUE

'She's been raised by wolves. If I get one step of this wrong, they'll turn on her.'

Freddy's second session in the bar with Novotný had left him seething, not least because the man had grown, as Freddy bitterly put it, 'far too comfortable with me'.

'He's filled with hate because nothing in his life has gone right since the war ended, although none of that of course is his fault. He wouldn't say where they were in 1945, but he definitely didn't want to come to Prague – he blames Jana for that decision – and the Soviet-backed takeover here has sickened him. He's clever: he's not stupid enough to say it out loud, but he loathes communists. He trotted out the old Nazi Party line that they're a threat to any country they get a foothold in. It was a test to see how I would react, I'm sure of it, so I nodded and said nothing.

'He was far less discreet when it came to his opinion of Jews though – I gather hating us isn't a problem here. God, Hanni, the language he used. It's been years since I've heard it, but it doesn't get easier. The demonising, and the way he got fixated on *parasite*... Everything out of his mouth could have come from a Goebbels-approved script. If they have been pouring that filth into Renny, if they – or he, because he thinks Jana is keeping secrets about her – find out the truth about her background before I can get her out of there...'

Freddy's description of Novotný's beliefs had been horrible to listen to. And his fears over Renny's safety had made it even harder for Hanni to keep counselling caution, especially as he had – as Hanni had expected – no interest in anything Jana might try to do to stop him. Hanni couldn't shake that concern away. Jana had proved how far she would go when she was desperate by taking a Jewish child in the first place, and then by hiding Renny's origins from her husband. She could fool him, but Hanni wasn't fooled by her at all, and she was determined to stay wary. Which wasn't difficult when Jana only had eyes for her daughter.

'She's a natural, isn't she? I knew she would be – that's why I was so thrilled when you suggested giving her a lesson.'

It wasn't difficult either to agree with that. The park close by the café was a small one, but it had enough interesting features to make it a suitable training ground, not that Renny had required much direction. Hanni had shown her the basics of how to focus the camera and frame a shot; after that she had left the girl free to choose the subjects that spoke to her. It was the same technique that Ezra Stein had employed, although the material ten-year-old Hanni had had to work with – a procession of torch-bearing Hitler supporters – had been far more challenging than the twists of the railings and the bank of snowdrops Renny was currently investigating.

'She really is. You must be so proud of her. She doesn't have any siblings does she? She's your only one?'

The question had come naturally, one woman to another. It hadn't been intended to probe or to trick, even if that was the reason Hanni was there. Jana's face instantly collapsed.

'I'm so sorry. That was the wrong thing to say – it was tactless. Of course she is or you would have already mentioned another child, and now I've upset you, which was the last thing I meant to do.'

Hanni was babbling, concerned that Jana might pull away from her. The right response, the friend's response, to Jana's sudden flood of tears was a consoling arm or an enveloping hug, but Hanni couldn't bring herself to do it. She pulled a handkerchief and a mirror out of her pocket instead and waited while Jana restored herself, waving brightly at Renny when the girl briefly looked up.

'You don't have any children yourself yet, do you?'

Hanni shook her head. She wasn't about to share news with Jana that she was still hugging to herself and hadn't yet divulged to Freddy, no matter how important it was to build at least the show of a friendship. Besides, Jana was clearly on the brink of a story that could be vital to Renny's history and Hanni didn't want to deflect attention from that. She kept her secret to herself and let Jana carry on talking.

'I hope that you can, if that's what you want. It wasn't so easy for me.'

She paused. It only needed a little nudge to keep her going.

'Was there a reason for that, if you don't mind me asking?'

Jana didn't mind at all, she was clearly desperate for any form of human contact. She stared over at Renny, who had moved on to examine the knots in a low-hanging branch. 'Me – I was the problem, not that I knew. I wanted a big family, and I thought I would have one. A nursery full of toddlers, a baby in the pram. And that was my job, that was what was expected of me.'

Her gaze shifted until she was looking over Renny's head, into the distance and a life that only she could see. Hanni knew better than to fill in the gap, or to worry at the echoes of her own mother in *job* and *expected*. Now that Jana had let go and started talking, she wouldn't stop.

'I had no idea that it wouldn't happen, that all my chances had been taken from me long before I was married.'

She paused again; Hanni nudged her gently again. 'Did something happen to you?'

The question shifted Jana's gaze further away. It was obvious that she was slipping out of the park and into the past, but that didn't prepare Hanni for what was coming. Or for the unwanted sympathy she felt.

'I wasn't born here. I'm not Czech by birth. I was born in Kukhari, a small village in Ukraine, as the first war was ending. By the time I was a girl and old enough to think about marriage, the world I knew had ended. My village was starving, my country was starving, bled out to feed Stalin's Russia with no thought for what would happen to us. And I don't mean starving because we had to live on the kind of rations the last war made us used to, I mean because there was nothing to be had. That shouldn't have happened. Ukraine was a land of farmers; there should have been plenty. But Stalin took everything we had, until we were forced to eat tree bark and grass and... well there were stories of dark things I don't want to think about.

'Thousands and thousands died, my whole family among them. Some say it was millions although that's not a number I can make myself believe. Yet I lived. I thought that meant I was lucky, but my body was damaged. By the hunger. By a farmer who drove a rifle butt into my stomach when he caught me trying to steal the bread he had hoarded. And I didn't know that I had already failed as a wife before I was even married.'

The bleakness in her words was overwhelming. The numbers were another set of numbers that ran past anything Hanni ever wanted to hear again.

Everyone who comes through our hands has suffered.

The Red Cross official who said that to Freddy had meant the refugees who had suffered in the war, but the tragedy that had ruined Jana's life had already happened before that conflict began. And its stories had been lost in the carnage which followed. Russia – the power which now controlled vast swathes of the East – had deliberately starved Jana's people and Hanni had never heard a thing about it. It was impossible not to feel afraid at the implications of *dark things*. It was hard not to feel desolate when the world was such a deeply scarred place. Or to feel sickened that a woman whose life had been destroyed by one murderous regime could so devotedly have followed another. She had to take a deep breath she hoped would sound like shock before she could speak.

'Failed? Why would you say that, Jana, when none of what happened was your fault?'

Jana's voice was as lost as the country she had grown up in. 'Try telling my husband that. I let him down and I held him back. I wasn't the right kind of wife.'

Not the right kind of wife.

How many times had Hanni heard Reiner throw those same words at her mother when grief had kept Talie pinned to her bed? When her mind had slipped away from the present and she had spent her days chasing after ghosts. When she *wasn't fit to play hostess* the way a good SS wife should. Jana had explained her whole adult life with one line, and the sadness in it was real.

But she is still with him. She will still defend him to the death if it means holding on to Renny.

Hanni wanted to get up and leave, but there was still one question left to ask.

'And Renny? I assume she's not yours then?'

She had picked the wrong word. Jana's body stiffened.

'Renny saved my life. When I found her, I found a reason to keep going. How can you say *not yours*? She is mine, in every way that matters. I raised her. Nobody else can claim that.'

Freddy had been right, although he had used the word

wolves in a more vicious way. Jana was a she-wolf: she would protect her young whatever the threat, or the cost. Hanni raced to apologise and defuse the situation before Jana decided she didn't want a friend after all. 'Of course she is. I've never seen a mother as devoted as you are. What else is important to a child but that?'

It was enough. Jana softened. *Devoted* relit the proud light in her eyes. The afternoon ended with smiles and a second film filled and Hanni's promise to develop Renny's photographs as fast as she could. Jana kissed Hanni on both cheeks as she left and whispered a 'thank you' that she clearly meant as a seal on their friendship. Hanni managed not to shudder.

She watched them go, Jana reaching for Renny's hand, Renny taking a moment too long to respond.

Renny saved my life.

Hanni got up from the bench, forgetting to put her camera away, and exited onto the street, her head filled with how to explain to Freddy what an obstacle Jana might be in a way that would make him listen.

Because her thoughts were miles away from Prague and its dangers, she noticed the group of boys milling on the corner and staring at her a fraction too late. She stuffed the camera back into her bag the second she realised she was still holding it and started to pick up her pace. Her efforts were pointless – they had already begun to close in. The café should have been within easy reach, but the boys were ready for her. They moved in a pack, circling, cutting off her escape.

'Come one step closer and I'll scream the whole place down.'

They took no notice; they didn't need to. The threat only held weight for a second or two, until the few people in earshot suddenly faded away.

'I mean it. Get back.'

It was bravely said. But the hand which wrenched her arm up and behind her twisted Hanni's bravery away.

Not everyone, thankfully, had left her to her fate.

The police van was on them while Hanni was still struggling, her body curved over the baby as she tried to protect what had been an idea and was now, in the face of the boys' threat, infinitely precious to her. Someone had seen what was about to happen and had raised the alarm. The gang was bundled into the van's dark interior under a hail of blows.

'Oh my God, that was terrifying. I am so glad to see you.'

Hanni was halfway through her stammered thank-yous before she realised that the danger she had walked into was a long way from done.

'Papers.'

The policeman had his hand out and no interest in her experience or her welfare. Hanni picked her bag up from the pavement where her shaking hands had dropped it when the police arrived, trying not to fumble as she retrieved her faked documents. She hadn't had to surrender them to anyone yet, except to the border guards who had been paid to have no interest. She had no idea if they – or she – would stand up to scrutiny.

'It was my fault. I was careless. Putting my camera on display like that, it was asking for trouble.'

She was babbling, partly from nerves, partly to distract him from her papers. It made no impression. He looked from the photograph on the identity card to her and back again before passing it to his colleague and addressing her in a manner which suggested nothing good.

'Where are you from? Why are you in Prague?'

Hanni gave him the story of a too-small village and a fresh start as succinctly as she could. She had no idea if he believed it.

'And it is normal is it, in Košice, to walk around with a camera? To take photographs of public, and perhaps not so public, places?'

Not so public, with all its implications of secrets and spying, was not what Hanni wanted to hear. The man's expression and his stance hadn't shifted, there was no visible threat, but his tone suggested that she was one wrong answer away from joining the boys in the back of the van. There was no point in trotting out the guidebook story she had used on Jana and Renny; Hanni knew that would crumble in seconds. She decided instead to opt for naïve and to trust that being foolish wasn't, or at least not yet, grounds for arrest.

'I do hope I haven't done anything wrong – that honestly wasn't my intention. But Prague is so beautiful, and taking pictures of beautiful places is my hobby.'

From the way the policeman sniffed, it was clear that being foolish could very easily be classified as a crime. Hanni's palms turned clammy. He still had her papers. She had no doubt that he was about to seize her camera, and then her.

'It is an expensive *hobby* though, isn't it? It's not one I've seen an ordinary citizen indulge in before. Who gave the camera to you?'

'I did, Officer. It was a birthday gift to my wife who, as she just told you, has quite the passion for architecture.'

Luca's arm was around her shoulders before Hanni registered that he was there. The words were polite enough, but the way he said *officer* made it clear that was a title which could be very easily lost.

'You don't have a problem with that, do you?'

Whether the policeman did or he didn't no longer mattered. He had stepped back the instant Luca flipped his lapel and revealed a badge that Hanni had never seen before but the two men now wishing they were anywhere else evidently had. One sight of the raised arm and the rifle embossed on the enamel and they turned instantly into Luca's subordinates. There was a raft of apologies. Hanni's papers were returned at lightning speed. They sprinted back to their van and were gone. And Hanni was left alone in the street with another man radiating fury.

'Well that was stupid. Why would you call attention to yourself like that? It was bad enough when you were playing teacher in the park, but then wandering about waving a camera that no one here would dare parade in public like a flag? I should have let those clowns take you: a few hours in a cell might have taught you the caution you apparently lack.'

He didn't let Hanni speak. The badge Hanni assumed marked him out as a Stasi officer was hidden again. His arm was no longer draped round her shoulders but shoving her across the road and into the café. When he pushed her over to a table and into a seat, the rest of the customers immediately left.

'This has gone on too long. I need your message for Reiner written now.'

He pulled a pen out of his pocket, plus a handful of black-and-white and cheaply tinted postcards which he spread across the checked cloth.

'But I haven't—'

'No.'

His fingernails were on her wrist again, the memory of the pain he had inflicted on her last time snapping off her words.

'Don't bother telling me that you don't have a plan, or you don't know what to say. I don't have time for it; I don't care. We're moving on my timescale now. You have five minutes to get this done or I'm marching you straight to Freddy and sending a squad after the girl. I told you: all the Eastern Bloc's police networks are interconnected. Never mind the GDR, she'll be on a train to Moscow tonight and adopted into a good Russian family before he's finished screaming at you. Is that what you want?'

Hanni couldn't speak or move.

Luca pushed the cards across the table. 'I'll take your silence as a no. Your father used a postcard to contact you the last time so we'll do the same. Keep it simple and give me something I can use so that he knows this is definitely from you. What are you waiting for? Choose a picture. If the scene means something to him that's even better.'

Hanni stared at the cards. Her mind was tumbling so fast, the views depicted on them all blurred into one. She was aware that Reiner had visited Prague a number of times, including when he was overseeing the filming at Theresienstadt and had visited the film production office there, but the only place he had ever mentioned spending time at was the Petschek Palace. Beyond the fact that it had once been a bank, Hanni had no idea what that building might look like but, from the way she had once heard him describing his work there – or more precisely how often he had used his whip in the vaults that had been turned into torture chambers – she doubted it was a location which would merit a postcard.

'Come on, Hanni, don't take all day. If there's nowhere you think he'll know, choose the one where you'd feel most comfortable meeting him.'

Where she would feel most comfortable. The idea was absurd. Hanni picked up a shot of the Old Town Square and immediately put it down again. There were too many narrow streets surrounding it, too many corners Reiner could turn into a trap.

Luca's fingers had started drumming the table, closing in on her wrist. She couldn't let him take control of her with pain again; she had a feeling he would teach her a worse lesson if she did, and she was not in a position anymore to take physical risks.

'This one. This one will do.'

The image was a black-and-white one of the city's castle, taken from the gardens which flanked its southern side. It didn't offer *comfortable*; nothing could, but it offered open spaces and that would have to do.

'Good. Now write something that will make him take notice.'

Luca passed the pen over the table. Hanni forced herself to pick it up without trembling. Any attempt she made to contact Reiner would make him take notice, but she still had no idea how to tempt him to Prague. He didn't trust her any more than she trusted him; he was certain to assume that any message was a trick. Besides, there was nothing she could offer him, nothing she had that he could possibly want.

Unless I tell him the news about the baby. The hope of a grandchild, part of his bloodline. What wouldn't he do for that?

A baby would matter to him, even if Freddy was the father, and maybe she could lie about that. And in that thought the idea came crashing down. She couldn't hurt Freddy like that, any more than she could let Reiner near their child.

Then if not the baby, what about me? Wouldn't that be almost as much of a coup for him? What was it he said in the early days of the Strangler case? 'With a bit of handling perhaps you could have been an asset, not a constant disappointment.' That was it.

He had delivered that judgement in his usual mocking tone, but Hanni had heard a grain of interest, and possibly hope, in it. That he wished he had tried harder to convert not to crush her had disgusted her then and it disgusted her now.

But it could give me a way in to him.

She picked up the pen and wrote quickly, before she could change her mind. When she handed the finished note to Luca, he raised an eyebrow and nodded.

I am a long way from home and in need of a father. I truly wish you were here.

He slipped the card into his inside pocket. 'That's not what I expected but, if I was him, I would definitely be intrigued.'

Hanni retrieved her bag from under the table. She had to be away from him and back to a place where she could think. But Luca wasn't finished with her.

'Hold on, what about the rest? The special sign that proves it's really from you.'

A change in fortunes heralded by a bouquet. Perhaps it will become a family tradition.

They were also Reiner's words, written on the letter which accompanied the bouquet containing red roses he had sent her when his fortunes had changed and he had left Berlin. The same flowers which had accompanied the postcard he'd sent her a few months later from the Harz Mountains. Frau Greber had reported that to Luca but she hadn't properly examined them or understood their real message.

Hanni got to her feet. She had to be gone the moment she issued the instruction: the thought that she was aping Reiner's tricks, and using a symbol that meant purity to him and horror to her, made her sick.

'Attach it to a bunch of red roses. And wrap sprigs of edelweiss inside the stems.'

Maybe Luca won't be able to take Reiner into custody as easily as he thinks he can. Maybe there'll be a shoot-out and they'll both end up dead.

It was a ridiculous, laughable idea, the stuff of bad B-movies. Hanni still wanted to believe it could come true. Reiner would answer her summons, she was certain of that: his ego would demand it. The challenge of entering a Communist-controlled country undetected would thrill him. The possibility that his traitorous daughter had finally realised where her loyalties lay was the kind of victory he would crow over for years. So he would come. And if he found out about her deception before Luca could strike, his rage would be boundless. There would be two men in a city too small to contain them who were determined to destroy her. Or two men she would have to destroy.

Hanni made her way back to the flat in a fog, trying to bridge the gap between what had to be done to keep herself and the baby safe and the impossibility of doing it. She couldn't imagine how a scene where she was the one in charge and where Reiner or Luca, or both, were utterly at her mercy would play out. There wasn't a single movie she had seen, good or bad, where it was a woman successfully wielding the gun. And there was nobody she could turn to for help; not Marek, who was the only other person in Prague that she knew, and certainly not Freddy. Not unless she wanted to add another furious man to the list.

She let herself quietly into the flat, hoping to be able to slip into bed and feign sleep before Freddy returned. She didn't have the energy left to cope with another dose of his rage.

She didn't get a chance: the lamps were lit and he was already there. But he wasn't pacing. And he wasn't waiting to pour out the poison Novotný had poured into him. Freddy was sitting on the edge of the sofa, his shoulders slumped and his head down, lost in a silence that was worse than his tirades.

Luca and Reiner instantly flew out of Hanni's head. She ran to him. When she dropped down on the rug and took his hands in hers, they felt too limp to contain bones.

'What has happened? What's wrong? Is it Renny?'

She had a sudden vision of a tiny girl being bundled into a train compartment by a granite-faced minder and the miles to Moscow stretching endlessly on. 'Tell me she's not gone?'

Freddy raised his head. His skin was baggy beneath his eyes; his eyes were strangers to sleep. Hanni's heart flipped over.

'Gone? No, why would you think that? I've been with Novotný again and this time it was worse – it was too much.'

That was bad, but it was steadier ground than the fear of a Russian adoption which Luca had planted.

Hanni pulled herself up and sat down beside Freddy. She didn't let go of his hands. 'Tell me what he said. No matter how rough it was.'

Freddy sighed and pulled her close for the first time in days. 'It wasn't rough, or not in the way you mean. He didn't launch into one of his rants tonight. He was quieter, more introspective. You said Jana was lonely, which is why she confided in you so quickly. He's the same. And he's lonely for family too, but not in the same way as she is. He never speaks fondly of her, or Renny; they're nothing but a burden to him. Tonight was all about the comrades he misses, the loyalty and the bond he once had with them. A bond he described as the only tie that should matter to a man, one that goes far deeper than anything to be found between husband and wife, or with children. He didn't say explicitly who he meant – he's very good at doing that, no matter how much schnapps I ply him with – but who else could he be referring to except the SS?'

Hanni couldn't hold back a shudder. 'That idea of ties stronger than family was at the heart of Himmler's philosophy. The SS were the Party's sword-bearers, the virtuous ones, bound by a lifelong oath. The carriers and defenders of racial purity.' She pulled herself back from repeating one of Reiner's endless monologues as Freddy frowned. 'That was what was said about them at Nuremberg, wasn't it? It's stuck with me; it must have done the same with you.'

His fingers wove tighter through hers. 'It's certainly stuck with Novotný; it's stamped through him. He admitted to me tonight that he's actually a German, although he didn't go as far as divulging his real name.' Freddy paused for a second. 'And I admitted the same thing to him. Don't look so scared. I had to, for the sake of the connection we were forging. And I didn't exactly say it, I was as careful with my words as he was, but I gave him the impression that I was... that I agreed with... that...'

He couldn't go on. His voice disappeared under a sob.

'It's okay. It's okay.'

Hanni pulled his head onto her shoulder and held him while he cried out his anger.

'But it's not. It's a betrayal of everyone who died at their hands. I let a Nazi believe that I'm the same kind of man as him. I should have cut out my tongue first – or his.'

'You did it for Renny.' She pressed her lips to his hair, then she found his mouth and she kissed him again. 'And surely that makes whatever you had to tell him, whatever you had to do, to get closer to her all right.'

He was out of her arms so fast she almost toppled. 'How can you say that? It doesn't; it shouldn't. How can doing the wrong thing to get to the right place ever be acceptable? Isn't that simply a lie to justify the worst kinds of behaviour? Isn't it a way to make any sin sound right?'

Hanni stayed where she was, although her body yearned to leap up and hold his. She had promised not to try and soften the world for him anymore or to offer him platitudes. So she held herself still and she waited while Freddy wrestled with the conscience that ruled him and she wished she could soak up his pain.

'I'd made them both into monsters. That's why I didn't want to hear about Jana loving Renny or saving her life. I'd turned them into Nazi child-snatchers, into cartoon characters. And now I've had to get to know him and he's real, and that's worse. He chose his path. Despite Germany's defeat and Hitler's suicide and all the unimaginable, terrible things that have been revealed to the world since the war's end, he still believes that path is the only true one. He would stand up and wave a swastika and reopen the camps tomorrow if he could. And all I keep thinking is, how many more men, and women, like him are still out there, hiding in plain sight?'

There wasn't an answer Hanni could give him to that. The only thing she could think of to do was try to turn the focus back where it belonged.

'I hate that you feel like this, I do, and that you've had to spend more time with him, but maybe there's something in what he said that we can use. Did he talk about Renny – about how she came to be with them? I'm asking because Jana's started opening up. She admitted today that Renny isn't their child, or not biologically. And I know you don't want to hear this, but she doesn't care about that. As far as she's concerned, Renny is her daughter in every way.'

Freddy's face twisted. 'To her maybe, but not to him. Yes, Novotný's as good as said that she isn't his. That her being with them was all down to Jana not being able to have a child of her own and getting obsessed with Renny, which he doesn't understand. He resents her and I think it's getting worse. He wishes that Jana had left her "behind", although he wouldn't say what that meant. Or that she'd chosen differently. And he's not a fool, although he thinks Jana may have played him for one. He suspects he's been lied to: she told him that the child belonged to a maid who died and that there was no one else to keep her, but he's not sure about that anymore. He thinks there's something "wrong" in Renny's background because she doesn't jump to his tune. And that's when he clammed up and it was too risky to push him. I could hardly say, *Didn't it dawn on you when you stole her from Theresienstadt that she might be Jewish?* Or ask if he remembered which train he put her real mother on.'

Hanni let him move through the agony of that before she asked him, 'So what happens now?' It was the first time all evening his eyes had brightened. The light shining out of them wasn't a healthy one.

'We're going to their house on Saturday. We're going to sit down together and eat lunch.'

Hanni thought she had misheard him. She'd been hoping he would suggest more meetings in the pub and the café, digging out additional information they could use and building stronger bonds. All she could manage was, 'What did you just say?'

'We're going to be their guests, this Saturday. He wants to meet you. He wants you to meet Jana. He thinks our families could be friends.'

Now it was Hanni's turn to pull away. 'Dear God, Freddy, you can't mean it. It's too dangerous. Jana and I have already met. How is that supposed to work?'

Freddy shrugged. 'It will be dismissed as a happy coincidence, or as fate if you like, proving that we are all the *fellow soldiers* he wants us to be.'

He was looking at the carpet. He was looking at his hands. He was looking at anything but her. Hanni's neck shivered.

'What are you planning? It's more than lunch, isn't it?'

He still didn't look up. 'I'm going to tell Novotný the truth – that Renny is my sister. I'm going to reason with him. I'm going to promise to keep the truth of his war and his past quiet if he hands her back to me. And if that doesn't work, I'm going to threaten him with the exact opposite and I'm going to take her away.'

'Just like that?'

He nodded. 'Just like that.'

Hanni stared at him, trying to reconcile the man who had been in tears on her shoulder a few moments ago with the man who was now all clenched jaw and curled fists. There was nothing calm left in him, if there had ever been anything calm at all. He had swallowed his rage and turned it into fuel. He didn't care about caution. He was blind to anything except getting his sister back, even if doing that blew the little girl's world apart. And she couldn't let him do it so abruptly and ruin everything.

'Please, Freddy, don't you see that this is a mistake? I thought we'd agreed to take slow steps. That snatching Renny away from her home without warning is a terrible idea. What if Novotný has better connections than you know about? He could stop us getting her out of the country. And even if he doesn't care enough to try and stop you, I swear Jana will. She'll fight you tooth and nail. Do you honestly want Renny to see that? I understand your desperation, truly I do, but this is the perfect example of the wrong thing and the right place. It's what you said no one should do.'

When he finally looked at her, she wanted to weep. She couldn't find her Freddy in his face.

'And I meant that; in an ideal world I still do. But this is a long way from an ideal world, and where have my principles got me? Novotný mightn't want to be saddled with a child now, but I bet she helped him get clear of Theresienstadt; I bet he played the family card on the road as cover. And Jana wanted a child so she took one. They shaped the world to fit them, so why shouldn't I? Why should I stick to the right side of things and carry all this pain? And you don't understand my desperation or you wouldn't keep telling me what I *can't* do. I'm done with that, Hanni. I'm done with listening to the way you lay down the law as if you hold all the moral cards. I'm done with pretending I agree with the way you think the world should behave. I'm doing the talking now, and I'm the one making the decisions.'

She had nothing to fight back with. *Moral cards* had swept all her certainties away. How could she tell him not to try and shape the world to his own ends when that was exactly what she had been doing ever since they had first met? Doing everything wrong because she wanted their love to be the right place. And then the word hit her: *love*. That was what this was all about, and that was what had been forgotten.

She took a deep breath and tried again. 'I am on your side,

Freddy, even when I don't sound like I am. I won't argue with you anymore; I won't lay down the law, which I never meant to do. But is this what you want? To physically drag a child who probably doesn't remember you away from the only home that she knows? I know it would come from love, but she won't. Don't you see that you could terrify her? Wouldn't it be better to come to some sort of accommodation with the Novotnýs if we can?'

That at least had some effect; Freddy's face crumpled. 'No, of course that's not what I want; it's the complete opposite. I don't want to frighten her. I want her to know that she will be, that she is, loved far more honestly by me than by the couple who stole her. And, yes, I want Novotný to show some compassion and let the child go.'

His voice instantly hardened again. 'But we both know the kind of man we're dealing with here, so I'm only telling you what will happen if he won't.'

What will happen.

Hanni knew Freddy's mind was already made up. That he wouldn't be able to stop himself, that he would charge in the second his plea for an unconditional handover was refused. That *what will happen* was a certainty in his head, not a last resort.

She was as exhausted as he was, and the despair she had been trying to hide suddenly spilled over. 'How can you do this? He's not going to show compassion, and you're not expecting him to. You're going to tell him that he's been raising a Jewish child for five years. He's a Nazi – he won't let that go. He'll want some kind of revenge. On you, or on his wife, or God help us, on Renny. You know all that and yet you still won't stop. Oh, Freddy, my love, can't you see what's happening? This isn't only about rescuing her; this is about making him pay.'

He was on his feet, his body rigid with fury. 'And what's so wrong with that? Why should he get away with everything he's done? Why should any of them?'

It was pointless trying to reply. Freddy was gone, the door slamming like thunder behind him. His parting words – 'Why can't you just support me? Why does it always have to be a fight?' – sucking the air from the room.

CHAPTER 13

15 APRIL 1950, PRAGUE

She was a stranger, so he has to be too.

Hanni hadn't slept all night; neither had Freddy. And neither one of them had acknowledged that the other was awake.

The flat had been a fraught place since Wednesday night. Both of them were wary of the other; both of them were still raw from their row. Both of them, however, were trying to breach the divide.

Freddy had softened a little. He had managed to step back from his anger and, whatever he had said about no longer listening to Hanni, he had taken some notice of her words. He acknowledged that Renny could suffer if his confrontation with her parents turned ugly or violent. He promised that snatching her would be his last, not his first, resort. Hanni in turn promised that she believed him, and she tried hard to make that promise true. It was a step or two towards each other, but it wasn't the reconciliation they both craved and couldn't admit to desperately needing. They were both still a long way out of reach.

To keep herself physically out of Freddy's way, Hanni had

commandeered the small bathroom and turned it into a dark-room, ready to develop Renny's photographs. She had stopped halfway through setting up the first chemical bath. There was no way now to get the pictures to the child. Freddy had asked her not to meet with Jana again before Saturday – he hadn't been unkind enough to say, 'I don't trust you not to warn her,' but the implication was there. And Hanni could hardly take the pictures to a lunch she was supposed to pretend was a happy coincidence. So she had packed her precious materials away and fretted instead.

Her brain had been spinning round the invitation to visit the Novotnýs since Freddy had sprung it on her. With the fear of what Freddy would do. With the fear of how Renny – and Jana – would react if he declared who he was and what he wanted. There had been so many *what ifs* competing for space in her head. It was two o'clock on Friday morning before the most frightening one hit her. *What if Luca is right? What if I know the father? What if he knows me?* The impossibility of where that could lead to had crept over her in the dark and frozen her limbs. There was nothing she could do to prepare for it except not go, which had her turning in circles again. There was no scenario in which leaving Freddy to go alone was a reasonable one.

She had tried to get a steer. She had asked Freddy to describe František to her hoping that would help, but his description – of a square-built, bullet-headed man whose muscles were starting to slacken – could have applied to most of the men she had encountered in Prague. She certainly couldn't match it to anyone from her past. There had been a core of SS men in Theresienstadt, and a wider group of guards whose background was predominantly German–Czech. Five years on and Hanni couldn't put a clear face to any of them, which was hardly a surprise. She had avoided contact with her father's colleagues as much as she could in the town, and she had wiped

those she had been forced to come into closer quarters with –
when Talie's ill-health had forced Hanni into the role of hostess
– from her mind. They had all been the same man to her.
Older, arrogant. With eyes that wandered over her body and
hands she kept well away from. Dangerous men who had the
rule of the world at their fingertips and cruelty running thick in
their veins.

*Who the years won't have changed, like they apparently
haven't changed Novotný.*

By the time dawn broke, Freddy had finally fallen into a
fitful sleep, but Hanni was wide-eyed. *She was a stranger, so he
has to be too* had turned from a mantra intended to soothe her
into a scream she could barely hold down. She slipped out of
bed wondering what Czech women used to dye their hair with,
wondering how she could explain such a drastic change to
Freddy. Wondering if plucking her eyebrows into a thin arc
would sufficiently alter her appearance or simply make her
look mad.

She was so preoccupied with finding herself a disguise, she
stepped on the card that had been pushed under the door
before she noticed it was lying there. It was one of the postcards
Luca had presented her with in the café, the view of the Old
Town Square she had rejected. She turned it over, not really
concentrating, still caught up in her panic about meeting
Novotný. Until she read what was written there and the
nonsense that was hair dyes and altered eyebrows disappeared.

The message was short and written – no doubt deliberately
– in the same cryptic style she had used to address Reiner.

*The package is on its way. Meet me in the café at noon today to
discuss the best way to handle it.*

There was no signature, not that it needed one. And apparently no awareness that Freddy might have been the one to pick

it up and ask awkward questions. Or there was, and this was a reminder of exactly who was in charge.

Hanni refused to acknowledge how much she wanted to curl up in a ball and hide. She crossed to the sideboard and dug out a packet of matches, her movements as slow and careful as if she was handling a grenade. She went to the sink and turned on the tap; she lit a match and she burned the postcard to ash without reading it a second time. The words disappeared but the burned smell lingered, even when she threw open the window. That would require an explanation. Her being late to the Novotnýs lunch – because ignoring Luca's summons was a far more dangerous option than doing what she wanted to and sticking close to Freddy – would require an explanation. Hanni had no idea what those would be. She wondered briefly if Luca was aware of the invitation, if the timing of this meeting was another way of pulling at her strings. There was no point in worrying at that either. There was simply a set of steps to be taken which she had to survive.

Hanni rinsed the sink again for something to do with her hands and stared out across the rain-slicked courtyard, at the shuttered windows of the other blocks which formed their tight square.

The package is on its way.

Her father was coming; he could already be here.

A shudder ran through her as the words sank in. The day should have changed. There should have been some sign to warn of his coming – a thunderclap, a swarm of dark clouds, a bell theatrically tolling. There was nothing except a cool April morning which had rolled over Prague in the same unremarkable way as the one before it and the one before that. Which would roll across the city in the same way tomorrow. With no concern at all for Hanni's tiny corner of the world, where everything was slowly collapsing.

. . .

'I'm not well. It's this stomach bug that's been plaguing me since Theresienstadt. Give me an hour or so and it will settle, I'm sure of it, then I'll come and meet you at their flat. I won't be very late; you can make my apologies.'

There was no bug, although there had been plenty of queasy mornings Freddy had been too caught up in himself to notice. She longed to tell him the real cause, to wrap his happiness with hers around them like a shield. She couldn't, not until Renny's future – and theirs – was settled, so the baby remained a sickness that was increasingly turning into an excuse. Freddy wasn't happy with her, but he also wasn't concerned enough to alter the day's plan and stay until she was well again. If Hanni had allowed herself even a second to feel, she would have been saddened by that too. Instead she kissed him and reminded him to take the bottle of wine and the box of pastries they had put aside for the occasion, and she let him go. Then she waited for ten minutes, which felt like a lifetime, hurried into her clothes and headed for whatever Luca had planned.

'He didn't mind going alone then? Or was he glad of a break from you? I gather that last fight was a lively one. The landlord would be within his rights to send you a bill for the door hinges.'

Hanni sat down and didn't answer. It was simpler and quicker not to feed his ego.

Luca grinned anyway. 'Fine. Let's play it your way and get straight to business. Your message worked. We've had word that your father crossed the border yesterday. He must have been delighted at how easy we made it for him. So now it's back over to you.'

Hanni had no idea what he meant, and her face showed it.

Luca's eyes sparkled. 'Oh, Hanni, did you think that your part was done with the message? Did you think I was going to wait for him to ride into town and then march out and bring him to justice, or lean out of a window and mow him down?'

His Wild West allusion was so close to her imaginary gunfight, Hanni couldn't hold back a 'yes'.

Luca burst out laughing. 'You really are such an odd mix. Self-delusional, brave sometimes to the point of stupidity and at the same time so ridiculously naïve. Come on – think it through. Reiner isn't the kind of man you can creep up on and surprise. And I don't want him arrested and stuck in a cell here where someone else decides to turn him into a prize. He'll have every antenna up when he gets into Prague, so you are going to meet him exactly as he expects. Then you are going to take him to a location where I control what is happening and where I'll do what you've never done and deal with him.'

'And then my part will be over?'

Luca nodded but Hanni didn't believe him. She knew that whatever she did for him would never be enough.

So maybe this is where I refuse.

Luca had stopped smiling. He looked at his watch and then up at her as if all her thoughts were visible.

'Don't bother stalling – it won't do you any good. Time's ticking, Hanni; too much is happening without you. Do you think your hot-headed husband has snatched her yet, without your calming hand to hold him back? Or maybe Novotný's done what his wife will be screaming for, put a call in to the police, and fought back. Which do you think would be the most fun for poor little Renny?'

He was right. There was nothing to be gained by playing games: Freddy had already been at the apartment for half an hour; any of those scenarios – or worse – were possible. And there was no point in throwing herself on Luca's mercy. She doubted that he had any.

'Where do I meet him? What do I say?'

'That's better. You've already chosen the place. You go to the park on the postcard you picked – I imagine Reiner will read that as part of the message – and you wait. You start tomorrow lunchtime and you go back each day until he comes. That might not be for a day or two. He might watch from a distance first. Fine, let him believe he's in charge. As for what you say at your joyful reunion, again that's your problem – you must have had some idea what you meant by needing a father here. So meet him there once, and after that you get him here.'

Luca handed her a piece of paper with the name of a pub in the backstreets near the castle written on it. 'I'll be there every night from tomorrow. Deliver him to me and you're done.'

Hanni was well aware that that wasn't true, but she nodded and pretended that it was. She let Luca leave the café first, or rather she said nothing when he decided to get up and go. She needed a moment to breathe before she went out into a city where Reiner might already be walking. And watching.

I have to face him. I could be sat opposite him tomorrow. Pretending that I want him to play a part in my life.

The thought of it was sickening. The story she was going to have to weave for him was unimaginable. And time was still ticking.

Hanni dragged herself to her feet. Her body was heavy, weighed down by all the forces crowding in. She headed out of the square and down Melantrichova towards the Novotnýs' apartment, expecting at any moment to hear a too familiar voice call her by the wrong name. And with her head so full of tomorrow, she completely forgot about the danger bound up in today.

CHAPTER 14

15 APRIL 1950, PRAGUE

Renny.

It was all Freddy could do not to say her name himself before Jana introduced her. Or to blurt out his relief that the child really was his little mouse and not – as he had increasingly begun to fear – some construct of his imagination.

It was hardly any distance from his apartment to the Novotnýs' home, but walking there alone, without the security of Hanni's arm through his, had shredded his confidence. By the time he reached the row of carved-up old houses which had seen better days, Freddy had convinced himself that he had been wrong at the school. That one small sighting wasn't enough to base an identity on. That he had been forcing the pieces of the puzzle together because the alternative – that he had deluded himself and was doing what Hanni had accused him of, grabbing desperately at the last child who could remotely be Renny – was too painful to bear. And then he had been ushered inside and there she was, his baby sister, all grown up and reaching out solemnly to shake his hand when instructed, and the truth had come flooding in. Whatever his last-minute fears, he had known all along that she was Renny

and he hadn't been frightened of that. What he was really terrified of, what almost had him shaking as he took the child's hand
and tried not to let his feelings crush it, was failing.

One wrong step and I'll ruin it.

Hanni had been right. There had, somehow, to be caution
in this. Jana's fingers were constantly hovering over the child;
her eyes never left her. Whatever he could persuade – or pay,
because that was surely where a man as bitter as Novotný
would lead things – the husband to do, Jana would fight them
both. Hanni had, once again, read the situation with her photographer's eye for detail and her warning that *he'll want some
revenge* could just as easily apply to the mother. Hanni had
seen where all the danger lay.

Which is all well and good, except Hanni isn't here.

That hurt more than Freddy knew what to do with. He
couldn't understand why she was behaving so unlike herself.
Hanni had used sickness as a means to avoid – or so he assumed
– a situation she didn't want to be part of. They had worked on
some very difficult, and unpleasant, cases together and he had
only seen her pretend to be ill once before, and that had also
been on this trip, at Theresienstadt. He hadn't been able to
fathom her actions then and he couldn't now. Why demand –
no, not demand, as good as beg – that he take his time and tread
carefully and then leave him to cope on his own when she knew
how hard he was struggling to do that? Why come all this way
and talk about *we* as if they were the team he longed for them to
be, only to abandon him at the worst hurdle? Nothing about
Hanni was Hanni anymore. That had left Freddy reeling.

He had arrived at the Novotnýs' house in such a state of
nerves that he over-apologised for her lateness and then
sounded as if he was unconcerned at its cause. Freddy was
confused and his explanation that she had been taken ill, immediately followed by, 'No, of course she's fine to be left for a bit
and come later,' had in turn confused Novotný. That hadn't sat

well with his host. Freddy had sensed the man weighing him up again, poking for holes in his story. Wondering if Freddy was something darker than he had first presented himself as: an agreeable stranger trying to make like-minded friends for his family in a new city. And that re-evaluating had put Novotný's guard up, which was the last thing Freddy needed.

So, as hard as it had been to do, Freddy hadn't clung on to Renny's hand when it was offered. He had let her follow her mother into the kitchen without comment and had focused his attention instead where Novotný expected it to be – on him and the frothing and too-large glasses of beer he had immediately poured for them both.

Freddy had no idea what they talked about after that. He was too busy raking the room for baby photographs he knew couldn't be there and building his case for reclaiming his sister. It wasn't until they were seated and Jana had served the first course – a dense garlic soup slathered in croutons – that Freddy could finally begin the task he was desperate to do and turn his attention more fully onto Renny.

She was as self-contained, or detached, as Hanni had described her. Encased in a stillness which to Freddy – whose experience of children was, admittedly, non-existent – seemed far too practised. And she was watchful in exactly the learned way he had feared that she would be. She didn't look at her parents. Except for the few moments when she glanced up and responded to Freddy's bland and school-related questions in the politely unengaged way that was clearly her default, her eyes appeared to be totally fixed on her plate.

They weren't. They were never still. She was doing what Freddy, and what every other survivor of a camp or a Third Reich prison he had ever met did: she was studying him and trying to determine what his presence meant for herself and the rest of the room. Freddy guessed that she had started examining him from the moment they met and had carried on doing so, mapping his face, mentally recording his details. And the more that she did that...

The more that she knows me.

It was a ridiculous notion. Freddy tried to convince himself that he had nothing to base his certainty on other than his own desperate desire. Except there had been a tremor – tiny, perhaps, but definitely there – when he had held her hand. And a frown had creased the corners of her eyes and tightened her mouth when she had first looked properly at him. And now, at the table, there was a searching – he could feel it. Wheels were grinding. Fingers were diving down to find memories that surely could be nothing more by now than shadows. Telling himself that it was his imagination which was at play, not hers, did not change that feeling. Or help him figure out how he was supposed to respond.

Freddy should have made a plan – from the day he decided to leave for Theresienstadt, or from the day that he had decided to follow the trail to Prague, or at least from this morning. He was fully aware of that. He should have done what a good policeman did before he confronted a suspect or a witness, especially if the person under question was a vulnerable one. He should have played out scenarios and second-guessed answers; come up with a strategy to deal with whatever outcome resulted. And he should not have proceeded without the steadying hand of a partner. Freddy was aware of all that too. And yet, whether through fear of casting a jinx on the search, or because he hoped that a plan would suddenly reveal itself – both of which he had chosen at different times to believe – he had still done none of it.

Which doesn't mean that it's too late to change tack. To make this lunch into nothing more than a first meeting or even to explore official channels. Either of those choices would make Hanni happy.

Except Hanni wasn't there. Hanni had abandoned him, and

making her happy wasn't at the top of his list right now. And as loath as Freddy was to admit it, they had become so separate that there was a possibility that, unless they found a way to resolve all the secrets that were causing the rift between them, he and Hanni might be done. The thought of that loss was unbearable, but he couldn't do what was needed to stop it until Renny was safe. Which meant that caution was no longer an option.

He put down his knife and fork after one bite of a cutlet that could have been cardboard for all that he tasted of it, and he gambled. 'I have something of a story to tell you. It's not going to be an easy one to explain, but I hope you'll bear with me: there are things that need to be said and heard. And once it's done, there are decisions that have to be taken.'

Jana was only partially listening – she was trying to persuade Renny to eat a little slower under the promise that there was plenty more food to be had. Novotný, however, had tensed.

Freddy kept his eyes on him as he continued, speeding up his pace to get through what he wanted to say before the inevitable explosion. 'I told you last time we met that I was German. That is true, but it is not all I am. My name isn't Bedřich Havel, as I led you to believe; it is Freddy Schlüssel; it was once Freddy Schlüsselberg. I am a detective from Berlin, and I am Jewish.'

There was a sharp intake of breath at that from Novotný. Freddy ignored it and ploughed on.

'As I'm sure you can imagine, that made my war, well, let's say a difficult one. I came out of it without my family, and for years I didn't know what had happened to them. I still can't place my brother Leo after his capture in 1943, but I know that my father Jakub and my mother Rosa and my little sister Renny were all snatched from Berlin and taken to the ghetto town at

Theresienstadt. That my father died there and my mother was deported to Auschwitz where she died too.'

'Stop it. That's enough.' It wasn't quite an explosion but it was a very clear message. Novotný was on his feet, his voice low and brimming with menace.

Freddy had expected a response like that, a physical one full of threat. Jana was frozen, her face drained of colour. He had expected that too. Their reactions were of no interest to him; the only person in the room he cared about was Renny. He had spoken quickly and he hadn't aimed one word of his opening gambit at her, but he had deliberately stressed all the names in case one of them might act as a catalyst. And one of them, or the combination of them, had worked. Renny was no longer staring at her plate; she was looking up at him and something – he would have staked his life on it – was dawning.

Freddy turned to her. He cut Jana and Novotný away and he focused everything that he was onto Renny.

'My sister Renny was barely more than a baby when the Nazis took her away from Berlin, although she would be nine years old now. I saw it happen. I saw my mother carrying Renny high up on her shoulders out of reach of the dogs and the soldiers. After that I lost sight of them, but I know that they were both taken to Theresienstadt and that my mother was taken away again from there, and my sister was left alone. She was put in a room full of other little children whose mothers had been taken, where the beds were packed in tightly together—'

'I said stop it! I said enough!'

Novotný was still on his feet, but he now had a knife in one hand and his other was curling into a fist. And Jana had woken up. Her arms flew around her daughter, and her mouth drew into a snarl. There was danger in every inch of the room, but Freddy didn't care. Renny was staring at him, oblivious to Jana's embrace, and her eyes were finally alive.

'The children were in that room with the aunties.'

The knife fell to the floor with a clatter as Renny spoke. Jana's arms fell to her sides.

'That's right, sweetheart. You remember, don't you? Because that little Renny, my little sister, was you.'

Freddy stumbled to his feet with his own arms outstretched. Waiting for the final flash of recognition that would give him his family back. Waiting to hear his name tumble out of Renny's mouth and the little body he had so often carried to hurtle itself into his embrace.

Except Renny didn't speak. She didn't move. The only parts of her that weren't frozen were her hands. They were at her throat, her fingers clinging on to a thin necklace that was fastened there. A necklace which made Freddy's heart flip when he saw it.

'That's hers – that's Rosa's!'

He took another step forward, his heart overflowing. But Renny still wasn't shouting with delight; she still wasn't running to him. If anything she was so pale she looked as if she was about to be sick.

You could terrify her.

Hanni's words again; Hanni reading the situation correctly again.

Freddy's empty arms dropped. He stepped back. He wished that he could cancel everything he had said; he wished that he could restart. He would have done anything, including denying himself, if it would wipe the shock from Renny.

'I am so sorry; forgive me. I did this all wrong. The last thing I ever meant to do was scare you.'

It didn't matter what he had meant. Her eyes weren't wide with joy because she had recognised him. Her eyes were wide and focused far away from him, on scenes he couldn't see.

'It wasn't supposed to be you. It was supposed to be her. I

was a good girl, like I was meant to be, so why didn't she come? Why are you here and not my mama?'

The question fell with a storm's force. Jana's heart cracked with a cry that swallowed the room. Novotný had the knife in his hand again. He was swinging it, screaming at Freddy to get out and leave them be. Freddy was hurling all the insults he had wanted to hurl in the bar. And Renny was...

Freddy was too slow, too clumsy to catch her. In the midst of the chaos, Renny was gone.

———

She had known him.

From the moment he came through the door and smiled at her. From the moment he took her hand. Somewhere deep inside, in a place where Renny never went, she had known him; she had sensed their connection. What she hadn't known was why or where from. Or what he had hoped to achieve by throwing everyone into a confusion of shouting and knives and blind panic.

Renny was a good girl – she knew better than to leave a table without asking. She knew better than to run out of the house on her own. But the rules she had so painfully stuck to for so long had disappeared when her father yelled. When he and Freddy – a name which had danced around her, like the others he had used, with a beat that was both strange and familiar – had leaped at each other and her mother had begun screaming about which one of them had the best claim. Being a good girl in the middle of all that hadn't felt important anymore. So Renny had run.

She ran blindly, oblivious to people and speeding cars, oblivious to all the dangers Jana had drummed into her. She ran because she didn't know what else to do. Because she couldn't bear the mess of emotions Freddy's story had unleashed. Or understand what it meant for her.

That little Renny, my little sister, was you.

If that was true – and all the scattered images pushing into her head of aunties and the room and the beds said it very well could be true – then he was her brother. And therefore the mother and the father and the Leo he talked about must be her people too. People she had no recollection of, or not in the way that Freddy wanted her to. That was a lot for her to make sense of, but he had said other things too. He had called himself Jewish. Brother was hard enough to comprehend but Jewish? The word her crueller classmates and her father filled with hatred when they said it, did that apply to her too?

Renny didn't know how she was meant to feel about anything Freddy had said; she didn't know what she was meant to do with it. All she knew for certain was that he had unravelled the world she had spent her whole conscious life in. He had said *room* and *beds* and the ward had flown back. He had said *Rosa* and *Leo* and *Jakub* and faces had reared up in fragments and fog, and the time and the place she thought she was in now had shattered. So she had run and then her feet had started to ache, and that carried echoes too.

Renny wanted to stop but she couldn't. She was running because all the broken pieces that made her up had suddenly started to shoot back together. Because some part of her had always been running. Away from the parents who might not be her parents, who had either loved her too much or not at all. Who she couldn't love the way she was supposed to, no matter how hard – or at least with her mother – she had tried. Away from the school where the other children had sniffed her out as different, where she didn't fit. Away from the images and blurred snatches that stalked through her dreams.

Away from this life that's not and never was mine.

That brought her up with a jolt, although the world kept

lurching. She grabbed hold of a wall, her lungs burning, her body off balance; her throat filling with all the screams she had never let herself scream. Nothing was sure anymore; she had no idea where she was going. All she knew was that she didn't want any of them, not right now. She didn't want her father's cold indifference or her mother's desperate need. And she didn't want this Freddy with his too visible pain, or not yet. The only person she wanted was *Mama*.

The thought came from nowhere; the name took her knees away. Renny sank down onto the cold pavement, her fingers instinctively reaching for her pendant.

It will keep me with you whatever comes next.

A key had turned, a box had spilled open; her mind was too full. But she knew those words mattered, that those words were true. That *Mama* wasn't simply a name she couldn't let herself say; that *Mama* was love.

'Renny, where are you? Come back please. It's all right to be scared – you're not in any trouble.'

There was distance between her and the shouting voice. There was street noise from the main road round the corner. She couldn't properly make out who was calling. Perhaps it was Freddy, trying to claim her. Perhaps it was her... in the light of all that she had just learned *father* was suddenly as impossible as *brother*, as impossible that Novotný might be the one offering her some kindness. Whoever it was, they were close and she didn't want them any closer.

Renny scrambled to her feet. There was a park another block away. There would be trees there, and quiet. She could manage another block. She could make herself a burrow and maybe, there in the silence, the battered memories would come to her in whole sections. And maybe there she could work out who she was, before everyone else decided to tell her.

CHAPTER 15

15 APRIL 1950, PRAGUE

The door to the Novotnýs' ground-floor flat was open. That was the first thing Hanni noticed was wrong. And there wasn't a sound to be heard from inside – no clinking glasses, no buzz of conversation; no child's voice answering all the questions she knew Freddy was desperate to ask. That was the second.

Hanni knocked. No one came.

She pushed the door wider and moved at a snail's pace into a narrow hallway that was dingy and dark. Paint which might once have been cream had turned a nicotine shade of yellow. There were no paintings or photographs to brighten the walls. Nothing about the place was welcoming; instead the hall wore the faintly sour air of neglect.

'Hello? It's Hana, Bedřich's wife. I'm so sorry I'm late. I hope you don't mind me making my own way in but the front door was open.'

Her voice was too high, her greeting forced and uncertain. She sounded like a woman expecting trouble.

Hanni hovered, staring from one closed door to another, trying to decide which, if any of them, might lead to the room where the family would entertain guests. The silence stretched without even the tick of a clock to break it. And then, just as she decided to try her luck with the nearest door handle, Hanni heard the sound she had been dreading the whole way to the flat. A sniff and a heart-wrenching sob.

What has he done? flashed through her head, followed by a series of images she had already played too many times on the walk to Šafaříkova Street. Freddy clutching Renny and holding the rest of the room at bay. Novotný tied up or lying beaten to a pulp on the floor. Freddy waving a gun. She shook herself as the pictures grew more hysterical. The sob had sounded broken, not terrified.

'Is there someone in there? Can I come in?'

She didn't wait for an answer. She pushed open the door. From the state of the barely touched and congealing food on the plates, the lunch had begun but it had not ended well. And the only person still sitting at the table was Jana.

Who will sob even harder the moment she looks up and sees me. Or fly for my throat.

'Goodness, what's happened here?' would have been the most sensible thing to say. 'Jana, are you all right?' would have been the most honest. Hanni couldn't risk either: she had no idea how much of the truth the woman now knew, and an empty and disordered room where there was no sign of Freddy hadn't featured on her list of possible scenarios. There was nothing to do but keep up her happy-to-be-here façade and try to buy herself a few minutes before Jana looked up and recognised her.

'I don't know if you heard me say through the door, but I'm Bedřich's wife. Is he still here or did the party end early?'

She was talking far more brightly than such an obviously abandoned meal merited. She wasn't surprised when Jana, whose head was still in her hands, treated the question with scorn.

'It didn't *end*. It fell apart when your husband decided to tell us who he really was. Which means that I know what *you're* after, so you don't need to put on that jolly act anymore.'

Jana's face was blurred, made soft and swollen by the tears which had turned her eyes red. It took her a moment after she raised her head to properly focus. When she did, her voice rose up in a howl.

'You? Oh dear God, where does this end? You're his wife? So the whole thing was a trick? You didn't care about me; you weren't my friend at all. You were hunting me down for the Jew! You're disgusting, the pair of you.'

She spat on *Jew*, a Nazi through to her bones, whatever lapse she had made choosing Renny. Jana's insults and hatreds, however, weren't the immediate problem: her high-pitched shriek was. The last thing Hanni needed was the neighbours alerting the authorities.

'I'd apologise for our deception but you have to admit you've done a good job of that yourself. You've as many secrets you don't want revealed as we have.'

She glanced round the room as Jana swore at her, properly taking in the upturned chairs and scattered cutlery. There had clearly been some kind of a fight: all that mattered was finding out who had won.

'But the two of us arguing won't help anyone. Where's Renny? Is she safe? Shouldn't she be our priority?'

Jana's face had lost its blurred edges. If there had been a knife close by, Hanni would have been on the receiving end of it. Luckily, whatever struggle had taken place had cleared the table of weapons.

'*Our* priority? That's rich. Until a moment ago, I thought you were a genuinely kind woman, interested in passing her skills on to my child. Until an hour ago, I thought my husband had finally found a friend who would listen to him rant about how miserable he is and spare me the ordeal. But none of that was true, was it? There's no kindness, there's no humanity in either of you. The only thing you evil pair wanted was to steal my daughter.'

Jana should have choked on *evil* or *humanity*. Hanni wanted to choke her when she said them, but she didn't have the luxury of getting upset. She had to stay calm, and she had to keep Jana calm until she found out where Freddy and the girl were. Renny was gone, so was Freddy, and the apartment was in chaos. Hanni didn't have time to spend on anything except working out how those three states were related.

'Fine, you know that Renny is my husband's little sister. And I presume he's told you that he's been searching for her, and his whole family, for the last seven years. And I know, even if I don't care, that Renny is also, in your heart anyway, your daughter. But the problem here, Jana, is that you were the one doing the stealing. We know where you took her from; we know who your husband was in the war. You don't have any rights to Renny, and you both have a lot to lose if your real identities come out. So the only thing to do now is to try to agree on the best way forward.'

Hanni stopped. She waited for the denials and the rage and the 'we saved her life; you owe us for that' – and for the harder to hear but equally true 'and I love her and I won't let her go' – to come pouring. Instead, there was a silence which lasted a moment too long, and a smile which made Hanni's heart race.

'*The best way forward*? You've really got some nerve. I presume you mean that Renny leaves us and goes with you and your husband? Well you'll be lucky – he's ruined that. He terrified her. He brought back all the bad memories I've worked hard to bury, and the poor child was so frightened, she ran. František is out there now, looking for her. And when he finds her, which he will, he'll tell her exactly who the monsters are. They won't be us, I can promise you that. What do you think this is, some fairy tale about a lost princess returning home to the king while the whole country smiles?

Don't be such a fool. There's no king here – there's a Jew stuck in the wrong country, fighting the wrong people. We've had Renny for five years; what do you think that means to her? Five years is a long time in a child's life, it's a lot of lessons, and Renny has always been good at her lessons. So she's not his, and she won't want to be now she's heard what he is. She's ours.'

The venom running through all of it and especially *ours* was worse than the smile. Hanni tried to regroup, but listening to Jana's cruel warning was too like listening to her father. And remembering that there were no boundaries that he and his kind wouldn't cross.

For the first time since she had entered the flat, Hanni's brain went blank with fear. 'Where's Freddy?'

Jana shrugged. 'Chasing after František? Lying in a ditch because he caught him up? Why should I care? He won't get Renny, whatever he tries. My husband loves me too much to allow that.'

But he doesn't. He hates you, and he hates her.

Freddy's description of Novotný's attitude to his family stormed back into Hanni's head. *He'd get shot of them both in a heartbeat.* Jana was deluding herself and that had to stop. And whatever Freddy had tried to do had gone wrong, which meant that he needed her to salvage the situation.

Hanni took a deep breath. It was time to take back control and remind Jana exactly who was at fault.

'Are you so sure of that? Are you sure that he wanted to take her from Theresienstadt in the first place, or was that all your doing? And are you sure he wouldn't let her go if the price was right, especially if he now knows that Renny is Jewish?'

Hanni deliberately stressed the last word in the same way Jana had. She hated the way it sounded, but it worked on Jana like a stab. Her face went from white to purple. Her mouth flapped open in a tirade of 'he won't care' and 'I won't let him'.

But before Hanni could ask how on earth Jana thought that would be possible, the dining-room door swung open.

'She's not ready to be found so don't start whining at me to get back out there. She'll come home when she's hungry. You know what she's like around food.'

Novotný couldn't have sounded any less concerned and he hadn't seen Hanni. Not until Jana waved her hand, gulped her words back together and began shouting.

'His wife's here, and she's as wicked as he is. She said you'd sell them my Renny.'

He didn't immediately deny it, Hanni knew she had summed him up right. She didn't get a chance to enjoy that. Novotný turned. And stared, and swore. And brought 1944 crashing back into the room with him.

'Friedel, welcome to my little gathering. No wife with you tonight? Well you have my sympathy with that. They're a burden aren't they, these *sensitive* women? Useful for nothing at all. Never mind, let me introduce you properly to my darling daughter, Hannelore. Maybe if you can be done with the first one, we could make her the second. She would benefit from a firm hand.'

Hannelore hadn't been listening. She rarely listened when her father introduced her to one of his fellow officers. She had learned to wear a hostess's mask when she had to deputise for Talie and to retreat behind its bright smile while Reiner flattered whoever he had decided to single out, for that night at least, as his favourite. She didn't react to the casual insult he aimed at her mother; there was always one of those. She didn't react to the overly stressed *darling* she knew amused him and he didn't mean. But his last words – the ones which seemed to be offering her up as some kind of consolation prize, or as a sacrifice, it was hard to tell which – broke through.

The man leering at her – Hauke Friedel, that was his name – was one of her father's most devoted acolytes. Hannelore had encountered him briefly in the house before, in the weeks before the UN delegation's visit. Unrolling drawings of fake shop fronts and cemetery plots, laughing at the tricks which were about to be played on the unsuspecting delegates. Now he was Reiner's right-hand man on the film sets, keeping the exhausted extras in line with his whip. He had copied that skill from Reiner. For tonight's drinks reception he had also copied the smartly cut black uniform her father wore when he was in the mood to be particularly intimidating, down to its brightly polished silver skulls. The thought of Hauke's hand anywhere near her, in any capacity, was repulsive.

'Come now, Hannelore, don't pretend to be shy. Poor Friedel has had his fill of neurotic women.'

Her welcome had been too slow, her dislike of the man too obvious.

Reiner's light hold on her arm tightened into a manacle. 'I know. Why don't you be a good girl and have the care of our guest for the night? Show him the garden, fetch him his drinks, be his devoted little slave. Wouldn't that be fun?'

She hated him. She hated his twisted idea of *fun*. She hated that he treated her like his property. And that if she didn't do as she was told, her camera would be gone, her freedom would be gone. Or she would be forced into the marriage he kept threatening her with, to Friedel if he could engineer it or to another man in a uniform who would be his double, and a life dedicated to raising the next leaders of the Third Reich. Hannelore couldn't bear the loss of her soul that would involve so she smiled and she played along with Reiner's games. She gave Friedel his tour and she fetched him his drinks, and she agreed with her father the next day that the flowers Friedel had sent her were not inappropriate for a married man but delightful.

And she hated herself more than she hated him. For being afraid. For being such a good girl.

He wasn't a stranger at all. František Novotný was Hauke Friedel, Reiner's second-in-command, the man who would have courted her at Theresienstadt if she hadn't hidden every time he came near her. The man who her father had delighted in referring to as her future husband. The shock on his face had already turned into a bemused delight. He didn't even bother to look at Jana as he issued his orders.

'Leave this to me. Go and clean your face up. The child will run away again if she sees you like this.'

Novotný's terse instruction to Jana had snapped Hanni out of her father's house, but it had left her in a worse place. There was no doubt that it was him. There was no doubt that he recognised her. Denying who she was would only prolong the danger. The only reason that she hadn't known Jana was that the woman had never accompanied her husband to the Foss home or to any official functions, so the two of them had never met.

And he would have swapped her for me in a heartbeat if he could. He looks as if he still would.

Jana sobbed her way out of the room, shoving Hanni as she went. Hanni stayed as still as a mouse, waiting for the first swipe of the cat's paw so she could at least get a sense of how sharp the claws were.

'Well, well, Hannelore Foss, you're still a sight for sore eyes. But is this true – are you married to Schlüssel, to a Jew? That's a turn-up I won't pretend I'm not sickened by. When that little bastard described his lovely wife, the last person I expected it to be was you. What a fall from grace. Your poor father's heart must be broken.'

Hanni flinched. She couldn't help herself. It was one thing

to swallow insults that were aimed at her; she couldn't ignore insults aimed at Freddy.

Novotný saw her reaction, and the knowing smile Hanni had already seen worn by too many men spread across his face. 'Wait a minute, there's something else here. What's the secret, Hannelore? It can't be your marriage. Even if you haven't told Foss, he'd know. He always knew everything and, whatever else has changed in the world, I doubt that has. So is it something you're keeping from your husband? It is, isn't it? You've gone as white as a sheet. Don't tell me you've been hiding your real self from him. Oh, that would add an interesting layer.'

He was fishing. She could have denied it, but Hanni was suddenly sick of it all. Sick of hiding her secrets and feeling Freddy slipping away. Sick of being pushed around by men with no conscience. Sick of keeping herself so tightly under control. Honesty, for once, felt powerful, and there was nothing left to lose: Novotný would realise quick enough that he had her life in his hands. So she stopped trying to keep herself under control. She let herself see red.

'How dare you speak about my husband as if he is nothing. I know what you were in Theresienstadt. I know what kind of man you still are. You are disgusting. You have blood so thick on your hands I'm surprised you can lift them. You're not fit to lick Freddy's shoes. He is a good and kind man; you are a killer and a kidnapper. So what if I'm hiding the truth from him? At least I've tried to live a decent life. What have you done, except hang on to past hatreds?'

His body tightened. Hanni braced herself for the blow, scanned the floor for the knife she would use if he tried it. But he didn't lash out – or not with his fists at least.

'Go on, keep going. Enjoy yourself. Every insult you throw adds another thousand to the price. You won't be able to afford the brat soon.'

She hadn't got him wrong. He would sell Renny in an

instant, but then, like Luca, he would never stop making them pay.

He'll bleed us dry, then he'll put her out of our reach anyway, because he can. Because all of them – him, Luca and Reiner – are cut from the same kind of evil.

A light suddenly snapped on. She had a gambling chip after all. Reiner, who Novotný clearly still believed was a hero.

Hanni unclenched her fists, dropped her voice and tried to look more like the girl he remembered. 'So you would sell her – I was right. And I imagine you would set the price very high. But does this transaction have to be based on money? What if I can give you something that's worth a lot more?'

She stopped, giving herself time to think up a plan that was more than one line and giving him time to catch up. Hauke Friedel had been a greedy man, his hand always out for the next glass of wine, the next slice of cake; the next wife. All she needed to do was follow his weakness.

'You're not happy with Jana or Renny or any aspect of your life here, are you? You told Freddy you hated living in Prague. Exiled from Germany. Stuck in what is barely more than a manual job. Stuck under Communist rule. Going nowhere. That's a hard burden to carry. But what if I told you that there were some parts of your old life that you could get back?'

She could almost see the cogs whirring. He was on the hook. He was wondering if the bait was her. Hanni smiled and let him imagine that for a moment. Anything to soften him up.

'It's better than what you're thinking, I can promise you that. You see, unlike you, my father got back to Berlin at the end of the war and he made quite a success of his return. And he's still as devoted to the cause as Freddy says you are. He's even got plans to revive it.'

That was the moment when he could have wriggled out of her grasp. When he could have asked how she was still close enough to her father to be privy to his ambitions when she was married to Freddy. He didn't. His face shifted exactly the way Hanni had hoped it would: the greed filled it. One more bite and he was done. So Hanni filled out her story.

'And here's the thing. Reiner is coming to Prague, tomorrow or the day after, to see me. Isn't that wonderful timing? Because if he knew that you, his most trusted second, was also here, eager to serve, ready to join him, well that would be the best kind of news. So what do you think? If I could deliver you a return to power and prestige and respect, how much would that be worth? Surely more than the ransom you could raise on a child.'

She had him. If she got this right, she had Renny. Novotný was sunk, although he pretended to carry on with the bargaining.

'And the only thing you want in return is the girl?'

'Not quite. I want my secret kept safe from Freddy. And I want you to keep a tight rein on Jana – she won't take kindly to any of this.'

She answered him as if keeping her secret wasn't as desperately important as it was. He dismissed that and Jana with a shrug.

'Good, then everything is settled. I'll set up a meeting with my father. I'll keep Freddy out of the way so there's no trouble while that all plays out – I'll tell him you've demanded a payment he needs to get and that you won't speak to him again until that's done. We all get what we want this way; we all get a better life.'

'Why are you here? Have you brought my pictures?'

The small voice made them both jump. They had been so busy discussing the idea of Renny, they had forgotten that the real one was gone. And now she was suddenly there, standing in the doorway, her hair and her dress splattered with mud. Looking at Hanni as if she might offer a safe haven.

For a moment, Hanni was tempted to go on with the

charade. From the look of the child, the last thing she needed was another adult who wasn't what they seemed. But she also didn't need any more lies.

'No, Renny, I haven't, although there will be plenty of pictures to take in the future, I promise. I'm here because I'm Freddy's wife. My real name is Hanni. And if you come and live with your brother, which is what he and I both want, you'll be coming to live with me too.'

The little girl didn't react to Hanni's revelation with the same level of shock Jana had. And she didn't drop her eyes the way that she normally did. She stared from her father to Hanni as if she was measuring them both up.

'Do you hate Jews?'

It was the last question Hanni had expected; she couldn't say anything but, 'What?'

'My father hates Jews. I think he would like me to hate them too but I don't know any. And lots of the children at school hate them as well, although they don't seem to know why. Freddy is Jewish – he said so. Which is why I want to know if you hate them too.'

She was holding herself very still, but Hanni could see the tension in the girl's narrowed mouth.

She doesn't want upset or anger; she wants facts. She's trying to understand who we are and what that makes her.

Hanni had never wanted to get an answer right so badly in her life. She ignored Novotný's furious scowl and she answered Renny from her heart.

'No, I don't hate Jews. Nobody decent does. Jewish people are no different to anyone else; there is no reason to hate them or to be afraid of them or to talk about them as if they are monsters. The people who do that are the bad ones. The people who do that aren't the ones that you should be around.'

The girl nodded. 'And Freddy is a good person?'

Hanni smiled. 'Freddy is the best.'

'Oh thank God you're back! I was worried half out of my mind. Come here, pet. Let me give you a hug.'

Jana burst into the room, her arms trained on Renny. But they were left grasping at air. Renny walked past her without a word or a look. A moment later they heard her bedroom door click shut.

'No.' Jana looked at Hanni, who looked away. She looked at her husband, who did the same. 'No. I won't let you do this, either of you. I'll take her away from here first. I'll—'

And then Hanni saw the vicious streak that she remembered had gone hand in hand with Novotný's greed. Jana was pinned against the wall before she could finish the threat.

'You won't. If you try anything, you won't just lose her, you'll end up wishing you had never been born.'

It was horrible to watch. Hanni's instinctive reaction was to run to the woman as Novotný let her go and she crumpled to the floor. She refused to let herself weaken. Jana was cut from the same rotten cloth as her husband. Hanni didn't want her hurt, but only Jana could stop that.

'I need you to swear that Renny will be kept safe or none of the rest of this happens.'

Novotný glanced down at Jana, who was sobbing far more quietly now. 'She won't cause any problems; she'll do as she's told.'

There was nothing else to be said. Hanni walked out of the room and past the closed door concealing Renny. She longed to bang on it, to burst through it and to snatch the child out of this poison-filled house. She kept moving. She had to trust him, the same as he had to trust her.

Hanni left the house. She walked away with a determined step. She didn't let herself start shaking until she was well out of sight. But then she couldn't stop. Reiner, Novotný, Luca and Freddy. Four men who needed to be managed if she was going to come out of Prague with the life she wanted intact. Four men who were all, to different degrees and in different ways, unpredictable and not men to be managed at all. Three men who were dangerous.

And only one of them who matters.

Hanni wrapped her arms round herself, pulled herself back under control and slowed down her breathing. She couldn't afford to attract attention, not again; she didn't know who was watching. None of what was coming was certain, except that Reiner was the lynchpin, the centre without which the rest fell apart, and that there had to be a sequence of events which she could control.

She started to try and work through some kind of structure as she walked, to find a rhythm that would get her through the days that were coming.

The first thing to do was to get Freddy out of Prague for long enough to set everything else in motion. That done – and it had to be quickly done – the next thing was to meet Reiner and tell him a convincing story about why she had summoned him to Prague. Then she had to persuade him to meet Novotný at the bar Luca would be waiting at and then... This was the difficult bit, the one which involved instructions she didn't want to give. If Luca got his claws into Reiner before he played his part in Renny's rescue, it would be game over. So she had to get Luca out of the picture. She had to persuade Novotný to... kill him?

She tried whispering the order but it wouldn't come out.

So I'll have to practise saying it till it does.

She didn't let herself dwell on that. Luca would be removed – that was all that mattered. Reiner and Novotný would meet. And finally, when all the other moves had been made, the last and the best one fell into place: it would be time for her and Freddy to finally make Renny theirs.

Although that isn't the last bit, not really. There's our return to Berlin, where I tell him about the baby, and I tell him

*all the rest. And then the final move of the game goes to
Freddy.*

That was a challenge for another day. What she had to do
in Prague had a shape; it was a plan. Hanni could do it. If she
didn't listen to the part of her – the logical, sensible, detail-
oriented and careful part of her – which said that it wasn't a
plan at all. Which said that the whole scheme she had cooked
up had too many complications where it could fall into holes.
That it was going to end in disaster. Hanni knew she couldn't
listen to the voice whispering that. If she did, she wouldn't be
able to do anything at all. The whole scheme was too big, so she
wouldn't think about the whole scheme. She would only think
about it one stage at a time. And the first stage she had to get
right was selling his part of the plan to Freddy.

'She came back. She's fine. There's no harm done.'

It was a lie, but one glance at Freddy told her that a lie was
all he would be able to handle. He was curled in a ball on the
sofa, still wearing his coat. His eyes were too big; his body had
shrunk. Hanni dropped her bag and wrapped herself round
him. It was a while before he could speak and a while longer
before he could do that calmly.

'I should have waited for you. I should have listened. But I
had to know best, I had to go charging in. I was too much for her
– of course I was. Throwing out names like rocks, hoping one of
them would hit and stir something up. Talking about beds and
wards and making her remember Theresienstadt. Then I
shoved Novotný, and he came at me. I don't rightly know what
happened after that, but there was a scuffle and a lot of insults
were shouted, and Renny was so frightened she ran. That was
my fault, Hanni – I terrified her. I flew after her, we both did,
but she wouldn't come.'

Hanni held him tight and kissed his hair and wished that

she could tell him that all would be well and that he wasn't to worry. It was better to let him talk.

'She recognised me though, or some aspect of me, I know it. I could feel it. So I stood up and I put my arms out, and I thought she would come flying into them. I thought she would be so happy to be found. Oh, Hanni, how did I get to be so stupid? I forgot she didn't know she was lost. I forgot that I was nothing to her. Or that she knows nothing about Jews, except what that monster has taught her.'

That at least was something she could reassure him about.

'I think when it comes to what being Jewish means, you should trust that Renny's got a mind of her own. I think she has the measure of Novotný.'

Hanni loosened their embrace and took Freddy's face in her hands. 'I saw her, my love. She's safe. And she asked me if you were a good person, which was the easiest question in the world to answer, so I think there is hope.'

She didn't tell him what had come before that. She didn't want to darken the new light in his eyes. The things that she was going to ask him to do didn't need his anger or fear. But they did need another lie. She forced everything out of her head except *right place*.

'Novotný will let you take her; I got that much out of him. But the price is a high one – twenty thousand korunas.'

It was a figure pulled out of the air, intended to be too extreme to be immediately or easily pulled together. An amount intended to buy time for Reiner to arrive while Freddy was tied up trying to pull the sum together. Freddy's stricken gasp made her wonder if she had overplayed it.

'I know, I know, it's madness. But I think he'll take less. I think he'll take half, if we could raise it.'

Freddy's body had slumped; his fingers were counting invisible calculations. 'How on earth can we do that? I couldn't raise that kind of money in Berlin, never mind in Prague.'

And here it was, stage one. Hanni took a deep breath and forced herself not to think any further.

'Which is why we have to ask Marek for help – and quickly. Go to the bar he told you about on Husova Street and leave him a message. Let him know that you've found Renny so now you have to go to Jirny and sort out her paperwork. Tell him that you need to leave tomorrow if possible and that there's a problem you need his help with, that you want to meet him there as well as his contact. Then, when you're in the village, ask him for help to raise the money. Or for a different way of ending this than cash if that won't work.'

It made sense, she could see that in the way Freddy's face cleared. And he liked the last part – which Hanni had added to deal with his fear that even Marek's extensive web of connections would struggle to gather together the amount needed in so tight a time – far more than he liked the thought of handing over a ransom. He still resisted her.

'But what about Renny? I could be away for three days, or more. I need to see her again, to explain myself and put things right. I can't go anywhere until I've done that. It's not fair to leave the poor child alone when I'm the one who's caused all this mess.'

'You have to.'

Hanni had been expecting Freddy to want to see his sister again, to try and repair the damage. She wished that he could – the little girl needed the surety of seeing him again as much as Freddy needed to see her – but there would be far more damage caused to everyone if he confronted Novotný.

It's only for a few more days. He'll be with her for good in a few more days. I can't let anything risk that.

'I'm sorry, Freddy but there's no other way. He's promised to keep her safe. And they need time to prepare her, and themselves – especially Jana – for what comes next if the handover isn't going to be any more traumatic.'

She had certainly overplayed that. Freddy was frowning, digging through everything he knew about Novotný's disinterest in Jana.

Hanni jumped back in before he could start asking questions her plan wouldn't hold. 'All right, that's putting it too kindly. I imagine he'll lay down the law and Jana will follow if she knows what's good for her. But, whatever happens, it doesn't need us two in the middle. Novotný wants the money more than he wants Renny, Freddy. We have to trust to that.'

It was a lie seasoned with enough of the truth to make it sound comforting. It got Freddy focused and out to the bar. It left Hanni wishing that she wasn't so skilful at fooling him and profoundly grateful that she was. And it worked. He was far calmer when he came back and far more optimistic.

The message to be ready to leave, that a guide would be waiting at Husova Street at ten o'clock and not a moment past that, came with a knock on the door the next morning. Freddy was packed in less than an hour. Stage one was done. By the time noon arrived, Hanni was in place at the park by the castle, the scheme still measured out in small tasks so that she could keep breathing, and Freddy – her first obstacle – was gone.

CHAPTER 16

17 APRIL 1950, PRAGUE

He didn't come.

Hanni sat on the bench staring out over the red roofs jostling for space below her and the vines stretching up to swallow them until the park and the view were nothing but shadows. He didn't come.

Which is good. Which means I'll have myself under control and I won't be scared of him when he does.

They were brave words but they didn't work; they barely bought her a few hours of restless sleep.

When Reiner finally slipped onto the seat at her side on Monday morning, commenting on the glories of the day's spring sunshine, nothing had changed. Not his elegant appearance. Or his mocking, controlling manner. Or the fear and the hate which ran like hot metal through Hanni's body the second he spoke. All it took was his, 'My darling Hannelore, what an absolute pleasure it is to see you again and what a story you must have for me this time to drag me all the way here,' for all his old threats and insults to surge back.

A Jew and a failure... could you have sunk any lower?

God help me, I'll put you on the next train myself.

And all her failed promises to reveal his crimes and bring him to justice flew in at their side.

Hanni had been determined to meet Reiner as an equal. One sentence from him and she was cut down to a powerless girl. That couldn't do. She wouldn't let it. So she didn't look at him after the first glance; she focused on the peach and pink blossom dancing over their heads instead. She focused on the dark green and the light and the twenty shades in between covering the trees. She let her body cool. She let him be done with his amusement that she was the one this time sending the bouquet. With his taunting, 'So are you finally ready to cast in your lot with me?' She let the air he had disturbed settle, until all he was left with was, 'So what is this really all about?'

Hanni had spent the hours waiting for Reiner to arrive deciding how best to answer that question. The moment he reappeared, she was glad she had a new card to play. Reiner was no fool. He had a liar's instinct for when he was being lied to, and no mercy for those who tried. Offering him news of the baby still repulsed her. She had grown used to the word *pregnancy*; she was almost ready for *mother*, but she had never understood *protect* more than she did now with this new life so dependent on her. So not the baby, and her second idea, pretending that she suddenly wanted to join him and work for whatever Third Reich revival he had planned, wasn't perhaps as repulsive but it wasn't a strong one. She was worried that he would see through her the minute the words went sour in her mouth and then dig until he discovered Luca's conspiracy. The thought of that was paralysing. But she had Novotný now, so there could be some measure of the honesty – at least at the start – that would be needed to win his trust.

'It's Freddy's little sister. He thought she'd died in the war with the rest of his family, but she's here in Prague. She was taken by a guard and his wife from Theresienstadt at the end of the war and brought up as their own. I want your help to get her back.'

She had his interest, but he wasn't as easily caught as Novotný had been.

'So that's what you're *in need of a father* for? I confess, Hannelore, that disappoints me. You marry him, which is enough of a disgrace in itself, and then you have the nerve to ask for my help to stick the Jew's family back together? Why would I do that? If they had been taken on my watch, there wouldn't have been any of them left to find.'

She had to breathe through it. She had to screen out the worst of him.

'I'm asking because there's nobody else who can do this but you. The guard who took her is your old deputy, Hauke Friedel. He's in Prague now, living under a false identity, and he's miserable trying to exist under a Communist regime. He wants his old life back, working with you for the... for the good of the cause. I told him that I would make that happen if he handed Renny over to Freddy. And he will do that, without the insane ransom he's threatening us with, if you tell him to.'

It was hard not to fill the silence Reiner left, but Hanni forced herself to wait and not to add details he could twist.

'Hauke Friedel, your old admirer? Well that's not what I was expecting either, although I did wonder where he'd got to. I can quite imagine he's unhappy here. When I knew him, he could only stand close to a communist if he had a whip in one hand and a gun in the other. How many more surprises are you going to bring me today?'

There was something in his tone Hanni couldn't read. Her heart began to flutter with the horrible thought that she had forgotten something. Then he stopped reminiscing and told her what that something was.

'I can see how Friedel would benefit from this exchange. I can see how the Jew would benefit too. But what do I get out of this? Except a reconciliation with my daughter that's a little too convenient, and a little odd given everything that has gone between us, don't you think?'

He was suspicious. That was to be expected but – when stacked against *what does he get out of it?* – his suspicion wasn't the main problem. What Reiner stood to gain was the first thing she should have thought about, and all she had come up with was the baby or herself, which were the last things she wanted to offer. She had been so busy working out Friedel, and Freddy's, side of the bargain, it hadn't occurred to her that Reiner's fell short. *What might he want? What might he want?* whipped through her head so fast it wiped away logic. And sense.

'It's not too convenient – you coming here is what I wanted.'

She picked up speed: if she gave herself a second to think, her mouth would clam up.

'I've been thinking more and more about family, about blood, and I thought, maybe, you and I could try and at least come to some kind of accommodation with each other. Work out a way to be closer. You said once you wished you hadn't pushed me so easily away. Do you... still think that? Is my being closer to you something you might want?'

She ran out of steam, and self-respect, and stopped. All she could hear as she tried to decide if Reiner's frown was confusion or interest was the other insult he had once revelled in.

How hopeless you are. You don't think, you don't plan. You could never be a danger to me.

Reiner's frown slid far too happily into a smile. It was as if, like Luca, he could read her thoughts.

'That's an interesting question, and it's quite a surprise that you're so fond of family all of a sudden, but let's not dismiss it. Let me give it some thought. But I'll confess, I'm not entirely sure how useful you could be.

'Take this matter with Friedel, for example. Now I'm here myself, why would I need you to broker a meeting? I can find him without your help if I want to. You need to offer me something better than that, or I'm going to start sensing secrets, and you know how much I hate them.'

Hanni wasn't surprised that Reiner hadn't instantly opened his arms and welcomed her in. She also had a nasty sense that she still didn't really know what he wanted, but he did. Which meant that she was the one on the back foot again, scrabbling to sweeten the pot and him.

'There's no secrets – why would there be? You're the only person who could help, so I reached out to you. And I can be useful, you just have to trust me.'

She took a deep breath and tried not to worry about how deeply he might probe. 'I've heard rumours that you're setting up some kind of a training facility. Preparing soldiers to fight for... what you believe in. To carry out more of the fire-bombings and the sabotage that's been happening in the East, which your name has been linked to. I can help with that. I've had police training, I know what the authorities look for when they're picking out suspects. I could be useful finding the kind of men who wouldn't stand out.'

'Could you indeed? That's interesting, and so is the fact that you've been listening to rumours about me.'

There was still a mocking tone, but there was no amusement. Reiner's tanned face had all the sharp angles of a wolf on full alert.

'The trouble is, Hannelore, that you're offering me your help, but you still can't name the cause you'd apparently be fighting for. That's a bit of a red flag, but we can come back to that too. What's really intriguing me is who you've been talking to. Who's been telling you such interesting tales about sabotage and camps?'

The way he was looking at her, as if he could strip her mind bare, was terrifying. If he got the slightest scent of Luca standing behind her, everything would fall apart.

And he'll make me – and Freddy pay – for putting him in danger.

Hanni knew what that meant. She had been seconds away from death at Reiner's hands before and she wasn't going to be there again. Or, more importantly, allow any such threat to get close to Freddy. Which meant that her story had to stack up stronger, whatever that took.

'I heard it at one of the newspapers I work for. One of the journalists had some photographs of a training camp in the Harz Mountains and he mentioned that your name was associated with it. Pictures of boys marching and wearing swastika armbands and learning how to strip rifles.'

The look on his face was one she rarely saw there, but it was one that had served her well in the past: there was admiration in it.

'You do have a capacity to surprise me. Maybe you're right, maybe I should have channelled that earlier, maybe I can use you now. You don't back down, do you, even when you've only got half of the story? There's certainly work to be done with "recruitment" as you put it, although in a more refined way than you appear to imagine. And now you look confused, so maybe I should give you a more accurate picture of what it is that I'm doing. It's not impossible that my name has been linked with a number of these so-called incidents. I imagine my previous life has put me on the GDR's watch lists. The attacks, however, are not my doing – not directly anyway, although I certainly applaud anything that derails the Soviet machine. Sometimes it's as simple as boys will be boys, and my boys are certainly guilty of that.'

He smiled and shook his head, the very picture of an indulgent father whose sons had been described as 'good-hearted little scamps'.

'Perhaps some of them have been setting fires and making bombs and lodging their protests. That's fine with me. But I'm

not co-ordinating them, and I'm not building an army. Or not
the kind you think. Swastika armbands, really? That makes me
worry about the word journalist, and I can tell you for certain
that those pictures must have been taken with a very long lens.
It's a school badge, a simple crest – a circle split into slightly off-
set squares. It may need a redesign if it's causing some kind of
moral panic, but it's hardly sinister. And lots of boys learn rifle
skills and practise drilling at school. It teaches them how to be
men.'

He leaned forward, as if he was about to confide a secret.
The woody notes of his cologne turned Hanni's mouth dry.

'You didn't think I'd stopped, did you? When my school in
Wannsee was discovered? Oh no. Whoever caused that to be
closed down did me a favour. It made me think bigger. Maybe
I'll get to thank them personally one day.'

Hanni didn't react. He knew the culprit was her, but he
didn't have proof and there was clearly far more fun to be had in
letting her fear the accusation and its consequences than actually making it. She wasn't going to be diverted by that; she
wasn't going to let him completely control the narrative.

'What did you mean by *not the kind you think?*'

Reiner leaned back, crossed his ankles and smiled at her.
'Good girl, stay focused, don't break. All right then, this is
proving to be quite entertaining, so I'll give you a little bit more.
Close your eyes. No, don't jump; indulge me.'

Hanni didn't want to do any such thing, but she could see
he wouldn't continue until she did.

'Excellent. Now I want you to imagine the sort of army that
you think I'm creating. Not a few boys practising drill in a wood
but a whole mass of them marching in ranks. It's not hard –
you've seen its kind before. Go back to being ten, on the balcony
at the Adlon Hotel. Imagine that procession, the one to honour
Hitler. You can see it, can't you? Filled with torches and singing
and the swastikas you're so obsessed with. And now imagine

that same procession with those same trappings marching under the Brandenburg Gate, not in 1933 but today. Because that's what you think I'm planning, isn't it? And now tell me what would happen if such a thing really took place.'

Hanni's eyes sprang open. 'There would be a riot. People would take to the streets in protest. There would be troops everywhere – American, British, Soviet. Berlin would become a battleground.'

Reiner nodded. She couldn't work out if he was more pleased with her or himself.

'Exactly. Nothing would come out of a scenario like that except street battles and arrests and international shame. So why would I build something so foolish, so visible? Oh no, Hannelore, you've totally missed the point.'

The look on his face was so knowing, it hit her skin like a vat of ice water. She wanted to get up and walk away; she already knew that the truth was worse than any of her imaginings.

His voice oozed on, pinning her down in its snare.

'My army – because you are right about that much, there is definitely an army – will be as devoted to National Socialist ideals as I am, but it will fight its wars quietly. I'm not building a training camp for foot soldiers; I'm building a forum for leaders. Yes, some lost souls who are badly in need of a little discipline have found their way to me, or they've been pushed my way by the Americans – the last thing they want to be doing is trying to "reindoctrinate little Nazis" as they so elegantly put it. Those boys are malleable, if impulsive and a little brutish sometimes in their actions. Firebombs would appeal to them. The rest will be more carefully chosen. They will be clever, right-thinking boys, from wealthy, right-thinking families. And not just Germans. This military occupation is going to be a long one. The American and the British commanders are bringing their families here, and they don't want the kind of schools that are currently on offer: sixty boys to every bomb-battered classroom and barely a dozen textbooks between them. They want schools whose curriculum is on a par with Eton and Harrow and the Ivy League, where their sons will be turned into scholars and gentlemen. And no one can offer that to them but me.'

His smile fattened; his shoulders broadened. Hanni had to force herself to stay still.

'And it's working – it's already started, my quiet revolution. There are two schools fully functioning now; soon there will be more. In Germany first and then, one day, all over the world. And my carefully honed boys, because they will be *my* boys, will win prizes and places at the top universities. They will get jobs in industry and education and government in all sorts of countries, and they will rise to the top, taking all their principles with them. Why wouldn't they? They will be groomed. They will be natural leaders. They will be so perfectly suited to running the show, who would want to stop them?'

Natural leaders. As precisely crafted and honed and as deeply indoctrinated as the commanders of the Thousand Year Reich were once destined to be.

Hanni could see them as clearly as she could see the blossom and the trees, and *natural* was so far from true it was monstrous. Reiner's vision was horrifying. And it was so cleverly worked out she knew he would do it. And that he would deny the idea of such a conspiracy as impossible if she threatened to tell it. Hanni could barely hold her stomach down. She retched.

Reiner laughed. 'But that is for the future, not now. I don't know exactly what you're planning here, Hannelore. I have a feeling there's something more at stake. But I'll go along with your little plan, for a while at least, although God help you if you're stupid enough to try any tricks. So I will meet with Friedel, but at a bar of my choosing, not the one you've no doubt got planned, and tomorrow night, not today as I'm sure you were about to suggest. Let's make you work a little harder for this.'

He was playing with her again. Hanni tried to hold her ground but she had nothing left to bargain with.

'How will that work? How will I know where to meet you if I don't suggest the place?'

His smile was so self-satisfied she longed to slap him, but the consequences of that were unthinkable.

'Well you could give me your address. No? I thought not, although I'm sure I can easily find it out myself. All right, then I'll leave you a note here in the morning, when I've seen which of my old haunts are still open. It's always best, I've found, to conduct meetings on my terms and on my ground. And I will help you get the child back, as long as you remember that, for all your ideas of what I might want in return, there's still a side of this bargain that doesn't hold weight. You haven't worked it out, Hannelore. I wonder if you even can.'

There was a spark in his eyes that was terrifying and set her mind whirling as fast as her stomach. She couldn't think of anything else she had to offer that she could possibly deliver.

'Can't you just tell me what it is? Why does it have to be a test?'

But Reiner was already on his feet, brushing down his coat, smoothing his hair. Totally in charge and walking away.

CHAPTER 17

18 APRIL 1950, PRAGUE

'He's changing the rules. You shouldn't have let that happen. And you shouldn't have agreed to this absurd schoolboy spy method of communicating. It's a good job I've been tailing him too.'

Luca was standing by the bench, holding Reiner's note. His stance, as well as his hectoring tone, suggested Hanni ought to be worried at finding him there. She didn't have the time to indulge that. If she didn't try to pull out some positives after a second sleepless night, she would start to unravel. So she turned it around instead, telling herself that Luca appearing had at least solved the day's first problem: how to tell him that the meeting venue had changed. Her non-committal, 'It was taken out of my hands,' did not improve his mood.

'And this bar he's picked is not a good venue. It's one of those old ones by the Petschek Palace which still has a reputation as being too sympathetic to the right. It must be one of his haunts from his SS days, which means he's sending a message. I don't like that; I don't appreciate this level of meddling at all.'

Hanni took the piece of paper with the bar's name scribbled on it and slipped it into her pocket. That was two positives. She had something to report to Novotný, and Luca was uncomfortable with the arrangement. That meant his guard might be down. She was so wrapped up in the possibilities of that, she forgot to be wary.

'How does that make sense? Reiner doesn't know about you, so if he is sending a message, then he's sending it to me. And yes, this is a power game; it's about establishing control, but what did you expect? I promised to bring Reiner to you; I didn't promise to change him.'

The blow came too fast for her to see it coming or to avoid the full force of its impact. The pain in her cheek and her jawbone made her yelp and then it made her furious, but not quick enough to retaliate. Luca caught her wrist in mid swing as she tried to lash back at him.

'Don't you dare. You're not my equal in this. I set the rules and you follow them. I'll be at the bar tonight, and there won't be any mistakes or any more changes, not if you want to come out of this with your life in one piece. And when we're all in place, you introduce me as a local detective who's been helping with the hunt for Renny. That should be simple enough to remember.'

Hanni took a step back out of his reach before she replied. He wasn't going to get a second shot at her.

'I'll say whatever you want, but he won't believe that story. He already thinks that he's on a GDR list. He'll work out quick enough that you're German and, when he does, he'll suspect a trap. If that happens, you'll lose him.'

Luca didn't raise his hand again; he shook his head instead. 'You're still not getting this, are you? I'm telling you what to do, not asking for your input. And he won't suspect anything if you play your part properly. All I need is the chance to sit down at the same table as him and buy him a drink. And all you need to do after that, whatever happens, is act like you're having a pleasant evening. Can you manage that much?'

Hanni presumed, if buying drinks was involved, that at least part of Luca's plan involved drugging Reiner. She didn't bother to tell him that Reiner would never accept his offer, that he would be the one standing the rounds and carefully covering his glass. That all SS-trained men were paranoid about poison. She nodded instead and let Luca resume his lecture.

'I know that the lunch at the Novotnýs' went badly. I know that the child ran, that Freddy has gone off on some wild goose chase in search of a ransom that's been set at an impossible amount. He'll never raise it, not here. So I'm your only hope, Hanni, and I'm one step ahead of you all the way. Don't be a fool and forget that.'

She agreed that she wouldn't and watched him walk away, his stride the relaxed pace of the overconfident. She wasn't the fool – he was. He wasn't one step ahead of her at all; he wasn't even by her side.

Hanni fastened her coat tighter against the air's sudden chill and headed back towards Lesser Town and the brickworks. Her cheek was still smarting. The speed at which the blow had come had proved how dangerous Luca could be.

But I can be dangerous too.

She could still see his tall figure in the distance. It was hard not to shout 'you don't know what you're dealing with' after him; not to laugh at his stupidity.

But when he's beaten and broken, then I will.

Luca might have had his spies in the bar Freddy had gone to, but he didn't know what had happened in the flat between her and Novotný. Better than that, he had no clue who Renny's father had once been and what his relationship was to Reiner, or he would have said so and made capital out of it.

When I choose to send someone digging. Luca had threatened to look into the family, but he hadn't done it. Whether that was because he didn't want the Czech police too closely involved, or because he had been so full of his own abilities that he hadn't marked Novotný as a threat, or because he wasn't the detail-clever man that he pretended to be, it didn't matter. Luca didn't have the whole picture, and Hanni did. That was a mistake he would pay for.

'Where is she? What have you done with her?'

Hanni hadn't intended to arrive at Novotný's workplace so late or in such an emotional state. Her confidence had been buoyed up by her meeting with Luca. She had intended to visit Novotný calmly, to give him the venue details for the night's meeting and only then to, carefully, bring up the subject of Luca. To elicit a promise of a beating bad enough to keep the agent away from the bar and out of action until everything was settled. She wasn't going to ask for anything more than that, despite her earlier decision that the only outcome could be *kill*. Hanni had learned, almost too late, when she was working on her first police case that she wasn't the type of person who was capable of ordering a murder, no matter the provocation, and that wasn't going to change now. Her meeting with Novotný had been perfectly planned but then – because of one badly made, impulsive decision – it had almost derailed them both.

Hanni had ignored the advice she had given to Freddy to stay away from Renny. She hadn't gone straight to the brickworks; she had crossed the Charles Bridge back to Vinohrady and had gone chasing after the girl instead. That might not have been the best idea, but the image of Renny asking about Jews and trying to understand what her future might be had haunted her. Freddy had been right: it wasn't fair to leave the child alone and vulnerable, trying to make sense of which family she belonged to, with nowhere to turn to except Jana's hysterics and Novotný's bad temper. The situation they had created was far too volatile, and the more Hanni picked at it, the more it felt like cruelty to the girl. So, buoyed up by her success at fooling him,

Hanni had gone from her meeting with Luca to Šafaříkova Street determined to reassure Renny again.

She had rehearsed her opening speech on the way. She had knocked on the door ready to deliver it, refusing to believe anything could get in her way.

'Just five minutes – that's all I'm asking. To explain in more detail why we did what we did. To tell her how happy she'll be when she comes to live with us.'

She had stood on the doorstep eager to launch into it the second the door opened, but nobody came. Not on her first knock or her fourth. Not so much as a curtain twitched. Hanni had been forced to walk away with the unsaid words burning her throat, determined to stay calm and to track down mother and daughter. Refusing to entertain the creeping suspicion that Jana might have taken the girl and run, exactly as she had threatened to do.

Hanni had managed to sustain that belief for almost twenty minutes, until there was no sign of the pair in the café or the park. Then she had checked her watch and realised that the child would still be in school. She had run there and spilled out a far less practised tale about being Jana's sister and needing to collect her niece for a last-minute, forgotten appointment. She had barely got over the threshold. She was met with a crisp refusal to let her anywhere near the classroom.

Hanni had been forced to walk away again, although it was becoming even harder to stay. She knew she was being watched out of the school windows. She presumed a phone call had been placed reporting a stranger displaying erratic behaviour. She had resolved to do better at Novotný's workplace, but the walk there was too full of laughing parents holding hands with their little ones. By the time Hanni reached Novotný's office – where 'I'm his sister' worked this time and got her grudgingly admitted – the dread that Freddy might have got so close to that kind of happiness only to lose it again had consumed her.

'She's not at school; she's not at home. What have you done with her? Has Jana really run?'

Her voice bounced round the cramped office and through the thin glass partition separating the foreman from the typing pool. Heads turned. A hand hovered over a telephone receiver. Novotný grabbed hold of Hanni's hands and smiled for his audience, but his growl was a long way from brotherly.

'What the hell is wrong with you? Do you want security called? Do you want questions asked about why I'm accepting visits from unstable females in a government-run workplace? How am I supposed to meet Reiner if I'm locked in a police cell?'

He pushed her into a seat and stuck his head out of the office door. 'It's nothing to be alarmed at. My sister is having problems with our mother who has grown sadly very difficult to manage and has quite forgotten herself as a result. I'm sorry to have brought personal issues into work; there won't be a repeat of it.'

The heads turned back to their work; the damning phone call wasn't placed.

Novotný sat down at his desk and scowled at her. 'I told you I would keep the girl safe, which is exactly what I'm doing. She's in the house. Jana won't take her away – she wouldn't dare. But she also won't send her to school, and she won't open the door to anyone. She's terrified you're going to be lurking outside waiting to snatch the brat up, and she wants to squeeze every drop out of what she's now rather dramatically calling her last happy days. To be honest, I'm starting to regret stopping her from running away. I want this sorted quickly, Hannelore. I want to be done with them. Is Reiner here?'

His hands were clenched, his forehead slick with sweat. Whatever state Jana had worked herself into since Saturday, it had pushed her husband to boiling point. He was bursting with aggression. Luckily, that was what Hanni needed, as long as the violence was unleashed in an alleyway and not in his home. Renny was safe – she believed that. But the window to keep her that way was closing fast.

Hanni leaned forward so that her face couldn't be seen by the typists and kept her voice as low as Novotný's. 'I know that you do, and I'm grateful that you've done what I asked and kept Renny away from harm. Jana is an obstacle to you, I understand that, but soon she won't be – she'll be part of your past. And what I came here to tell you, what I should have started with, is that the meeting with Reiner is arranged. It's set for tonight. He's delighted at the thought of working with you again. Your future is ready and waiting. But I have an obstacle too, one that could get in the way of all our plans, and I really need your help to shift it. There's a threat to my father from a man who will, at best, arrest him ,but I think he plans worse. And I can't stop him alone.'

Threat worked – it pulled on all the old loyalties. And when Hanni explained that the danger came from a communist agent, Novotný immediately sprang up and wanted to set out on the hunt straight away. That was exactly the result Hanni wanted, as long as she could rein him in.

'Go after him tonight on his way to the bar, not now. You have to stake out the area first and see what can be done. You know what the police are like here – they have eyes everywhere, and none of us can afford to get caught.'

Hanni was so relieved that Novotný had agreed, and so absorbed in making the evening work to the timetable in her head, she didn't pay attention to Novotný's reactions as she described what she thought would be the right, and the wrong way, to stop Luca. Which meant that when he frowned and asked why she was doing all this, why Reiner wasn't dealing with the problem himself, she brushed his question far too easily away.

CHAPTER 18

18 APRIL 1950, PRAGUE

Hanni was exhausted. Her body was no longer her own. The nausea caused by her pregnancy had thankfully passed but it had given way to a weariness that engulfed her from nowhere and turned her limbs into lead. All she wanted to do was sleep and nothing would let her.

The timing of the baby could not have been worse. Hanni needed her wits to be at their sharpest. She needed to be focused on the intricacies of her plan. Instead, her head was muddled and her thoughts kept drifting to pictures of a little girl with Talie's bright blue eyes or a little boy with a shock of dark hair like Freddy's. So the timing wasn't at all what she would have chosen. But as for the baby itself? Hanni was already falling in love with it. Which meant that she had to be even more careful to protect herself, and the child, from her father. Reiner might hate Freddy, but a grandchild, especially if it was a boy, could be a very different proposition.

The thought of him finding out about her condition, the image of Reiner leaning over a cot with his hands outstretched, had almost kept Hanni away from the night's rendezvous.

There was no visible sign of the baby yet but she couldn't shake Novotný's *he always knew everything* out of her head.

Hiding away, however, was not an option, not when she was so close to achieving her goal. One more night and everything would be resolved. One more night and she would be able to welcome Freddy home and present him with his sister. She could manage one more night.

Buoyed up by the thought of Freddy's delighted face – and glossing over the explanation for Novotný's sudden switch from blackmailer to human being that she would need to give him – Hanni forced herself out of the bed and through the quietening streets that led to Wenceslas Square, an area of the city she did not know well. Like Luca, she would not have picked it for a meeting place. To reach it, Hanni had to walk along Politických vězňů and past the Petschek Palace. She doubted that was a coincidence. She assumed that Reiner had followed her and found out where she lived and that her seeing the palace, where he had once wielded control with his whip, was part of his plan for commanding the rest of the night.

The building itself was a square hulk of a thing which straddled a whole corner block. Beyond the columned entrance which all its neighbours shared, it had no interesting architectural features that would merit a second look. If it hadn't been for the name of the street – which Hanni was able to translate as Political Prisoners – a passer-by with no knowledge of the place would be unlikely to wonder at its history. Hanni didn't have that luxury. She knew all too well from Reiner's boasting what the palace had once been.

During the Nazi Protectorate of Bohemia, the building had housed some of the Gestapo's worst torture chambers. Thousands of prisoners had been processed – to use her father's clinical term for the misery that was unleashed there – through its basement torture cells, and countless numbers of those prisoners had died in agony there. If there had been any justice in the accuracy of the RAF's bombs, it should have been pounded to rubble in the last months of the war. It hadn't. It had survived the whole conflict completely intact. Hanni imagined there was a message from her father in that too.

The area had put her on edge, and so did the bar. It was as dark as the one Elias favoured in Mitte and no more welcoming.

As soon as Hanni entered the smoke-coated interior, she understood Luca's discomfort at the change of plan: it was most definitely not the kind of place where government men would venture. There wasn't a portrait of Stalin anywhere on show, and the only photographs on the walls contained images of men whose uniforms she didn't want to examine too closely. It was also not a place that could be easily put under surveillance. The bar was housed in a cellar with only one point of access, and the lane that led to it was narrow and unlit and lined with crumbling, neglected buildings. The only consolation Hanni could take was that the location could play to Novotný's if not Luca's favour. It didn't look like an area the police would bother with or where a scream would merit attention. It looked like a good place to deal with an obstacle.

Which, please God, he will do. Then he and my father can make whatever deal they want and I can be finished with all of them.

It was a disturbing feeling to want someone other than Reiner to be the night's target. To know that she had, by letting Novotný loose on Luca, protected her father from the kind of capture and punishment she had been hoping would be his fate for the last five years. And to accept that she hadn't merely protected him, she had brought Reiner another fanatic who would further his cause. It was hard for Hanni to walk down the last few steps into the bar's gloomy interior under the weight of that. In the twists and turns of her battle against Reiner, he was now firmly on top. There were betrayals in allowing that – of herself, of his victims, of Freddy – which Hanni would one day have to face. But they weren't betrayals for now. Now was about trying to claw herself into a stronger position. Except, when she reached the bottom step from where she could pick out the faces of the bar's few customers, it was difficult not to feel that she had already failed.

'Hannelore, are you here by yourself? That is a shame. I was hoping that you would arrive arm-in-arm with Hauke. All the little lambs returned together to the fold.'

Reiner had arrived first, which Hanni had been determined to do and her tired body hadn't let her manage. He had selected a table which gave him a view of the bar's darkest corners, and he had taken the seat which gave him command of the room. A bottle of wine sat open at his elbow; there were three filled glasses waiting. Everything about him screamed, *I'm the one in charge.*

'Why are you hovering? Are you looking for someone? Don't tell me that dear Freddy is lurking in the back ready to pounce?'

Hanni had automatically started scanning the room for Luca, Reiner had immediately noticed. She sat down with a 'No, of course not' that he laughed at and took refuge in her wine.

'That was a silly thing to say, forgive me. I keep forgetting that he doesn't know who I am. So there will only be the one joyous reunion tonight then.'

She didn't know if that was intended as a question, but that was how she heard it. The sudden certainty of *he knows he's in danger from someone, even if it's not Freddy, and he doesn't care* knocked everything else out of her head. Luckily, Novotný's arrival saved her from having to speak.

'Reiner Foss. I cannot tell you what an honour it is to be in your presence again.'

He was far more self-possessed than the growling man who had been forced to apologise for Hanni in his office. There was

no blue serge bagginess about him tonight; Novotný's appearance was immaculate. His black suit was sharply pressed; his
white shirt was crisply starched. The ensemble was as close to
his old uniform as he could have managed without adding a
swastika pin.

*And he doesn't have a hair out of place or a mark anywhere
on him.*

The shiver that ran through her as Novotný accepted Reiner's invitation to sit down was an unnecessary one, or so Hanni
chose to believe. The man would hardly have walked in dripping blood. He would have been very careful to wipe away any
evidence of whatever punishment he had meted out to Luca –
that was, after all, something he was well practised at. But even
allowing for the ease with which she imagined he could unleash
violence, Novotný was remarkably self-composed.

'You found this place without meeting any problems then?'

It was as close to a question about Luca's condition as
Hanni dared ask. Asking it also allowed Novotný to step into
the hero role and spin Reiner the story of the communist
agitator he had saved his old boss from. Hanni had assumed that
he would be desperate to do that from the moment she asked
him for the favour. She had encouraged him by insisting he
didn't mention that the tip-off about Luca and his plans had
come from her. All she would then have to do was turn the
relief of knowing Luca was out of the picture into a convincing
portrayal of shock.

Except Novotný acted as if her question had no subtext. He
didn't say anything but 'yes'. Then he turned to Reiner and the
two of them began rolling back the years, speaking in a German
they made no attempt to hide, which told Hanni all she needed
to know about the character of the bar they were sitting in. And
she couldn't find a way in to the conversation that would allow
her to ask anything else.

'So, Hauke, all this reminiscing has been delightful, but I

understand from dear Hannelore that you would like to come home to Germany? That is good news – that is where good men like you should be. So let's make it happen. If you can arrange the papers you will need to cross safely over the border, I have a role which could have been designed for you.'

For the first time since he had appeared at the table, Novotný looked unhappy to be there. 'A visa and the travel documents aren't a problem; there are plenty of people here willing to provide such things. But that has a cost, and so do the bribes, which will have to be paid at every level.' He looked into his glass as his face flushed. 'And that, I'm afraid, is where my difficulties start. I simply don't have the funds.'

'Which is not an issue I want you to worry about.'

Reiner plucked an envelope out of his pocket and passed it across the table to Novotný. 'This will cover everything you need, provided of course that you are the only one who is travelling?'

Novotný nodded, confirming everything Hanni needed to know about Jana's future. She thought for a moment he was going to lose control as he looked at the thickly stuffed envelope, but he blinked and recovered himself, and launched into a litany of thanks which Reiner lapped up.

This was what he wanted, Novotný in his debt. He's bought the man's loyalty forever.

And Novotný still hadn't made eye contact with her. Something wasn't right, although Hanni did not want to imagine what that something was. They had been at the table for almost an hour and there was no sign of Luca. Novotný had to have dealt with him as agreed.

'Well, now that's all settled, you should go and start putting your affairs in order. I don't plan to stay in Prague for more than a couple of days. The air here doesn't suit me. Let me walk you to the door while we tie up the final arrangements.'

The two men got up, Novotný reaching for his coat. Hanni

only just managed to stop herself from shouting at them to wait. The meeting had come to an end far too abruptly, and it was leaving her agenda behind.

She scrambled to her feet a moment after they did.

'But what about Renny? I mean, I'm glad this has all worked out for you, but when do Freddy and I get her? Shall I come with you now? Shall I take her tonight?'

Once again Novotný took no notice of her and he left it to Reiner to reply. Reiner waved Hanni back down as he put a hand on Novotný's shoulder to guide him away.

'Goodness me, what is the hurry? You and I have barely had a chance to speak about anything other than the practical, and we have so much still to catch up on. The handover of the child will be managed – don't worry about that. Pour yourself another glass of wine why don't you, and then I'll be back for a nice little chat.'

Hanni didn't want a chat, little or otherwise. The only conversation she was interested in was the one Reiner was currently having with Novotný at the bottom of the stairs, but she couldn't make out a word of that.

It's nothing. He's going to sit and torment me about Freddy and, when he's had his fun, he'll let me go. I can hold myself together through his mockery for a little bit longer. I've done it often enough before.

And Hanni could have done it again. If Reiner hadn't smiled so unpleasantly as he sat back down. Or raised the glass he had taken to the door with him in a mock toast and wondered – in a voice that suggested that he was thoroughly looking forward to whatever came next – how long they would both have to wait.

The answer was barely a matter of minutes. Just long enough for Reiner to say, 'Well isn't this nice,' and for Hanni to know that it wasn't.

Luca came down the stairs a little too quickly, a little out of breath; a little less composed than the man who had delighted in giving her orders. He was also scanning the room in the same obvious way Hanni had done when she first entered. And Reiner once again was watching, although he made no visible sign that he was interested in the bar's latest customer.

Hanni's heart sank when Luca appeared and she realised that Novotný hadn't done anything to stop him. That could only mean that Reiner had made arrangements of his own. Arrangements that Hanni was potentially a very unwilling part of. Now Luca was flustered and making mistakes, trying to play catch-up on a scene he couldn't read and proving what Hanni had already begun to suspect – that her schemes had somehow run past her.

She took a sip of her wine, which had begun to taste metallic. There was danger seeping all around her, but she couldn't work out where it would strike first. Reiner was pulling the strings, that much was certain. And Luca was a second away from a pretend sighting of her which would reveal them both as frauds. She had to pivot and buy time. She had to find some way to counter the suspicion, or Novotný's warning, that Luca's arrival in the bar was her doing. So she put down her glass and took charge.

'Luca, is that you? What are you doing in this part of town? Isn't it rather out of your area?'

She turned to her father before the agent had time to reply. 'This is Luca, the guide who brought us from Theresienstadt to Prague. He's been an incredible help with the search for Renny. No one knows the city like he does.'

Reiner must have known that wasn't true, but there was a chance he might believe she'd been duped and that would hopefully keep her, and her child, safe. He switched on a bland smile which allowed Hanni to complete her part of the bargain and beckon Luca over to their table.

'Luca, this is my father, Emil. He's also come to help us with Renny. And I know I probably should have told you that, given how well you've been managing the search and the police for us, but I didn't expect your paths to cross.'

Her voice was deliberately light, as though the two men meeting was a bonus and not in any way dangerous. It momentarily threw them both off guard, which was what she had hoped for. Every moment she could keep the truth at bay was a moment she could look for an escape. Luckily Luca decided to play along.

'It's an honour to meet you, sir.' Luca shook Reiner's hand. 'Hanni's right, this isn't my normal stomping ground, but I had the kind of business in the area that's brought on a thirst. Why don't I buy us all a drink?'

There was a pause while Reiner smiled at the offer. A pause in which Hanni could see the wine flow from the bottle and the drug slide in and her father falling in a stupor from his chair. But then he shook his head and the moment for hoping was gone.

'That's kind of you, but it's not necessary. This place is an old favourite of mine from years back and they still keep a couple of cases of the wine that was my drink of choice in... happier days. The landlord would be offended if I ordered anything else, and the price he charges me is too good to upset him.'

The bar was his. Reiner illustrated the point with a flick of his hand which instantly brought them fresh supplies. And he kept his glass well out of Luca's reach.

There was no escape and there was no way of redirecting the night the way she had hoped it would go – or changing the evening's victim into Reiner.

Hanni sat back as the conversation between the two men became a game in which neither of them was willing to concede a point. Reiner probed at Luca, Luca probed at Reiner; nothing of any value was said. There was a confrontation coming, but Hanni couldn't yet determine which way it would fall. Both men were on full alert. Neither was prepared to issue an outright challenge, although Hanni suspected that Reiner would have the bar's backing if he did. And so, from the way he kept trying to manoeuvre his chair to ensure that there was nobody behind him, did Luca.

He did attempt to manipulate things. He tried to catch Hanni's eye. At one point, he gripped her knee under the table as if he was about to tap a message onto it. She moved her leg out of his way. She didn't let him hold her gaze. She presumed he had some powder or liquid or a pill concealed in his pocket, but if he couldn't deliver that into Reiner's drink, she wasn't going to be the fool who would try.

She also did not attempt to leave, and not only because Reiner would have refused to let her go. She couldn't let this play out without knowing who would be left broken and who would walk away and what hand that left her holding. So Hanni let the conversation wander on until one of them decided to bring it to a close and she could see her way forward.

'And that, I think, is my night finished if I want to have a clear head in the morning. Hannelore, can I see you safely home?'

It was a relief when Reiner finally stood up – at least it broke the tension. He did it so quickly Luca was left scrambling, insisting that he also needed to head home. Which meant that he didn't react to Reiner's use of *Hannelore* or notice – as Hanni did – Reiner's smile when Luca failed what had, she presumed, been a test.

Nobody spoke as they moved towards the door; she didn't yet have a plan. At Reiner's insistence, Hanni walked up the steps first, trying to pretend that didn't make her uncomfortable. She emerged onto a street that was empty and a darkness that was even thicker than the bar's gloom. There wasn't a sound, not even the distant rumble of traffic. Every instinct was screaming at her to run.

She slipped her hands into her coat pocket where they could cradle her stomach and ignored her brain's pleading. She kept her pace steady, stepping to the side so that the two men's longer strides forced them rather than her into the front. Nobody looking at Reiner and Luca would have sensed the menace Hanni could feel radiating off their bodies. Their shoulders were relaxed. Neither of them had a hand in a pocket where a weapon could be.

What if they're working together? What if the target is me?

It was a nonsensical notion – there was nothing that the two men could possibly have in common – but the shadows and the silence made even nonsense seem horribly real.

What if I've put the baby in harm's way?

The thought of that made her stumble and gasp. It was the smallest sound, but it sent ripples through the still air. Hanni realised too late that she had unwittingly created the conditions they had both been waiting for: a disturbance, a distraction which would divert attention the wrong way. The men turned, one a fraction quicker than the other. Hanni saw the difference in speed, but the darkness was so solid she couldn't tell who was who.

There wasn't a struggle. There was a brief flash of silver across the black which could have been a cufflink, or could have been a blade. There was a second when one set of feet seemed to rise onto its toes. For an instant the world froze as if a camera lens held it. And then it swung back into life and a body crumpled to the ground.

Get out of here. It doesn't matter who's won; you're a witness – they would both see you dead for that.

The words whipped through her head, but her body didn't hear them. She had to know who was down. So instead of turning, instead of running away, Hanni stepped forward. She tried to see who was still standing.

And a moment later, the person still standing wasn't her.

CHAPTER 19

18 APRIL 1950, PRAGUE

The blow had knocked her dizzy and knocked her over, but it hadn't knocked her out. That mattered. Whatever came next, staying conscious mattered. She was prey now, but not every hunter brought the prize home.

An arm yanked at hers, pulling her to her feet. Hanni forced herself to match the pace that was set for her, to move as one with the man who dragged her up and across the slick cobbles. She couldn't fall; she couldn't let herself be punched or kicked. She had to keep pace with whatever was happening, and she had to co-operate if she was to have any chance of staying alive and keeping her baby safe.

'Get in there. Get down on the floor.'

In there was behind a door which slammed open with a force that suggested it was heavy. It was a room whose contours Hanni couldn't make out. The floor she was pushed onto was gritty and uneven and embedded with an acrid smell that instantly made her eyes water. And the voice giving the orders was Reiner's.

'I'll have eyes on you at all times so don't move until I tell you to. If you try to run, I will kill you. Do you understand?'

She couldn't see his face in the darkness; she didn't want to. When she managed a 'yes', he ducked out into the alleyway again.

Hanni did as she was told. Even though the door was now partly ajar, she didn't move – Reiner wasn't a man who made empty threats. She ran her hands along the wall behind her instead and stretched out her legs, trying to make some sense of the space he had put her in. It wasn't a home, or it hadn't been for a long time. She couldn't tell if it was a workplace or a warehouse or a broken-down ruin. There was nothing behind her except bare brick, and the dirt piled and thickened round her feet the more she pushed at the floor. There wasn't a sound inside or out; there wasn't any promise of help.

When Reiner reappeared, she quickly curled up again.

'Get up. Move forward ten paces and move slowly.'

He knew where he was, which didn't bode well, and he was dragging Luca behind him. Hanni couldn't see more than another dark shape, but she could hear the rattle of Luca's breath and the groans as a hand or a leg, or his head, crashed against the hard flooring. He was alive. From the way Reiner was handling him, Hanni didn't imagine he would stay alive long.

'Down there. Go.'

Her eyes had adjusted a little. She could make out the top of the staircase, but she couldn't calculate the angle of the drop.

Reiner was growing impatient. 'I told you to go down it. Unless you want me to give you a push.'

He would do it too, and he wouldn't care what kind of mess the fall made of her.

Hanni reached out for the railing, wincing as the first splinter dug into her palm. The top step she trod on felt steady enough; the second had a softness in its middle that almost caught her out. She gripped the rail tighter, no longer feeling the splinters cutting into her hand. Three, four, five. Half a dozen more and she was at the bottom in one piece. She allowed herself a small sob at that.

'Stand back against the wall and keep away while I bring him down.'

Reiner knew the staircase's tricks. He moved over it with a far more certain pace, leaning his weight to the side of one step, skipping over the next. Luca hit every one of them. His breathing was shallow and ragged by the time he reached the floor.

'Get in there.'

Reiner pushed her through another door into another room which was just as dark as the first. The smell – which was run through with damp and carried the scent of wet earth and rot in it – confirmed that it was a cellar.

Hanni had never liked being underground, and cellars were places that reminded her too vividly of the long, lonely hours she had spent hiding from marauding soldiers in the last days of the war. Her hands had turned as slick as the stones outside; her breathing was a match for Luca's. Her brain screamed at her to get out, to try and find the door and the stairway and to hell with Reiner's threats.

She moved to do it, but before she could manage more than a groping turn, a light switched on. The room instantly flooded with a brightness that turned them all from shadows into flesh-and-blood people.

Hanni froze. She forced her pulse to settle, her breathing to slow. Light had to be good. If she could see the room, she could properly find her way out. If Reiner could see her, she could bargain with him. Except that was the moment when Hanni caught sight of Luca and she forgot about running or bargaining; all she wanted to do was weep. He was still alive despite his rough ride down the staircase, but there was a gash across his forehead that was steadily dripping blood, and his nose was a pulped mass. And nothing about Reiner's stance suggested that he was a man interested in making bargains. His feet were planted wide; his coat and jacket were off. As Hanni switched her frightened gaze from Luca to him, he began rolling up his shirtsleeves.

'Stop. Don't touch him.'

She didn't know where her courage had come from. Perhaps it was because, faced with Luca's broken body, she could all too easily picture how her own death would go and she wasn't ready to accept it. Perhaps she simply could not bear to watch what was coming. Whatever the reason, she embraced it.

'I can tell you who he is, and what he wanted with you. There's no need to hurt him any more than you already have.'

Reiner liked her better when she was brave, she couldn't have got that wrong. Hanni kept her eyes firmly on him. She waited for him to remark on her daring, as he had done in the past when she had fought back. She waited for the admiration to appear on his face that in the past had made him rethink his handling of her. *I've beaten him before, I can beat him again* surged through her head like a current. Until she saw the way he was looking at her and realised that the stakes had been set at a higher bar this time. That there was nothing in his expression but contempt. He carried on rolling up his sleeves.

'I have no doubt that you can, given that you were the one who was leading him to me. But I already know who he is. Hauke told me, and he told me he suspected that you were working together. He's the final piece of the puzzle, isn't he, our little Stasi friend here? The real reason why you summoned me to Prague. You were the one casting the net; he was the one planning to trap me. That wasn't hard to work out – when you decided to ask Hauke to hurt our friend here but not tell me, you gave yourself away. Just like all the other times you misunderstood the depths of my men's loyalty.'

He gave his sleeve a final turn and stepped closer to Luca's prone body. 'That was quite a move, Hannelore; it was worthy of me. You had what you needed so you decided to remove what you didn't. I should congratulate you on that.'

He shook his head as Hanni started to burst into something she hoped would become an explanation.

'Don't waste your breath. We are done with lies, you and I, don't you think? For the moment, what I'm interested in is his side of the story.'

The kick he accompanied that last word with was swift and precise and aimed squarely at Luca's stomach. It brought Luca spluttering and screaming back to life. It sent Hanni's arms clinging tight around her own body.

Reiner followed the first kick with a second which cut deeper, keeping his eyes on Hanni as he did so. His meaning was clear – he might as well have said 'do you want some of the same?' He only paused the third strike when she shrank back onto the floor again and began silently crying.

Luca was conscious now, but although he was clearly in terrible pain, he wasn't ready to give in or to die. He pulled himself into a half-sitting position and shuffled back against the wall away from Reiner's boot. His body was as hunched and bent over as if he had aged forty years, but when Reiner began asking questions – who he was, how long he had been in the Stasi, what he was doing in Prague – the only thing he offered in return was the name which Hanni if not Reiner knew was a false one. It was Luca's chance to be brave now, to face his interrogation with a soldier's response. Unfortunately, his body was in no state to sustain the effort that needed. It only took Reiner a few more precisely placed kicks – and the promise to hunt down every last one of his family unless he talked – to break him.

The story Luca gave Reiner was the same one he had given Hanni – the Stasi agent tasked with catching a former Nazi who he would drag back to the GDR and turn into a scapegoat. It was a shorter version and there was far less grandstanding, but it presumably married with what Reiner had already been told as he didn't question any part of it. But he didn't fully accept it either.

'But why you? This wasn't an easy mission. I might not have come; I almost didn't. I could have been stopped at the border or picked up by the Czech secret service before you got your hands on me. If you'd failed, which you very easily could have done, you would have gone home in disgrace, and your bosses are no more tolerant of mistakes than mine were. So why take it on? Are you really that loyal to your hopefully very short-lived country?'

Hanni saw it before Reiner did, that last moment of courage surging through Luca that refused to let him be a victim, refused to let him die a coward. She recognised it because she had felt the same instinct herself; it was a totally alien emotion to Reiner. He was staring down at Luca with his usual mocking smile on his face. Luca couldn't match that, but he stopped clutching his stomach; he managed to keep his head up.

'Short-lived? No, don't underestimate us. We're part of something bigger than your failed Third Reich. Stalin has a reach across the East which I swear will one day extend to the West, and I will cheer for it when it does. You didn't get picked up at the border or by the police because you were too clever. You got across because I paved your path here. I was running you from the second you climbed down from your mountain. I've been the one in charge all along.'

It was a courageous speech. It cost him a broken arm and a mouthful of blood and lost teeth, but Reiner couldn't smash the fight out of him. Luca kept talking and talking, pouring out his hatred and unable to stop, although his mouth was swollen and his eyes were pinholes of pain.

'You see I know who you are; I know all about you. You were the perfect Nazi even before you were sent to pretty up Theresienstadt, a monster from the start. You oversaw the implementation of T4, the euthanasia programme, didn't you? And then you joined the Concentration Camps Inspectorate, making sure their killing programmes ran just as smoothly. You volunteered for every obscene job that was available. How much does your daughter know? Did you take her to Sachsenhausen and show her how good you were at your job? That was a real success story, wasn't it? You purged Berlin for the Olympics with that one, filling it up with *criminals* and keeping all the good Berliners safe in their beds from the communists and the Jews. I spent eight months there in 1936, as one of your *guests*, but I bet you didn't know that. I got a taste of your whip there, although I don't imagine for a moment that you remember my face as vividly as I remember yours. So yes, I've been hunting you because that's my job, and my job and my country is everything to me. But I've been hunting you for longer than that. Because I loathe you. Because nothing would have made me happier than your death.'

He stopped. The effort of speaking for so long had run down the little strength he had left and his eyes were flickering. Hanni had disliked him and feared him since the first day they had met, but in that instant – as he finally showed something of the man he was behind the communist zealot – her heart lightened towards him. Luca wasn't simply a machine dedicated to a cause; he was a man who knew suffering, who had been indelibly marked by it. And Reiner was looking at him in the same way that he had looked at her a few moments earlier, with an expression of utter contempt.

'I would have had more respect for you if you'd told me this quest was driven purely by your political beliefs, but you're another one who can't divorce himself from the personal. It's a weakness I wouldn't have tolerated in any of my men.'

Hanni had never loathed her father more. Luca's story meant nothing to him, and he had no idea what it had meant to her. Sachsenhausen was where Ezra Stein had died. Where she had always suspected he had been taken on Reiner's orders. Her father had been orchestrating her life since the first time she had stood up to him when she was ten years old and had refused to apologise for talking to a kind man on a balcony. No one was safe from him; no one would ever be. Luca's story had meant nothing to him and neither did his life. The man was dying, but Hanni could see in Reiner's face that his dying wasn't done, that it would stretch out as long as Reiner had the mind to stretch it. She couldn't allow that. She couldn't stand witness to that. She couldn't be her father's daughter.

Hanni pulled herself back up off the floor. She ignored Reiner's 'What the hell do you think you are doing?' and walked towards Luca. He was slumped on the ground again, no longer able to support himself. She took his head in her lap and wiped the blood from his eyes with her sleeve. Reiner wasn't going to let her walk away easily from this; the odds were that he wasn't going to let her walk away at all. So she was going to do something good with her last moments. She was going to spare Luca any more pain, whatever that cost her.

'Get away from him, you stupid girl. You as good as arranged for his death a few hours ago. You can't atone for that now by weeping all over him.'

Reiner's contempt cut because it was true. Hanni didn't look up at him. Luca's eyes were locked onto hers, full of fear and searching for comfort.

'Perhaps I did, but it was your death that I wanted.'

Hanni was done with lying, and she was done with being afraid. She held Luca tighter and waited until she was calm before she stared up at her father.

'Luca would have killed you, I'm sure of that, and I would have cheered my lungs out when he did. I stopped him from doing that tonight, or I tried to, but I didn't want to. I only let you live because I needed your help to get Renny back, and, yes, I had to stop my life with Freddy being blown apart. But when

Luca first ordered me to bring you to Prague, when he forced me to go through with it, I really hoped that he would murder you. I lay awake and I pictured it.'

She waited for the boot, for the blow to her head that would finish her, or the blow to her stomach that would end all her dreams. From the look on Reiner's face it was coming, but then there was a strangled gasp and Luca started to speak.

'She's right. I was going to do it. I told her I'd arrest you, take you back. It wasn't true: I was always going to kill you. I came to the bar to do it tonight.'

Reiner shrugged. 'That's hardly a revelation. But you didn't try very hard, did you? Or maybe the Stasi's training methods leave a lot to be desired. You should have got there first; you should have bribed the barman to do the job for you. It's all basic textbook stuff, but no. Instead of being prepared, you were late.'

The oddest expression flashed across Luca's face. If his mouth hadn't been such a mess, and the situation hadn't been so bleak, Hanni would have thought he was smiling.

'I know what I should have done. But here's the joke, my bosses stopped me. They wanted to know the state of my progress with you, so they sent me a message which I had to reply to and—'

'Your bosses made you late. Oh the delicious irony of that: bureaucracy saved me, and it will literally be the death of *you*. That would have made an even more perfect anecdote if it was true, but there was no one on the end of the call when you finally got through, was there? It was Hauke who called and delayed you, you fool. It was my plan that brought you here. You were never running me – you don't have the brains.'

Reiner didn't simply smile this time; he burst out laughing. His amusement was a moment's distraction from the scene on the floor, but a moment was all Hanni needed. She reached into Luca's jacket pocket, hoping she had picked the right one because there would be no second chances, hoping that he hadn't chosen powder as his weapon. Her fingers scrabbled through the cloth, ripping at it until she found what she needed. She pulled the ampoule out, stuck it into the back of Luca's mouth and clamped his jaw shut.

'It is done. It is over. There's no more to come.'

Her voice was as gentle as she could make it, but the newspaper reports of the pill's ability to grant a quick death to the war criminals who had chosen a coward's way out were wrong. The cyanide didn't work as fast as Hanni wanted it too; it took longer than a handful of seconds to stop Luca's heart. His death wasn't painless; it came with contractions that rocked his body and flooded horror through his eyes. It was dreadful to watch. But then he was gone and he was safe, and there was a kind of peace in that.

'You little bitch.'

Reiner wasn't laughing anymore. He was looming over her, his face blazing. Hanni closed Luca's eyes and pressed a hand to his cheek before she replied.

'I've taken him out of your power. I've let him die with more speed and more kindness than you would have done.'

'You never learn, do you? You always have to get in my way.'

Reiner stooped. When he straightened, there was a brick in his hand. Hanni braced herself. She wasn't going to beg; she was going to be brave for one last time. If she had to die, so be it. But then her body and her instincts and her love for her unborn child took hold and the words she had sworn not to say to him were out.

'I'm pregnant.'

The brick dropped.

His hand still rose. The world still turned black.

CHAPTER 20

19 APRIL 1950, PRAGUE

It was hard to surface – she didn't know if she would make it back up.

The fog surrounding her was dense enough to be solid. It filled her ears and blurred her eyes. Hanni couldn't be sure which parts of her body would move and which parts would scream in protest if she tried. Her head ached with a throb that ran from her forehead down the left-hand side of her face to her chin. She was scared that if she did anything more than breathe, she would crack into splinters and break. And yet somehow she was alive.

The shock of that thinned out the fog. She was alive. Reiner could have killed her but he hadn't. That opened her sore eyes, although the world stayed out of focus. It gave her hope, until another thought followed and the fear rushed back in.

What if he's playing games? What if this is just a delay and he's locked all the doors and left me down here to die.

That was a terrifying thought. That pushed her off her back and up into a sitting position. Which was a mistake. None of her was ready for that. Now the world wasn't only out of focus, it was spinning.

Hanni lay down again and closed her eyes, which was a less frightening thing to do now that she knew they would reopen. She began to explore the state he had left her in far more carefully, stretching her fingers, bending her knees, rolling her shoulders. Nothing was broken. She moved her hand to her stomach. Nothing was tender. There was no evidence to suggest that the baby wasn't still safely there.

She opened her eyes again, blinking until they could stand the light and she knew that the room would stay steady, and worked her way upright. It was a very gradual process. She started on her knees, sliding her hands up the wall for support. The relief that she was not only alive but could move sent a surge of energy through her. Yes there were doors to get through, and a staircase that was a death trap, but she could navigate those. She had to. But then Hanni stood fully up and turned round, and the night's horrors came roaring back.

Reiner hadn't only left her behind in the cellar; he had left Luca too. The agent was lying spread-eagled on his back, his arms and legs flung out in the pattern his final convulsion had twisted them into. It was hard to remember that the death she had given him was the better one. Hanni didn't want to do it, but she forced herself to go over to the body, instinctively scanning the floor as she did so to see if Reiner had left any evidence of himself behind.

As she crouched down beside Luca, she was grateful she had at least closed his eyes the previous night. She was also glad that no one who had loved him would see the terrible way Luca had died. His cheekbones and nose were shattered, he had bitten through his lip and the skin visible beneath the bruises was a deep cherry red. A faint and bitter almond scent hovered around his mouth. Whoever Luca had been was long gone.

Which is partly my doing.

There had been nothing but mercy in her heart when she

had slipped the pill into his mouth and crunched his jaws onto it. Looking at him now, it still felt like murder.

Which it was, no matter the motive or whether Reiner performed the last act or I did. And if I am the one who is found down here with him...

For the first time since she had concocted the plan that had failed her, Hanni had no idea what to do next. There was no sequence to work out for this. The adrenaline which had pumped through her when she was squaring up to Reiner had vanished. Luca's death could still lead to hers. Reiner might not have been able to bring himself to kill her – or might not have been able to kill his unborn grandchild – but he might have called the police. Hanni had no idea how long she had been unconscious. There could be a van already on its way; there could be policemen massing outside. There was nothing to suggest that anyone but she and Luca had ever been in the cellar. Which meant that she had to get up from Luca's side and get away, making sure as she did that there was no trace of her left anywhere near him.

Hanni scrambled to her feet, ignoring the throbbing in her head. Her bag was still where she had dropped it and her papers were all safely inside. There was nothing she could use to wipe away fingerprints, but surely the basement was too filthy for that to be an issue. The main thing to do now was not panic. The cellar door was open; she had to trust that the outer one was too, unless this really was some elaborate scheme to make her believe that she would survive when she wouldn't.

Hanni refused to let that thought take root. She fled, heading for the staircase. She was on the third step, her foot balanced at the side of it to avoid the rotting middle, when the reality of the situation hit her. She couldn't leave Luca.

She stopped, even though she was desperate to keep on climbing. She couldn't leave him discarded on a freezing-cold floor as if his life amounted to nothing more than a pile of rubbish. Not when she had seen so many who had died in that miserable, inhuman way.

The tears she had been fighting for days suddenly burst out in a wail that should have brought a crowd of rescuers running. Her conscience wouldn't let her leave him behind, and she couldn't carry him either. She was as trapped as if the door was locked and the staircase was a mirage. She couldn't get Luca out without help and she hadn't a clue where to turn to find that. Who could she possibly explain him to? How could she explain her part in his death?

Marek.

Hanni clung on to the handrail as light edged into the horrors gripping her brain. Marek. Who knew the way the city worked and had already, or so she hoped, helped Freddy. Who had enough respect for him to hopefully help her. She needed Marek.

Hanni went as quickly as she could up the rest of the staircase, remembering the sequence Reiner had used to get safely across it. The building's main door was heavy, but it wasn't locked. Reiner had meant to keep her alive. Hanni didn't trust that at all, but she didn't have the time to worry at why. She slipped out into the alleyway, emerging into a watery daylight that smelled of fresh rain. There was thankfully no one around; she doubted there was ever anyone around for long in such a miserable place.

She closed the door behind her and checked her watch, but the glass had smashed when she fell and the hands were stuck. She didn't know if it was morning or afternoon or when the bar, which was the only point of reference she had for Marek, would open. She didn't know if he was back in Prague.

Hanni set out anyway. Someone would listen to her; she would make sure of that. Someone would find him. They had to. Hanni had no plan to replace the one to beat Reiner and Luca, the one which had failed her. All she wanted was for

Freddy to come home and for them and Renny to get out of Prague as fast as they could. And – whether it was superstition or exhaustion or because her conscience had ducked too many times now for her to ignore it when it pricked – she was certain that none of that would happen until she gave Luca a better kind of ending.

'I don't know what kind of a place you think this is, but we don't let the homeless in. And if it's a policeman you need, you won't find one here. I suggest you go back to wherever you got yourself into this state and sort it out.'

Hanni stared at the barman, who had taken one look at her and stepped back from the counter. Until she entered the Tygra, she had been too focused on what she wanted from Marek to give any thought to her appearance. People had shied away from her as she walked to the bar, not that she had taken much notice: people often shied away from each other in Prague. But for someone to comment, to think that she lived on the streets or to recognise that she was the victim of some kind of a beating in a city where no one commented and no one got involved, or not overtly, in anyone else's business, suggested that she really did look out of place. That was the last thing Hanni needed if anyone was going to take her seriously and send Marek a message. So she drew herself up as if she was wearing furs and didn't let his challenge derail her.

'I don't need the police and I'm not homeless.' She stuck out her chin and scanned the scruffy room and its equally scruffy inhabitants. 'But if I've offended your standards in some way, perhaps you could direct me to the ladies' restroom where I can freshen up.'

That sent a roar of laughter around the room. It also relaxed the barman enough to win her a smile. He nodded at a door at the back of the bar and threw a heavy key across the counter.

'Here – take this. There's a bathroom through there, second door on the left, where you can fix yourself up a bit. It's hardly the Ritz but hopefully Madam won't be too disappointed.'

He gave her a mock bow, but he carried on grinning and, despite the state she was in and the dangerous and illegal favour she had come to ask for, Hanni's confidence trickled back.

The bathroom he directed her to wouldn't have passed as a broom closet in the Ritz. It was tiny and none too clean, but, after one look in the flyblown mirror, Hanni was amazed he had let her use it or let her into the bar at all. Her hair was red with brick dust. Her cheeks were smeared with dirt, and there was a dark purple bruise spreading along one side of her face. Her coat too was plastered with muck and with splinters, and her stockings had run into holes. People hadn't shied away from her because they were wary of strangers; they had been shocked or afraid at the sight of her. If the police had stopped her, she could have easily ended up in a cell.

Hanni washed her face in the freezing cold water and shook out her coat and did her best to repair the damage to her hair and face, although the only tools at her disposal were a grey sliver of soap and a comb she didn't dare inspect too closely. When she went back to the bar, at least the barman didn't grimace this time. She handed him back the key and got straight to the point.

'I have to see Marek. It's urgent.'

The barman was immediately on the defensive again. 'If this is a domestic, I don't want to know, especially not if it involves him. None of my customers would come back if they thought their women could find them in here, and I'm not going to go upsetting the one with a temper, no matter how pretty you are.'

It wasn't the best answer, but it at least confirmed that he knew him. Hanni tried again.

'You don't understand. I'm not somebody's woman, and I'm

certainly not his. Marek has been helping me with a search for a lost child. Tell him it's Freddy's wife, Hana Havelova, from Terezin. Tell him I've another job for him. If he's got a temper, he won't appreciate finding out that you kept him away from good money.'

Terezin had made the barman pause, although he was still reluctant to do as she asked. Hanni answered his 'I don't know where he is; it could take hours to track him down' with a very definite 'I can wait' and secured herself a table with the best view of the door. She ignored the comments from the men slumped at the counter until they gave up trying to impress her. Eventually the barman stopped watching her and went away, although when he returned, he was shaking his head. Hanni ignored that too. She continued to sit, refusing to wince at the pains still rippling through her jarred body.

After an hour of sitting in silence, the barman appeared at her table with a plate of thick stew. 'Eat that; you look hungry. He'll be a while yet.'

Hanni wasn't just hungry, she was ravenous. She polished the plate's contents off in minutes and held it out with a smile for a second helping. By the time Marek finally arrived, Hanni had eaten two more platefuls, the best part of a basket of bread and drunk a glass of cold beer which tasted like heaven. She was more than ready to deal with his scowl.

'I don't like being summoned like this, so you'd better tell me quickly what you want from me. Your husband is on his way back; he has the papers and half the money you sent him to get, which wasn't an easy thing to drum up. Don't be asking me to try and get the rest of it.'

Freddy was on his way home. The thought of that was a joyous one, even if the decisions Hanni had made while she was waiting meant that the joy would likely be short-lived. That was for later. Now she knew that he was safe and that he was on his way back, the world felt like hers to control again.

'I don't want money, but I do need your help.' She waited while Marek decided to stop looming over her and sit down. 'And I have a story to tell you.'

She did that as quickly as possible, keeping the account of what had happened to Luca as concise as she could. And – because she didn't know how closely Marek had been in contact with her father in Theresienstadt – she deliberately skirted round the subject of Reiner and didn't mention his name. All she told Marek was that the killer was an ex-Nazi like Novotný, who was trying to make capital out of Renny's discovery and that she had inadvertently got caught in the middle of Luca's attempt to catch him. It was a flimsy story, to her ears at least, but Marek didn't question it. She doubted he would have been so willing to stay if she had told him the truth.

To her relief, he let her get through the whole explanation without interruption. When she finished, he produced a packet of cigarettes and watched her carefully while he lit one.

'I don't understand why you're bothering. Why not leave him in the cellar? If he died the way you said he did and he's a Stasi agent, the police will hush it up. If there's no leads, then they won't come looking for you, and it makes no sense for the Nazi to contact the police when the murder also implicates him, especially if he's the war criminal you've said he is. And if no one finds Luca's corpse but the rats, what does it matter?'

'It matters to me.'

Hanni shook her head as Marek pushed the cigarettes across the table.

'I can't leave him there to rot. That's what a Nazi, a monster, would do. Whatever else Luca was, he was a person; he was someone's son. He deserves a proper burial, even if it is a poor one. I can't give you a better reason than that, I'm sorry, except maybe to say that I've hidden too many things and told too many lies in my life, and I'm done with it. Treating Luca with respect is a new start for me. And when Freddy comes back and he has Renny safely with him, I'm going to go to the police. I'm going to tell them about Novotný and his accomplice and all about their plans to destabilise the East. Which, as I learned from Luca, might not be true but will be believed. I'm going to make sure that they're caught at the border and they never see daylight again.'

Marek drained his beer and waved for another one. 'And that's very noble of you, but you do know that they will arrest you too? You knowing a Nazi is enough to make you a Nazi here. It won't just be the two of them missing daylight.'

Hanni brushed the breadcrumbs off her coat and stood up. 'I don't care. There's been people in the past that I should have denounced for their crimes and I didn't do it because I was afraid the authorities would arrest me too. That decision had awful consequences for people who deserved better, and there's been too much fear and far too many things I've had to keep hidden since. But I'm not afraid anymore. I'm already in a prison – the only difference is that I built this one out of secrets and lies. If honesty has a price, I'm ready to pay it. So will you help me? Will you do what I asked?'

Marek shrugged. 'If that's what you want. And because Freddy is a good man. I don't know what you are.'

Hanni knew better than to offer any response to that except *thank you*. She left the bar at once, without looking back. Despite Marek's barbed comment, she felt lighter than she had since she'd left Berlin, since the night of her exhibition.

With all the love we have for each other, can't we fix anything?

Freddy's words from Theresienstadt had come back to her as she had sat alone in the bar. They had been out of step with each other for a long time, longer than he knew. But they loved each other deeply, Hanni was certain of that. And love had to conquer all in the end, otherwise all of the songs and the stories that swore it did were lies. Hanni didn't want to listen to lies anymore, and now that Luca's burial was arranged, she wasn't going to tell lies anymore either, or keep secrets or leave silences. She had tried to bring Reiner to justice and people had paid for that. She had stopped trying and people had paid for that too. So now it was time to bring their battle into the light and be done with it. Not with overcomplicated plans but with a simple stepping forward instead.

This is him and this is me. We are not the same person, my father and I, but I understand if you can't see the difference yet.

It was the most honest way she could say it. And now the decision to tell Freddy everything was made, it no longer felt frightening; it felt like a release. It felt like the right backdrop for the new world they were building. Renny would soon be out of Novotný's hands for good. Freddy was coming home and so was his little sister. And Hanni was going to tell him the truth; she was going to trust that, together, they could fix anything.

When Hanni finally got back to the flat, it was close to midnight and the moon was streaming in silver slices through the thin curtains. She sat in the bath for a long time, soothing her sore skin, washing the night's traces away; whispering welcoming words to the baby. Then she crawled into bed, where the exhaustion hit her the moment she wrapped the covers around her, sucking her down into a sleep that was deeper than anything she had known in weeks. A sleep that was perfectly, beautifully dreamless.

CHAPTER 21

20 APRIL 1950, PRAGUE

She was so beautiful. How had he let himself forget that? And how had he allowed his fears over Renny to spill out into the fights and the mistrust that had set all the old barriers back up between them? After all the struggles they had been through to bring their lives together, to go backwards like they were now doing felt like a crime.

Freddy lowered himself gently onto the empty side of the bed. Despite the fact that he had been travelling through a night which was still not over, he was too wide awake to sleep. He had come back alone, after Marek had been called back to Prague quicker than Renny's transit papers were ready. He had spent the bumpy truck ride into the outskirts of the city and the silent walk through its centre replaying the events of the last few weeks and wishing he had handled them all very differently. Whatever came next with the Novotnýs and his sister, a great deal had to change.

Ever since he had caught sight of Renny's photograph on the wall in the gallery, Freddy had been living half caught in the past, and buckling under all the pain and the shadows that had brought with it. He had seen threats and conspiracies everywhere. He had seen Hanni as the enemy. He had been afraid of what he would find if he scratched too deep, and he had let that fear warp everything he knew to be true about her. It was a sad and destructive way to live, and it couldn't continue. Not when the love and the family he had longed to find – the sure place in the world he had dreamed of reclaiming through all the terrible days and nights in Buchenwald – was finally within his grasp. He couldn't ruin that, so he had decided somewhere between Jirny and Prague not to.

I'm going to live in the present. I'm going to look forward to the joy that is coming, not backwards into the hell that has been.

When Marek had given him the money he had miraculously pulled together to enable Freddy to buy Renny back from Novotný, the world had steadied for the first time in weeks. Nothing was going to threaten that balance again. Freddy's mind was made up. He was going to do again what he had told Marek he had learned to do once before: to stop stabbing at hurts he couldn't change, to stop reliving the days filled with pain. Above all, he was going to be grateful, and especially for Hanni. Who wasn't the enemy; who was the love of his life and his best friend.

And who really was very beautiful.

Freddy reached out a hand to stroke her hair and bent across the patched coverlet to whisper, 'I'm here and I love you.' He stopped himself a second before his movements woke her.

Hanni looked so peaceful. She was lying on her side, her face turned away from him, with one hand cupped under her cheek and her hair spread out in waves across the pillow. She was sleeping the kind of deep and dreamless sleep that looks more like an enchantment. Freddy couldn't remember the last time he had seen her so untroubled. Sleep had become a fitful place for them both. The bed had become a cold space where they turned away from each other more often than together. A few days in the quiet village – along with the depth of kindness Marek had shown him before he headed back to the city – had cured Freddy of poor nights and had made him long for a happier bed again. And now it seemed that something had worked the same magic on Hanni. He didn't want to disturb that, especially as he had come to suspect that uninterrupted sleep was something Hanni badly needed.

'Let me run through that again. She's fanciful and not her usual practical self. She's been ill when she's never ill, and you can't gauge her moods right. Dear God, man, are you really so caught up in yourself? It sounds to me like your wife is about to make you into a father.'

Marek's response when Freddy had shared his confusion over the state of his marriage had winded him. But the more he thought about it, the more sense his words made. Hanni had been behaving so oddly since they left Berlin because she was pregnant, and she didn't know how to tell him. Her reticence to share the news made perfect sense given the situation they were currently in. It was an explanation Freddy was more than happy to grab on to and not question. It wasn't as if they had even had a conversation about having a child of their own – they were too new in their marriage. And Freddy had never thought about himself as a father before; he had been too busy associating family with what he had lost. But to have a baby with Hanni? He had to ease himself up off the bed before his determination not to disturb her was trampled beneath a far greater urge to scoop her into an embrace and shout out an exuberant 'put me out of my misery and tell me' which would have woken the whole block, never mind Hanni.

He got up instead, slipped out of the bedroom and went back to his rucksack and the travel documents and ransom money which he had already checked a dozen times and would check a dozen times more. Marek hadn't said where the money had come from or how he had got it, and he had given Freddy a year to repay what – although it was only half of what Novotný had asked for – was still a huge sum.

That had been the other revelation of the trip to the countryside: the change in Marek. It was hard to reconcile the man Freddy now knew with the man who had been so hostile when he had led the way out of Theresienstadt. Marek was still gruff but he was kind beyond measure, and he too had finally chosen to move on. When Marek had confided that he was leaving Theresienstadt for good, not just to reintegrate himself back into the world, but to play a part in the recreation of his lost home town, Freddy had had to hastily swallow an unexpected rush of tears. A good man had come back; a good man was learning to let the hurt go. Another scar in the world was healing.

And tomorrow it's my turn to mend the last rip in my life.

Freddy grabbed himself a blanket and settled down on the least lumpy of the apartment's sagging armchairs. By tomorrow evening, Renny would be with them. It was hard not to cheer out loud at the thought of it. Once Novotný had the money, which Freddy would take to him as soon as the hour would reasonably allow it, that would be it. He – no, they; him and Hanni – would bring his little sister home and then the healing would surely be done. He could see Renny now as clearly as if she was already sitting there, cuddled on the sofa between the two of them as they told her about Berlin and how good their life was going to be there. As he told her about Leo and Rosa and Jakub and how loved she had been and how loved she would be. He had got so much wrong, but he was going to get so much right. They all were, his new family – Hanni and Renny and the baby.

Freddy was still smiling at that image as he drifted off into sleep.

.   .   .

He spotted the piece of paper which had been shoved under the door almost as soon as he woke up; its white lines were pristine against the dirty brown of the carpet. If there had been a knock when it was delivered, he hadn't heard it.

Freddy levered himself out of the chair, wincing at the twinges which immediately plucked at his neck and his shoulders. He couldn't wait to get back to their Berlin apartment, and to their far more comfortable furniture.

According to the clock on the wall, it was close to nine thirty but – from the watery quality of the light filtering into the room – he assumed the morning was another grey one. He was tired of that too. He wanted Berlin's blue skies and its April streets, ripe with cherry blossom. He also wanted coffee that was smooth and rich and didn't leave him with a mouth full of grounds. And a *Pfannkuchen* – his mouth watered at the thought of that treat – covered in powdered sugar and bursting with thick plum jam.

He was dreaming of those delights when he picked up the note and brushed the carpet's dust off it. It was a single sheet of paper, folded over. There was no name or address on the front. The message inside – which was signed *František Novotný* rather than admitting the truth of the writer's real identity – was short and straight to the point.

I am leaving Prague today. The child is waiting for you. It would be better for you to collect her sooner rather than later.

It was really happening. Freddy had to brace himself against the wall as he read the note a second time. There was no mention of the ransom money, which made him hopeful that Novotný was so fixated on leaving the city – a possibility Freddy hadn't considered – he would settle for the reduced amount. The rest of the note, however, was more worrying. Although it didn't specifically say that Renny would be left behind on her own if Freddy didn't get there in time, it implied it. Or – given that the first line said *I* not *we* – it implied that Novotný's plan could be to leave her in Jana's care when he left.

Which could be worse, because surely Jana will run away with her the moment her husband walks out of the door.

Breakfast was forgotten. As was any improvement to his dishevelled appearance except a splash of cold water to wake himself up. There was still the possibility that this was a trick – that he would get to the apartment, hand over the ransom and Renny would already be gone. The fact that he had put his trust in a Nazi suddenly seemed like the most stupid decision that Freddy had ever made.

He grabbed his rucksack, checked the contents again because he couldn't not check them, and was almost out of the door before he realised he had forgotten the most important thing – he had been running so fast, he hadn't thought about Hanni. He dropped the bag and pushed open the bedroom door, ready to rouse her. Hanni wasn't the kind of woman who spent hours making herself fit for the day. Once he read her the note, she would be out of bed and into her clothes in minutes.

'Hanni, are you awake yet?'

He paused halfway to the bed. She wasn't. It didn't look as if she had moved during the night. She was still so sound asleep, he could barely hear her breathing.

I have to protect her now too, in the same way I have to protect Renny. I have to make her days easy ones.

It was a strange thought to be having about Hanni. She had never asked for anything like that from him; he couldn't imagine 'look after me' coming out of her mouth. But he could do that for her this morning at least. Hanni didn't need to be at the Novotnýs' apartment, watching Jana's hysterics as the child she had pretended for too long was hers was removed. She also didn't need to be there trying to make him stay calm – she had done plenty of that already. This – letting her sleep, shielding her from the unhappiness that Renny's leaving the Novotný home would inevitably unleash – could be his way of returning the care Hanni had unfailingly shown him. And thanking her for it. She didn't know that he was on his way back from Jirny, so he would leave her to wake up in her own time, then he would bring her the best surprise. The delight on her face as he came home and Renny followed him into the apartment would be wonderful.

Freddy crept out of the room without waking her and went back to the note, scribbling his own words under Novotný's message. Then he picked up his rucksack and left the flat, closing the outer door behind him as quietly as he could.

The street he emerged onto was already bustling. Unlike Berlin, where the shopkeepers wiping down their windows and sweeping their piece of the pavement would have had a comment or two to throw his way, nobody looked at him. He smiled at them anyway. He wouldn't miss this any more than he would miss the poor coffee and the heavy bread. There was a weight of suspicion and control clamping down around Communist-run Prague that he didn't want to feel anymore. He would be glad to be gone from the city with its worn-out streets and its worn-out people.

He grinned as he realised that they could leave tomorrow. Marek had promised before he left to act as their guide on the route home, a journey Freddy knew would be a far happier thing than the one they had made to come here. By Sunday, the three of them could be in Berlin.

There was enough in that to keep him smiling all the way to Šafaříkova Street.

'There are a few small matters to complete and – well, I'm sure I don't need to explain the whole situation to you, but there's a bit of a way to go yet to settle Jana. Why don't you wait in the kitchen? You can sit with Renny for a few moments or so until we're ready for you.'

It wasn't a trick then; she was still here. Despite the sense of relief that brought, Freddy was nowhere as close to comfortable as Novotný seemed to be. The chance of finally being rid of his unwanted daughter had put the man in a far more cheerful mood than Freddy had ever seen him in. That only made him more loathsome. But he was offering time alone with Renny, and that was a welcome bonus to the day, so Freddy nodded as he was ushered into the flat. He didn't care about the matters Novotný still had to deal with – he doubted that there would be any paperwork recording the handover, or the ransom, so he assumed they had something to do with the man's leaving the city. All Freddy wanted was the business concluded and to be certain that there were no pitfalls coming.

'What about the money? I've got as much of it as I could but it's not the whole sum you asked for.'

He pulled the envelope from his rucksack and held it out and then didn't know quite what to do when Novotný raised his hands as if the payment wasn't of interest.

'Leave it in the kitchen. It would be far easier for Jana if we make this look more like a transfer of care than a transaction.'

There was something not right in the man's words or his manner. Freddy couldn't imagine why Novotný would start to worry about his wife's sensibilities now when they had never bothered him before. Or why the money Hanni had assured him was key to Renny's return was suddenly so unimportant. Or why Novotný's plans had to delay his. But those weren't what was really getting under his skin. The thing making his hands itch was the smirk on Novotný's face. It was one that Freddy had seen before but couldn't quite place. Until he did and his stomach contracted.

He is a Buchenwald man, an Auschwitz man.

That had been his first impression of Novotný; that was

how he had described him to Hanni, and now that first impression came back, blaring with warning signs. The smirk was the one the Buchenwald guards had worn in the moments before they were about to unleash a particularly vicious game as they called it – or torture to use the prisoners' more accurate term. Freddy was missing something – every one of his policeman's instincts was screaming that at him, but his instincts couldn't tell him what it was.

'What are the small matters you mentioned?'

But Novotný didn't answer; he opened the kitchen door instead and all Freddy's police training fell away. Renny was sitting alone at a small table and, when she saw him walk in, she smiled. Freddy was so wrapped up in the wonder of that, he didn't hear the door closing behind him or Novotný's heavy footsteps walking away. And he forgot everything that had been worrying him the instant she spoke.

'You look a bit messy.'

Freddy glanced down at his crumpled clothes and laughed. 'I suppose I do. I've been travelling all night. I went to get the papers you're going to need to leave Czechoslovakia and cross into Germany, and I was so eager to get here, I forgot to clean myself up. Do you mind?'

The little girl shook her head. The smile was still there, but it was a tentative one, and she was holding herself in a very rigid position. Freddy desperately wanted to put out his arms and gather her up into them. He resisted; he remembered the need for caution.

He sat down opposite her and put his hands on the table, doubting that she would take them but hoping that she might at least loosen her tightly held fingers. She didn't.

'Are you scared, Renny? Of leaving here, of coming with us?'

She didn't answer him immediately: Freddy managed not to jump in and take charge of her answer.

'I don't think so. I think that I've been scared before – there's been memories coming back to me, of *them* – the men in the uniforms who used to come into the room and take some of the children away – and of the dogs, and of being without people who should have been there. When I remember those things, I feel shaky and sick. But I don't feel like that about leaving Prague.'

The way she described her feelings, or lack of them – as if she was watching herself from behind a glass – was so bleak it made Freddy want to sob. He didn't ask her if the opposite was true – if she was excited. He didn't think he could bear it if she didn't understand what he meant. It was hard not to look at her and think, *Something is broken.*

But I'll fix it, I swear. If she'll let me.

She had fallen quiet again, but her lips were moving as if she was practising a question. Freddy leaned a little further across the table and moved his hands a fraction closer to hers. She still didn't reach out, but her fingers unknotted.

'What is it, Renny? What do you want to ask me?'

It was obvious that asking questions wasn't something that had played a big part in her life. He could see her screwing up her courage.

'When Hanni was here, I asked her if you were a good man, and she said that you were. Is she a good person too?'

That was far easier than he had expected. He couldn't keep the joy from his voice.

'She's better than that. Hanni has the biggest heart and so much love in her. I don't think she's ever done a bad thing in her life; I don't think she's capable of it. She takes such good care of me, and she'll do the same for you. You will grow to love her, I promise, and she will very easily love you.'

The answer seemed to satisfy her – the smile came back a little stronger. But it was obvious that there was still more to come.

'Go on, sweetheart. Ask whatever you need to and I'll answer the best that I can.'

This time she glanced towards the door before she spoke. 'I thought you would say that about her. I hoped that you would. But my—' She checked herself. 'The man who I've been calling my father is very bad, isn't he?'

Freddy nodded.

'What did he do?'

For a moment, Freddy wasn't sure what Renny had said, and then he wasn't sure how to answer – she was only nine years old; whatever she had seen, there was a limit to how much detail he could bear to load onto her. So he tried for simplicity instead.

'He was once with the German army, the most ruthless part of it. He worked as a guard at the prison town you were kept in after you were taken from Berlin, and he hurt people there who didn't agree with him.'

'Like Jews?'

'Yes. And he helped send a lot of them to their deaths.'

Renny's gaze was fixed so firmly on his, Freddy couldn't look away. 'Did he kill our mother?'

The use of *our* should have been heart-warming. In the context she had put it, the word tore through him.

'I don't know if he was the one who gave the order for her to be taken away; he may have been. If it wasn't him, it would have been someone like him, with the same twisted beliefs and the same hatreds.'

Renny let that sink in, then she nodded. 'There were a lot of them, weren't there? The men who took people away; the men who hated others and liked killing. I think the other man is one of them too.'

It took a couple of seconds before Freddy caught up with what Renny had said.

There's something not right; there's something I'm missing.

His neck prickled; his instincts began screaming again.

'What other man, Renny? Who are you talking about? Is there somebody else here?'

But before she could answer, the kitchen door swung open again and Novotný was standing there with the same smirk on his face, apologising for the delay and announcing that they were finally ready. And he laughed with far too much amusement when Freddy asked, 'What for?'

The room they followed Novotný into was the one where the disastrous lunch had taken place. It looked very different. The table had been pushed back, the curtains were drawn and there was only one small lamp lit.

As Freddy's eyes adjusted to the gloom, he could see that Jana was already there, sitting on one of the dining-room chairs which had, bizarrely, been set out in two rows in front of a white sheet which was stretched out and tacked onto the wall. She didn't look up when they entered; she curled in on herself. She also wasn't alone: there was a man seated in front of her who Freddy assumed was the one Renny had referred to as *the other*. He was elegantly, and expensively, dressed in a pale grey suit, and he had the same air of being in command of whatever space he was in as Novotný had displayed in the bar. Or more of it – as soon as he saw Freddy and Renny enter the room, he immediately assumed the host's role.

'Welcome to our little entertainment. We've kept the best places for you and the child.' He gestured to the two spare seats next to him; he did not introduce himself.

Freddy hesitated, trying to gauge the level of threat the stranger posed and why there had been a slight pause before *entertainment*. He wasn't in the mood to be ordered about or to engage in guessing games.

Just as he was about to decline the invitation with 'why

don't you tell me what's going on here first?', Renny's hand slipped into his.

Whatever it's about, she can't be frightened. This can't be a repeat of the last time.

Don't cause a problem if that will escalate a situation you don't yet understand was Freddy's constant message to overeager young policemen, and it was good advice. He kept quiet as he led Renny to the front. He settled her into the seat furthest away from their beaming host with a whispered, 'We must be going to pretend that we're all at the cinema,' which won him a brief smile. Then he took his own chair, ignoring the man's 'How touching' but not the unpleasantness in it. Whoever this man was, he was keen to provoke a reaction, and Freddy wasn't ready to give him that yet. Not that he seemed concerned – he stretched out his long legs and called to where Novotný had taken up position at the back of the room beside a loaded projector.

'Excellent. So now that we're all here, perhaps we can get started. Hauke, can I leave the honours to you?'

The use of Hauke was a warning shot. Freddy turned to call the arrogant stranger out. Before he could do so, there was a click and a soft whirr, and a circle and a set of numbers counting down from ten appeared on the sheet.

I think the other man is one of them too.

Renny's words, combined with the very comfortable use of Hauke, sent a sudden shiver through Freddy.

They're playing with us.

He had no idea why they would do that or what the game could possibly be, but he wasn't prepared to take chances. His hand flew up ready to clamp across Renny's eyes in case the kind of images from the death camps which had been shown after the trials at Nuremberg flashed onto the makeshift screen. But then the reel started and he dropped it again. The film was nothing like the one he had expected. The opening shot wasn't a heap of broken bodies but a group of children singing in perfect harmony. And the one after that featured a jazz band playing in the sunshine while a clapping audience sat on a terrace drinking tea.

'I don't understand what we're watching.'

The man at his side – who Freddy realised when he looked at him properly seemed oddly familiar round his eyes and his mouth – smiled, but he didn't turn from the screen.

'Keep watching – you will. So will she.'

Freddy glanced down at Renny. She was staring at the screen as a rather balletic sequence of men swinging hammers in a foundry unfolded. She didn't appear worried in any way; she seemed fascinated by the synchronised movement and the stirring music that accompanied it. The scene switched again – this time the actors were painting delicate figures onto pots and moulding sculptures out of clay. It was all pleasant enough, but it was rather mundane, and Freddy couldn't see the point of them both sitting through it when they could be heading for home.

'I'm sure this is all very interesting, but there are still a lot of preparations—'

He stopped, forgetting what he was about to say as the scene shifted again and the camera panned out to show a row of single-storey wooden barracks with narrow front doors and side windows. He held his breath, ready to rescue Renny if anything worse appeared, only letting it go when the camera swooped back inside another bustling workplace. There were none of the sights he had been worried she might see. There were no skeletal bodies and starved, terrified eyes. The people sewing dresses and cutting out shoes were well-fed and smiling. The men working in the forge displayed better muscles than Freddy could claim. The women's dresses had stars pinned on them, but the clothes were pretty and clean. They were also wearing necklaces and earrings, and their hair looked as if they had all just come from the beauty parlour. No one was dressed in the striped uniform he had been forced to wear in Buchenwald. No one looked brutalised or beaten. The children cheering at the football match and playing on the roundabout or running through the gardens were laughing like children laughed every-where, and the flowers they were pointing at – even without colour – were beautiful. And that was the moment, as a child bent over a rosebush, when Freddy understood.

This isn't beauty; it's an illusion – a web of lies and false images.

It wasn't true. Nothing on the screen was true. If Freddy hadn't had Hanni's words to guide him, Renny's reaction would have told him that. She was pressed into his side. Her body was trembling. He could sense that a less self-controlled child would have climbed onto his lap. And she was lost in the screen, watching a group of children playing with their toys in a spot-less and spacious room, and quietly whispering, 'No.'

'It's such a shame that we didn't have the equipment to play you the soundtrack. I would have loved to see how the little one reacted when she heard the narrator say Theresienstadt.'

The man – who Freddy now knew wasn't playing at all – had raised his voice on the name. Renny didn't turn, but she stiffened so fast Freddy was afraid she wouldn't be able to draw breath. He rose and reached out for her.

'You can stop this now. We don't need to see any more.'

'Oh but you do, Herr Schlüsselberg, you really do.'

He didn't need to clamp his hand around Freddy's arm to pull him back down. The use of that long-ago name did the same trick.

'No more jumping up please, and do keep your eyes on the screen. You don't want to miss her starring moment.'

Her.

There was such a finality in it. Freddy knew who *her* was before the image appeared. Something in him had known all along. He still wanted to weep when the film swept on. Novotný was suddenly in shot, wearing a black dress SS uniform. The man now sitting beside Freddy and Renny was there too, and his uniform was even more immaculate. They were waving at a group of prisoners – because Freddy now knew that was who the actors were – as if they were all the best of friends. And standing between the two men, one of her arms linked through one of theirs and smiling as if the world truly was as delightful as the film portrayed it to be, was Hanni.

'Who are you?'

Freddy didn't turn as he asked the question. The familiar features – which were even more of a match when they were writ large on the screen – had finally made sense. He didn't want to see her eyes in the wrong face. He knew that if the man decided to extend his hand in some pretence of friendship, he would have broken his fingers whether Renny was watching or not.

'Reiner Foss. SS Obergruppenführer Reiner Foss if you want to use my full title, which I'm more than happy for you to do. I am Hannelore's – forgive me but I really loathe this Hanni she uses now – father. Which makes me – and this I can assure you gives me no pleasure either – your father-in-law.'

Freddy desperately wanted it to be a lie. He knew that it wasn't. He desperately wanted the world to return to the hopeful, happy place it had been only a few moments before. He knew that it couldn't. Then he wanted to howl. He wanted to run. He wanted to put his head in his hands and be sick. Instead, he was frozen, staring at the screen and still seeing Hanni's laughing face flanked by silver skull badges even though the film had moved on.

'She told me that her father was with the Red Cross.'

Reiner's laughter bounced round the room. 'Did she indeed? Well Hannelore always was very good at telling stories, in one way or another. It was her skill doing that with her camera that caught Goebbels' eye and got her a photography scholarship.'

'You said she was good.'

Freddy couldn't work out for a moment who had spoken. He was trying to make sense of *Goebbels*. He was so lost in this brutal reshaping of Hanni, he had momentarily forgotten his sister was there.

He turned, his movements as slow as if the room had slipped under water. Renny was no longer pressed into his side. She had climbed down off her seat. She was standing in front of him, and her face was so pinched she looked ancient.

'You said that she had never done a bad thing in her life. But she was standing with *them*, and she was laughing. I don't understand. Which one is the truth? What you said about her or the picture that was up there on the screen?'

She was desperate for reassurance, but Freddy had nothing to give her. He couldn't think how to make something so wrong right again. His silence let Reiner step in.

'Look at me. You are allowed.'

The speed with which Renny responded was terrible to watch. Her body snapped into position like a soldier called to attention. Her gaze fixed itself on Reiner's face, although not on his eyes. Those were sparkling.

'Well done, you remembered how to do it. It's fascinating how deep the lessons run. Now then, who did I say Hannelore was?'

'Your daughter.' Renny's voice was completely expressionless.

Reiner smiled. 'And would I tell a lie?'

She answered him at once. 'No, sir, you wouldn't.'

When he patted her on the head, her eyes turned blank, but she didn't move.

'You are a good girl, Renny, and so was Hannelore. She always did what her father said. I wonder if you might have seen her in Theresienstadt – she liked to wander around taking pictures. But perhaps you are too young to remember.' He leaned down so that his face was level with Renny's. 'And now you are going to live with her and the baby she's having. Are you looking forward to that?'

Renny shook her head.

Reiner started to laugh again. 'Oh dear, now we have a problem. It's time for you to leave with your brother, my dear. Off you go now.'

A shudder ran through the little girl's body. She stepped back, Reiner's hold on her broken.

'I don't want to.'

Her words pulled Freddy out of his own trance. 'Renny, sweetheart. You don't mean that.'

She wouldn't look at him. She flinched from his hand when he reached out to touch her.

'I do. I don't want to go with you. Not if it means I have to live with her.'

Freddy knew that his heart was broken. It had split in two when Hanni's face had appeared on the screen. Now he felt it. Renny's words ripped through him, tearing into the wound whose agony had already crippled him.

'Oh dear, the child has a mind of her own after all. What shall we do for the best here?'

Reiner's parody of concern was obscene. Freddy's fists curled, ready to beat him to a pulp or strangle him. But then he caught sight of Renny's stricken, frightened face and he let his hands fall. He couldn't make this better, but neither would he make it worse by plunging them all into violence. He let Reiner carry on talking and he prayed that Renny would remember how much he loved her.

'Could we take her with us, Hauke? What do you think, Renny – would you like that? Or maybe you would rather go with Jana. Come on now, hurry up, don't try my patience. Who are you going to choose?'

Jana had stood up at the sound of her name. The longing in her bruised face and in her voice when she whispered, 'Renny, darling, come with me please,' could have melted stone.

Freddy was so terrified that the woman's plea would be familiar enough to work, he stopped trusting that Renny knew where her heart lay and blurted out the same words.

Renny didn't answer. She took another step back. She looked at Freddy. She looked at Reiner and Novotný. She looked at Jana. She looked at all the adults who had lied to her, or caused her pain, or promised to make everything right in her world when all they had done was make it wrong. She didn't linger on any of them. Her body shrank. Her eyes flickered, as if she was searching for something only she could see. And then she shook her head, and her face grew hunted and lost.

'None of you. I choose none of you. I don't want to go with any of you at all.'

CHAPTER 22

20 APRIL 1950, PRAGUE

Hanni woke slowly, emerging from sleep and the blankets with a body that finally felt like her own again. She wasn't sick anymore; she wasn't exhausted. Her mind wasn't whirling, chasing after strands that were impossible to pull together. She was also ravenous again and conscious that there was nothing in the house to welcome Freddy – or Renny – home with.

She got up and dressed. The bruising from Reiner's attack ran down the side of her cheek like an ink stain, but she patted make-up over it and styled her hair in a wave that at least covered the worst of the damage. She might not look fit enough to face the world, but she was.

She went into the living room running lists through her head, wondering if there was anything in Prague that might come close to Freddy's beloved *Pfannkuchen*. It was only when she pulled the thin curtains aside that she realised the room was not how she had left it. There was a blanket thrown over the back of the armchair, and its cushions were dented and pushed out of shape. Freddy was home! The thought made her heart leap. It must have been late; he must have looked into the bedroom and decided not to disturb her. And he surely wouldn't have left her to sleep if he had been worried about anything. That made her heart leap too.

'Freddy, where are you? Are you here?'

The apartment was silent and empty. Hanni was too well rested to be troubled by that. She presumed he had seen the empty state of the kitchen and gone out to buy breakfast. She picked up the blanket and folded it away and began gathering up cutlery and crockery. She would lay the table and make coffee. Food wouldn't make anything she had to say more palatable, but sitting down together and sharing a meal might carry enough echoes of happier days to make him at least stay and listen.

She didn't see the note until she went to put the coffee cups on the table. It was Freddy's name she read first, and the first line of his message.

You looked so peaceful and lovely, I couldn't bear to wake you.

Her heart soared higher. He had been happy to see her; he had looked at her with love – things might not fall away so fast if he could hold on to that. Then she caught sight of the second name and read the message that hand had written, and the morning's light disappeared. It didn't matter that the rest of Freddy's message was in the same happy vein as his first line – *I've gone to get her. I've gone to bring her home. We'll both be with you very soon, my darling.* His words had lost the power to warm her.

Freddy's joy danced off the page. Hanni sank down on a chair and wondered how long that joy had lasted. *I am leaving Prague today* might have been written by Novotný, but it had Reiner's hand behind it; so did *sooner than later*. Hanni didn't bother to try and convince herself that she was seeing threats where there were none. She didn't try to convince herself that the note had no deeper meaning beyond *it is time to come and collect Renny*. She had stood up to her father. She had spoiled his pleasure and unleashed her hatred of him, and he had let her live. She had been a fool to think that wouldn't have consequences.

Hanni put the note down. She picked up her coat and bag. She had no idea how long Freddy had been gone, or what had already been revealed to him. She didn't waste time railing at the heavens for playing such a cruel trick at the very moment when she had been about to admit everything. *You had five years to do this, to go to him and be truthful* had drowned out any self-pity.

The streets were busy when Hanni stepped out onto them. She moved through the crowds and around the queues without seeing anybody. Freddy was at the Novotný apartment. She presumed that her father was also at the Novotný apartment. The only thing that was uncertain in that mix was how much of her life there would still be left to salvage.

The door was closed; the curtains were drawn. The flat was as quiet as it had been when she had last visited it, but this time there was an immediate response when she knocked.

'In you come – we've been waiting for you to show up.'

Hanni followed Novotný through the hallway and into the dining room without speaking. That room was no longer set for a meal; instead the chairs had been laid out in two rows. Jana was slumped weeping on one of them. Her face was a patchwork of purple and blue, and one arm was crossed and held tight over her chest. Hanni tried not to look too closely at her – there was no help she could offer Jana even if she had wanted to. Not when the other occupant of the room was, as she had expected, her father. And not when he was smiling.

'Hannelore, here you are at last. A little late to the party perhaps, which is a shame in some ways. I would have liked to watch your expression as your husband finally had his eyes opened about you, but I imagine the retelling will have its own entertainments. How are you—'

'Stop it.'

She didn't have time for Reiner's games. She no longer cared if she upset him or what that might lead to. She was no longer afraid of him – she had left that emotion behind in the cellar. She wished that change had come sooner.

'Where is Freddy? Is he still here?'

Reiner shook his head. 'You're showing rather a lack of manners, my dear, but I'll let it slide for today. No, he is not. He is gone. I'm surprised you didn't bump into him on the way here, or hear the two of them at least. The child was wailing like a banshee by the time they left.'

He has Renny. That part at least has gone to plan.

The joy of that, for a moment or two, wiped away her misery at what else might have happened. Freddy had his sister back; some part at least of his heart must be safe. But then the rest of Reiner's words sank in.

'What do you mean? Why was she wailing?'

Reiner didn't answer; he glanced round the room instead. Hanni knew she was being directed, which she hated, but she followed his gaze anyway. She had barely looked at the room itself when she had first come in – now she couldn't make sense of it. The rows of chairs, the sheet pinned to the wall, the projector; the gloom. It was obviously set up like some kind of home cinema, but she couldn't imagine why.

'What have you been showing him?'

Reiner's smile widened. 'A little history lesson, that's all. A rather fascinating documentary that never got the distribution it deserved when it was made, but one that you might remember rather well.'

Hanni's hand flew to her heart. The beat she could feel had to be an echo. There couldn't possibly be any more of them to come.

'The film from Theresienstadt. You showed him the film from Theresienstadt.'

Reiner clapped; Novotný laughed. Jana carried on holding herself tight and weeping as if there was no one else in the room.

'I did. He struggled to understand it at first, then he seemed rather bored by it, which I'm sure dear old Gerron would have been terribly insulted by. Oh but then you appeared on the screen and goodness did he wake up. Do you remember that scene, the one you featured in? You were standing between Hauke and me, and you were in one of your moods. I had to order you to laugh, which you did. You wouldn't have won any prizes for your acting, but your dear husband definitely bought it.'

'Why?'

There were so many questions and none of them had answers she wanted to hear, but she had to ask that one. Reiner raised an eyebrow as if to say, *Don't you know?* Hanni struggled not to cry, to keep breathing. It was nothing but a game to him: he would make her tease out the information she needed until the pain stretched her to breaking point.

She found the back of a chair and clung on to it. If she let herself picture Freddy watching her on film, laughing as the prisoners were forced to act out lie after lie, she would crumble. She couldn't do that – she had to hold on to some measure of control.

'Why did you show him that version of me? You know it wasn't true. And why did you tell him – because I presume that you did – who you were? There was no need. You'd got away with Luca's murder. You've got your disciple back with you. You could have left Prague without stirring up any of this. You could have given Freddy his happy ending. So why did you blow our lives apart instead?'

Reiner wasn't smiling anymore. Hanni waited for the

contempt to come. She didn't know how to react when he sighed.

'Oh, Hannelore, why are you always one step behind? I told you, didn't I, that there was still a side of this bargain that didn't hold weight – a bargain can I remind you that you, not me, set in motion with your first challenge when I came back to Berlin all those years ago and have kept prodding at ever since. You dragged me to this miserable city, you got my help to recover the child. I told you that there was something I wanted in return, and it wasn't the knife in the back that you had planned for me.'

'And I asked you what that thing was, so I could deliver it, but you wouldn't tell me.'

Her anger made no impression on him. Instead of responding in kind, he gave a sigh that was theatrically weary.

'How did you ever get work with the police? I know you love detail – you bored me to death with your nonsense about that when your grandmother encouraged your photography lessons, but you have such a weak grip on the bigger picture. Do you never join up the dots? Think for a moment. You've been battling against me now for five years. Why? What is it that you've been so desperate for me to do?'

The answer to that was so easy, it was out of her mouth before she made the connection. 'To pay. You've got away with all your crimes and I wanted to make you pay.'

'Exactly.'

Reiner nodded to Novotný, who immediately left the room. When Hanni didn't say anything else, because she didn't know what he was still waiting to hear, he rolled out his hand in a ghastly echo of Luca in the café and added, 'And so...?'

The truth had been there all the time. He had never wanted her on his side. He hadn't been hoping that she would stop pursuing him and give up.

'You wanted the same thing from me.'

Novotný reappeared carrying two small cases.

Reiner got to his feet. 'And finally we get there. Yes, Hannelore. I wanted you to pay. For trying to have me killed, which you've now attempted twice. For Wannsee. For thinking that you were my equal. You started all this, my dear. I told you time and again that, if you stayed out of my life, I would stay out of yours, but no. You had to turn our relationship, a relationship I also told you long ago meant nothing to me, into a contest. But the problem with contests – for you anyway – is that I always make sure that I win.'

Both men had their coats on and their cases in their hands. Hanni wanted them gone. She couldn't be in the same room with her father a second longer; she couldn't breathe the same air. And she could never use the word *father* to describe him again, not now when there was no pretence of anything between them but hatred.

I should have listened to him; I should have let him go when he first came back wouldn't leave her head, and no amount of *but that was the cowards' way out* would calm it. Her body was shaking, ready to tip into shock, but she couldn't let it. There was something else pushing at her, a question he hadn't yet answered.

She ran into the hall and onto the pavement as it suddenly flew back. 'Wait!'

Reiner barely turned.

'You said Renny was wailing when they left, but you haven't told me why. Why was she upset if she was going with Freddy?'

His glance was a fleeting, disinterested thing. Her life was clearly nothing more to him now than an afterthought.

'Because she didn't want to go with him. Because he lives with you, and you are one of *them*.'

Hanni sagged against the door frame as her father walked away, flinging a 'Good luck with my grandchild' over his shoulder that would have made her sick if she had had the time to consider it.

Them must have been Renny's word. Hanni didn't have to think too hard about who it meant. Renny had grown up in a town ruled by death and deportations. She had learned skills to protect herself and survive that no child should have ever had to learn. *Them* might be the soldiers or the guards or the SS, any of the men who had made the selections and terrorised the town and controlled her young life. Whoever she had applied it to, it meant monsters.

And what brother would let his little sister anywhere near a monster?

There was a shriek from behind her as Jana's pain finally erupted. Hanni didn't turn; whatever Jana was feeling was of no consequence. She had to get home. She had to try and convince a devastated man and a broken little girl that – whatever life she had once been caught up in – the Hanni they knew now was good.

The shriek came again, high-pitched and haunted. Hanni slammed the door to block out the noise, and she ran.

The first thing she saw when she burst into the apartment wasn't Freddy. It was her rucksack, packed and propped up by the door. Before she had time to panic at that, Freddy came out of the kitchen. His shoulders were hunched; his face was haggard. He managed to look at her, but he didn't ask about her bruises. He didn't say a word.

'I was going to tell you all of it today. Who he was, what he did. How I tried to stop him.'

He didn't believe her. She hadn't expected him to. The silence stretched thick enough to blot out the room.

Hanni ploughed through it. 'And I know I should have done that years ago, but I was so desperate to be someone new. And I had this plan. My—' She stopped and shook the word away. 'When Reiner escaped after the war and reinvented himself, I was going to reveal his crimes to the world. I was going to bring him to justice. And I was going to bring that as proof to you that I wasn't him, that I was different, better. I tried to do it, I really tried. But I failed every time. I'm sorrier than I can say about that, and I'm going to do better this time.'

She stopped. It was the truth, but there was no weight in it. She sounded like a child who was only protesting their innocence because they'd been caught in the crime.

She waited for Freddy's rage, his shock and recriminations; for his disgust. His expression didn't change. When he finally spoke, each word cost him a physical effort.

'Who is he, Hanni? Tell me all of it.'

It sickened her to do it, but she ran through Reiner's story, from start to finish, as succinctly as she could, including her failed attempts to destroy him. There was no colour left in Freddy's face by the time she was done.

'Why didn't you tell me before? Why didn't you trust me enough?'

It was the most obvious question to ask, and the last one Hanni had ever considered. She shook her head, but the gesture was for herself not him.

'I thought you would look at me differently. I thought you would never get past it. And when I tried at Theresienstadt, the timing wasn't right. I couldn't bear to hurt you.'

The pain in his eyes was too raw to look at. 'But they weren't your choices to make. Maybe I would have walked away and hated you, or maybe I would have been able to separate you from him and carry on. But now we'll never know, will we? You didn't give me a chance, Hanni – you made all the decisions for both of us, and you never gave me a chance. That's what I can't move past right now. All the times you failed to ruin him, did you never consider that I could have helped you, that we could have destroyed him together? And now it's too late – he's won whatever battle you two were fighting and we have lost. Unless you have some new miracle plan to turn it all round. Do you?'

There was no hope for them. *Right now* didn't mean he would forgive her tomorrow or any other day. *New plan* didn't mean *for us*. Trying to turn anything he had said into hope would have been a lie, and there was no room in Hanni's life now for those. The only thing she had left was the truth.

'Yes. I'm going to the police. I'm going to tell them who Reiner and Novotný really are and make sure that they're arrested before they get to the border.'

His face didn't soften. He shook his head. 'No, you're not. You're pregnant – your father confirmed it, although I had already guessed. If you go to the police here they will arrest you for being a Nazi too and, if the reports of their methods are accurate ones, that would prove a very serious danger to my child.'

'You know?'

Hanni only got one step towards him before Freddy raised his hands and stepped back.

'Don't. Don't mistake my wanting to keep the child alive with any concern for you. If there was any way to separate your well-being from the baby's, trust me, I would do it.'

It was the cruellest thing he had ever said to her. It was almost impossible to hear it and stay standing. And his empty eyes told her that there was nothing she could do or say that would make him wish the words unsaid. She still had to try.

'I'm so sorry, for everything I've done wrong and for all the pain I'm causing you. I should have been honest from the start, I know that. I should have trusted you to be the good man that you are. You might not want to hear this anymore but I have loved you almost since the first day we met. And I have hated and feared Reiner, and everything he believes in, for almost my entire life, from as soon as I knew what he was. I am not him,

Freddy. I was a child caught up in the life that he chose for me and my mother. I loathed that life. I swear that I have never been the same sort of monster as him.'

'Really? You hated everything he believes in? You loathed the life he gave you? Did you explain that to Goebbels when he gifted you a photography scholarship?'

Her words fell away as the shame rushed in. 'I hate myself for that, I do. I wish I hadn't accepted it, but I was young and it was my dream and—'

He didn't let her finish.

'Were you as young as my brother was when he died in a stinking cattle car? Or as young as I was when all my dreams of being a lawyer were snatched away from me because no one in the Third Reich was giving scholarships to Jews?'

Now the silence was Hanni's. It was wrong of her to keep talking about love. There was nothing she could say that would balance the lives men like Reiner Foss had forced them both to lead. Whatever excuses or apologies she offered, her family would always be part of the machinery that had killed his. There wasn't enough love in the world to fix that, and she had no right to beg him to try. The only one with any right to speak now was Freddy.

'I can't do this, Hanni. I can't stand here looking at you, wondering how deep the secrets go. Wondering how many other favours you accepted in pursuit of your dreams. Wondering if the woman I loved ever existed. You've always been good with explanations – with *stories* as your father put it. You've saved my neck by being more articulate than me. But I'm done with your clever words. Even if I could somehow find a way to forgive you, Renny can't. She's in the bedroom, finally asleep after crying herself sick at the thought of living with you. So she can't do that. There's no future now that includes the three of us. There is me and there is my sister. There is no other choice but that.'

She would have begged then, whether it was fair to him or not. She would have dropped to her knees and promised him anything for one more chance. Except, as Freddy stopped speaking, there was a sharp knock on the door.

'It's Marek.'

Freddy gestured to her rucksack as Hanni stumbled over 'What?' and 'Why?'

'He's come to take you to the border and set you on your journey back to Berlin. You can have the apartment until the child is born – I don't want to be near any trace of you, and I'm going to give Renny a proper fresh start.'

'No, Freddy, please. Surely there's more to be said? More to be done? Can't I at least see her and try to explain?'

Another knock cut her frantic questions in two. Freddy strode past her, making sure that their bodies didn't touch, and opened the door.

'No, Hanni, to all of it. Whatever we were is done.'

He held the door wider. He stopped looking at her. Marek picked up her bag. Hanni was in the hallway before she realised what was happening, with Marek furiously telling her to get a move on. She couldn't take a step.

'Freddy. Freddy, please.'

The door was cold against her cheek.

'Freddy, I'm begging you. Don't let this be it.'

Her voice was too thin to cut through the wood. She wanted to believe that he was on the other side, his skin inches from hers. But the silence was too deep, and Marek was at her side, his hand pulling at hers. She still couldn't leave the door. Surely if she called out to him one more time, he would come to her? And then there was a noise that turned Freddy's name to ash on her lips.

The cry coming from the apartment wasn't the madness-tinged shriek that had burst out of Jana. It was more terribly human than that. It was filled with tears that would take months to shed. It was filled with a despair that was far bigger than the man trapped helplessly inside it.

'Don't let this be it. Please don't let this be it.'

She couldn't stop saying it. Nobody cared. She carried on anyway, long after Marek had prised her off the door and pulled her away.

CHAPTER 23

APRIL 1951, VIKTORIAPARK, BERLIN

They had edged slowly back towards each other for the baby's sake, but their foundations were shattered. The picnic blanket Hanni had spread on the grass in the park was the narrowest one she owned and yet they still clung to its furthest corners, keeping Leo as a chubby round barrier between them.

Leo.

Freddy had cried in the hospital when she had suggested that name for their son. That had been the first and the last show of emotion Freddy had offered her since she had been torn away from him in Prague. It was also only the second time she had seen him. The first had been the transactional passing of a suitcase through their apartment's front door in the days after he and Renny had returned to Berlin. There had been months of emptiness after that, until she had sent him a message when the baby was born, desperate for him to visit, not certain that he would.

When the nurse at the Charité Hospital had bustled onto the ward with a brisk, 'Tidy yourself up, Frau Schlüssel – your husband is here,' Hanni had struggled to match *husband* with the mess their relationship had collapsed into. But that was how he had introduced himself then.

And that is who he remains now, no matter how far away from me he sits.

They were still married. Neither of them had sought to change that. Neither of them had brought up the question of their marriage at all. Hanni guessed that, on Freddy's part, that was because he was hiding, burying his head in the sand to avoid making a decision to formally end their union, although he acted as if that ending was inevitable. She preferred to view their silence on the topic as a lifeline, their rings and their joint names still binding them together. As Leo also now did.

At six months old, Leo was a solid, smiling bundle of delight, and both his parents adored him. And despite everything that still sat so raw and painful between them, Freddy had become a regular visitor since his son's birth. Hanni knew that their coming together was a finite thing. That soon enough he wouldn't need her to accompany him to the park or anywhere else, that he would pick up the baby from her and go. She hoped that they would have the summer at least to play happy families in.

In the first terrible days after Reiner's betrayal, Hanni hadn't believed that there would be any more summers to come. If it hadn't been for the baby forcing her to keep a hold on the world, she wouldn't have survived at all. Those days were thankfully a blur now, but snippets still came back on long nights when Leo wouldn't settle. Her clawing at the door as Freddy howled on the other side of it. Her collapse and Marek abandoning any idea of making her walk to the border and dumping her unceremoniously in the back of a borrowed truck instead.

She had very little memory of the train journeys that followed, or of her arrival back in Berlin. She had spent most of the first week in a sleep that had devoured her days. After that, she had slowly come back to herself, and the reawakening had been worse. Her first thought had been to get a gun and hunt down Reiner; if she hadn't been pregnant, she would have done it. That she couldn't had unleashed a fury in her that was worse than the tears which had left her barely able to eat. She had stormed round the apartment night after night, making herself ill picturing scenario after scenario filled with revenge, all of which were hopeless. The rage had make her sicker than the misery.

'But you clung on somehow, didn't you, little man, all through the worst of it?'

She didn't realise she had spoken out loud until she saw the shock on Freddy's face.

'I'm sorry. I was thinking about when I first came back from Prague and how bad...'

She stopped; she was floundering. They never spoke about the past. They never spoke about anything except Leo. They behaved towards each other like two acquaintances who had no desire to make the move from a politely maintained distance.

Except that's not true, because I love him, and if he would only lower the shields he's wrapped round himself, I swear he still loves me too.

The thought was too much. The certainty that he would never lower his armour turned the world empty.

Hanni reached out to scoop Leo up, to take some comfort in the wet kisses that were his new trick. But Leo rolled over as Freddy also reached out for him and suddenly their hands connected with each other, not with the gurgling baby.

Their fingers had done this too many times to listen to their brains shouting, *Stop.* They were laced in each other, their hands tracing old patterns, before either of them could pull away.

'I can't.'

Freddy said it, but he was staring into her eyes for the first time since Prague, and everything but his words were saying, *I could.*

It wasn't only their hands that remembered. Their bodies instinctively leaned in; their mouths found their match. He had never tasted so sweet.

The park stood still as they melted back into each other, but Leo didn't. He rolled back across the blanket and into their knees, his tiny fists grabbing at the air, catching hold of Hanni's skirt. When the two of them broke apart, their hands finally finding and tickling the delighted Leo, Hanni could feel the connection between them still crackling. Until she looked back into Freddy's eyes and saw only sorrow there.

'You can't.'

She didn't put it as a question; she didn't ask why. The reasons were the same as on the day he had packed up her rucksack – it was Reiner holding him back and, if somehow it wasn't Reiner, it was Renny.

Freddy had said very little about his sister except on the long quiet night after Leo had been born and they had sat staring at their child in an unspoken truce which had lasted until morning. Renny wasn't adjusting to life in Berlin; Renny wasn't adjusting to life at all. It was Hanni's offer, as she held her new baby and wanted everything to be right with the world, to meet her and to help and Freddy's 'How can you do that when you caused all this misery?' which had sent them back into their solitary corners. They had never discussed Renny after that, and they had never once discussed Reiner.

Which is wrong. We have a child. We have a past together. We have to try to heal this.

Perhaps it was the longing she had tasted on his lips when they kissed; perhaps it was the sight of their baby or because it was spring and the rest of the world was blooming. Whatever the reason, Hanni could no longer swallow the unasked question.

'You can't, but you want to – I can sense it. Just to know that would be something to hold on to. Is there really nothing left between us?'

She picked up Leo as she said it. The baby was tired; he immediately nestled into her shoulder. Hanni kissed his soft hair and breathed in his scent. She looked over his head at Freddy, who was gazing at his son with adoration, and their problems suddenly, stupidly, no longer seemed real.

'And don't you want this? Our family back together?'

It was *family* that broke the spell. The second she said it, Freddy scrambled to his feet.

'I have to go. I've got an appointment with Elias.'

The 'No, you can't meet with him again; it's too dangerous' was out of her mouth before she had time to stop it.

Freddy froze. 'What are you talking about? What's dangerous about Elias?'

Leo had fallen asleep. Hanni got up slowly so as not to wake him and transferred his warm body to the pram. She couldn't tell Freddy the reason. It would be another sin to lay at her door. She had to leave. But Freddy was blocking her path.

'You can't say that and then walk away. You have to explain what you mean.'

Hanni didn't know where to start. She hadn't told him a thing in Prague about Luca – everything had fallen apart so fast there hadn't been time. But now, with what she had inferred about Elias, there was no longer any hiding from that part of the story. She took a deep breath and kept the account as concise as she could, and she didn't react to Freddy's sharp intake of breath or his curse as she finished.

'There was a Stasi agent on our trail, or on my trail, when we left Berlin for Czechoslovakia. He was after Reiner, but he used me as a way to get to him, and he had a network of informants to help. One of those informants was Elias.'

Freddy's face sagged. 'That's not true – it can't be. Elias is my brother. He would have warned me if the Stasi were digging around. He wouldn't have let me – or you for that matter – go off into that kind of danger.'

Hanni began rocking the pram as Leo stirred. 'I think he did try to warn you at our last meeting, or as best as he could. But the Stasi blackmailed him – they arrested his girlfriend. They didn't give him any choice.'

Freddy stared at her. She could see him making rapid connections.

'Marianna. They're not together anymore. There was a baby, he said, but she lost it and then she left him. He's not the same man he was when he was with her, although he pretends that he is.'

He stopped and frowned and made the connection Hanni didn't want him to make.

'And that happened because the Stasi needed you to get to your father? What happened to Marianna was another tragedy your lies caused?'

Hanni wanted to say no but she couldn't. There had to be nothing but honesty between them now, even if that made the path back to him even more impossible.

'I didn't know and I'm so sorry for them both. But yes. If the hunt for Reiner had a hand in her losing the child then what can I say except yes? The Stasi went after Elias because they wanted Reiner. And they did that because I was a coward and had never brought him to account.'

Freddy didn't argue. He stepped back from her.

'Your father is everywhere. He almost cost me my sister. And if what you're saying is true and Elias is an informer, he's cost me my best friend too.'

Hanni prayed for him to add, 'And he cost me you.'

He didn't. Instead, Freddy looked at the sleeping baby and his face collapsed. 'Reiner is poison, and I can't get free of him because I can't get free of you.'

The agony in his voice was too much. Every step towards each other simply dragged them through more pain. It was a life sentence he didn't deserve. Hanni looked at her son, who she had loved since she had first known that he was coming. She looked at the man who she had loved for far longer than she had dared say.

He is poison. It was true, and she was the one who had carried him into their lives. She might not know where Reiner was now, but she knew that he would come back – he always did – that his shadow was stuck firmly to her. And that was nobody's burden to carry but hers.

'Then I'll go.'

She hadn't planned to say it. The idea of walking away from her child broke her heart; the idea of living without him was unimaginable. But the thought that Reiner might harm her son simply because he was her son was worse.

'I'll go. What else can I do? As long as I'm near him, or you, then Reiner is a threat, isn't he? So I'll leave Leo with you and I'll go. I'll set you both free.'

She pushed the pram towards him. She knew that she was still breathing, but she didn't know how that was possible. She couldn't imagine that she would keep breathing long.

Freddy watched the pram roll towards him. He put out a hand to stop it, but he didn't pick up Leo.

'Go, Freddy. Don't make this worse. Don't make me think I can protect him. It's the only way, don't you see? You'll be happier, and so will Leo without the threat of that man always hanging over you.'

Freddy stopped staring at the pram handle; he looked up at her. His face was broken. 'No, Hanni, don't saddle me with that guilt. Don't make me that cruel. Don't you understand what you've done to me? If there was a way I could take Leo away from you and live with myself, believe me, I would do it. If there was a way I could banish you from both our lives, I would do that too. But that wouldn't make me any happier than it would make our son, and taking him would destroy you. Don't you get it? The thing that I'm stuck with, the thing that's killing me? It's not that I can't get free of you, Hanni. It's not *can't* at all.'

He laughed as he said that and it was the bitterest sound she had ever heard.

'Even though it should be easy given everything that you've done, it's not. Because the problem isn't that I can't get free of you; the trouble, God help me, is that I don't want to.'

Hanni had spent a year imagining hearing him say, 'I can't live without you.' She had dreamed of hearing those words every time he visited their son. In her head, the moment had been full of joy. And now Freddy was saying exactly what she had so longed to hear, and his words were full of nothing but pain.

She couldn't reply. *I don't want to* was too fragile. The words could as easily become *but I will.* So when he turned and walked away, Hanni let him go. He cared for her as much as he ever had, but the scars ran so deep there was nothing to be done. There was no plan for this; there was no easy answer or markers to guide her. She stood on the pathway totally lost.

And then Leo woke up and stretched out his arms and stared at her with Freddy's eyes. Hanni smiled at the baby; Leo smiled back. His smile was his father's and it was hers. He was the best of them both, the bond that would always bind them.

The world turned again, the balance shifted. And the heartbreak of *there wasn't enough love in the world to fix this,* which had torn her and Freddy apart in Prague, turned into *yes there is.*

A LETTER FROM CATHERINE

Dear reader,

I want to say a huge thank you for choosing to read *The Girl in the Photo*. If you did enjoy it, and want to keep up to date with all my latest releases, just sign up at the following link. Your email address will never be shared, and you can unsubscribe at any time.

www.bookouture.com/catherine-hokin

As anyone who has read my previous novels will know, I love the research part of the writing journey and this book was no exception. I was lucky enough to be able to visit Prague, which is a city steeped in history – what is now the very proud Czech Republic had its brief periods of independence in the twentieth century overshadowed by the German occupation in World War Two and its years spent under Soviet rule during the Cold War – and it has a wealth of museums which are all worth a visit.

That was a marvellous experience, but what I particularly enjoyed reading and writing about again was the Stasi, the GDR's secret police, a topic I have previously touched on in *The Secretary*. My first encounter with them was in the German film *Das Leben der Anderen*, and I have spent many hours since at Berlin's fascinating Stasi Museum, which is housed in the old headquarters of the Ministry for State Security. If you get a chance to visit Berlin and want to get a sense of how tightly controlled Eastern European society was, I would urge you to go there. If you can't, do watch the film, which is now a firm favourite of mine (I have a poster of it above my writing desk) – you are going to be meeting them again in the final part of Hanni's story so it's best to be prepared...

And while you are waiting for that, I hope you loved *The Girl in the Photo*. If you did, I would be very grateful if you could write a review as it makes such a difference helping new readers to discover one of my books for the first time. I'd also love to hear what you think, so do get in touch more directly. You can do that on my author Facebook page, through Twitter, Goodreads or my website.

Thank you!

Catherine Hokin

 facebook.com/Cathokin
twitter.com/cathokin

ACKNOWLEDGEMENTS

And while I'm thinking about research... this novel, along with all the others I have written, wouldn't have happened without the wealth of sources I have been able to draw on to add flesh to the bones of my characters and their world.

I cannot list every resource I have used because that would take up far too much space and many of them overlap with my previous novels, but there are some I would like to specifically cite here. For the background to post-war Europe: *Bloodlands* by Timothy N. Snyder, *Savage Continent* by Keith Lowe, *The Long Road Home* by Ben Shephard, *Poisoned Peace* by Gregor Dallas. For issues surrounding children in this period: *Children of Europe* by Dorothy Macardle, *The Boys* by Martin Gilbert, *Rock the Cradle* by Marie Paneth, *The Hidden Children* by Jane Marks and the article 'The Search for Displaced Children in the Aftermath of World War II' which Dr Verena Buser of the University of Applied Sciences Potsdam and Western Galilee College, Akko, Israel very kindly gave me access to. For life in post-war Czechoslovakia: *Prague Winter* by Madeleine Albright and *Under a Cruel Star* by Heda Kovály, and for the Stasi, *The History of the Stasi* by Jens Gieseke. All are excellent, and if anyone wants to watch a film about this period, *The Search* starring Montgomery Clift is superb.

And now to the thanks which can sometimes read like a copy and paste because the names are so often familiar but truly isn't! They go as always to my agent Tina Betts for her unfailing support and to Emily Vega Gowers, my thoroughly delightful editor who has once again done wonders with my words and worked magic on the cover. To the Bookouture marketing team, especially Sarah, who is a wizard when it comes to blog tours and publicity. To my son and daughter, Daniel and Claire, for all their love and support and for pretending they're still reading the books, and to everyone at the Edinburgh Writers' Forum who literally cheer on every success; good friends make the job less lonely. And last, but never least, to my husband Robert for the coffee and the cheerleading and knowing when to hide. Much love to you all.